Centuries ago a my. five clans; feuding, hiding, magic and science. Now a. ...... uj ust mechanical 19th century, only the five clans united can hold back the blood-red tide of industrial apocalypse.

Unless they dive into it laughing. I did say 'mad'.

Quest of the Five Clans

Book 2: *the Moon Tartan*
Raymond St. Elmo, 2018

'To be now a sensible man, by and by a fool and presently a beast! Oh, strange! Every inordinate cup is unblessed, and the ingredient is a devil.'

Othello, Act 2, Scene 3

Chapter 1

In which the hero is surprised by himself

I returned to the city to kill a man. Not a thing to boast. I dislike violence. As does Heaven, one hears. Though sky and earth tolerate each day's spilled blood. Perhaps they sigh up there, for what must be down here. So also, I.

But had I returned? I walked familiar streets and doubted. Someone industrious had erected a grand imitation, complete with actors playing favorite roles before stage-settings of house and store, church and stall. I fought an urge to kick a tenement wall, send the theatre façade toppling backwards. I considered choosing a door at random, rushing within… I'd find myself in empty rooms showing bare closets, unfinished walls. I'd startle actors lounging in cheap costume of merchant and soldier, beggar and priest, discussing how they played some difficult role requiring *accent* and *motif.*

Nonsense, I know. The city always seems false. One of its truest characteristics. It is a construct meant to give the idea of something beyond summation of mud, marble and brick. The name is irrelevant. *Lud, Londinum, Llundain.* Those comic stage-villains the Vikings called it *Lundenwic.* I think of it as *Londonish*; that is to say: the city not itself but something like itself.

Consider the Great Cathedral. A gathering of gargoyles, a lacework of arches. Stone and colored glass melding harmonious as the music that pipe-thunders within, ebbing like breath into gentle chant, rising up again to thunder. Each cathedral part a master-work joining in math-perfect dance: statuary and symbology, theology, poetry, music and light. Observe how the pillars and stone buttresses take deep breaths, then lift high the beautiful dome. A covered-dish for a holy feast offered up to the table of Heaven. One sees the ambition of each separate part to reach something greater than mere pieces joined.

And yet, loiter the pigeon-shat cathedral steps and behold a jumble of parts grasping for a heaven that remains mere sky. The dome reaches the upper layer of city-smoke, no higher. Enter the ornate doors, wander the lace-work of chapel-caverns cluttered with statues standing guard for the epitaphed dead. Every wall, every floor set with plaques to give name to dust and bone, squirreled behind and beneath the stone.

The total stands as sign to the idea of a holy mountain, never becoming the thing itself. And just so, the city of *Londonish*. Behold the idea of a great metropolis, a crossroads of peoples and commerce, waves and roads leading to markets and waysides. Boulevards of grand design, alleys of dim and dangerous mystery. Palaces, mansions, ministries, grand houses, row-houses, hovels and warehouses and whorehouses, taverns and shop upon shop upon shop, markets, wharfs, garrisons, churches, chapels, gardens and rivers glinting with

3

sunlight, swords, silver buckles and dead fish. Stage props for the dramatic production: *Capital of Empire.*

Now walk the High Street and mark the faces of passersby. Patently, these are players on a stage, called together to portray some story that puzzles them as much as you. Study each fish-monger, scissor-grinder, self-important messenger, drunken idler, farm-wife come to buy, farm-boy come to gawk. One gives these faces the benefit of doubt, when one is kind. They must be more than they seem. They do the same for you; taking face and clothes not for measures of your soul, mere cloth wrapping flesh, flesh wrapping the truth within.

Just so, I walk today wrapped in disguise. I fled this city a condemned traitor. I returned as Italian sailor, swiftly transmogrifying to Irish tinker, then on to my present disguise. I do not hide my face from mirror or conscience. I know the soul beyond the glass. But at the moment I hide my face from *Londonish.*

But if I am one thing feigning another, while eyeing the impersonation of a great city, should I not suppose my fellow men may do the same? Of course, these can't all be spadassins under proscription. Merciful God, the street would erupt in blood. Still, the world's a wide stage with plentiful parts to play. Everyone has a script. Enemies, foes, fears for which a mask must be prepared, a semblance presented to hide the face of truth.

You yawn, think me philosophical. But for a *spadassin* under proscription this is daily toil and bread. I grant each man a doubt to identity, knowing any may be other than what they seem. That slack-jawed farm-boy may be a French spy. The pox-faced scissor-grinder an agent for the Magisterium. Why does the self-important messenger keep passing, face hid beneath such a wide mad hat? Does the fish-monger reach into her basket for pistol, instead of herring? Face, clothes, basket and bearing, smile and eyes may be true signs of the soul within. Or again, may conceal a deadly truth.

Consider that burly dandy with wild hair. He lounges on the cathedral steps, enjoying the day. Note his well-tailored but scruffy waste-coat, cotton breeches tucked into fresh-scuffed boots. Mark the tilted hat, peacock-feather cocked. His slight rapier, such a delicate weapon for a man designed by nature to be an axe-wielding bear.

Passersby smile at his jovial enjoyment of stone and sun and pigeon. Some look twice, seeing a face they know: the spadassin Rayne Gray. These nod their heads in approval, else scowl and hurry on. He makes no mind of either opinion, scratches his broken nose in thoughts that make him grin. A dog passes; snarls. Gray shrugs in amiable live-and-let-live.

What a picture he makes. A dangerous man, yet soul undimmed by the scars on hand and face. He watches the world with no desire but to share all the sun-lit day. He is not Rayne Gray. But he is impressively *Rayne-Grayish*.

In point of fact I am Rayne Gray. Spadassin, wild hair, broken nose, etc. Though at the moment I am disguised. As the self-important messenger, if you wondered. And I feel entirely displeased with the day, the sunshine and this cheap-jack stage-play fraud sitting on the cathedral steps with my face. An idea of me, but not me. No philosophical point but personal insult. I am the thing itself. He is mere semblance. Not the thing itself, only something like the thing.

So also, the great grand city of Londonish.

I had returned to kill a man. In disguise, I being an outlaw considered dead. A convenient status when one wishes to commit what is technically a crime. Well, not technically. Homicide is clearly against the law. Excepting only war, execution, duels or when the particular Caine is of sufficiently higher social rank than the unfortunate Abel.

But plans shift, in war and vengeance. Contemplating this man who ostentatiously adopted my face and persona, I decided I stood on the edge of a trap. Time to pull back, consider.

No one shouted at this creature, though clearly they thought him me. The supposition of my death must be outdated. As well, the proscription and death sentence. Clearly I could now sit in public and smile at all, when only months before I was in chains, crowds shouting for my evisceration or vindication, in accord with the moment's mood. Someone had been busy with pardons and soothing words. Alderman Black and Magister Green, of course. But why?

I must be meant to stare astonished, then march up the cathedral steps in outrage. Demand his name, assert with thumps to the chest that I was no actor but the reality. A fascinating trap. I would have rushed forwards, once. When I was six or seven.

No; I will watch till the man grows bored. Wanders away to pee in an alley, or report failure to his employers. Patience. The real Rayne Gray (which is me) once waited in a pitch-dark basement with a deadly foe. Each listening for the other. We held silent all the night, backs to wall, ears pricked for steps, for shifts of weight, for snores. At last the lesser man sighed; at which point I ran him through. Patience is more than virtue. It is a hunter's license.

We would see who was hunter here; and who the prey. If this fellow with my face shows greater patience, I'll find myself a new name, award him mine.

In what may be a long wait, I should narrate something else. Hmm. I was trapped in a well of corpses once. But that story is unpleasant. No, while waiting, I shall tell of my recent honeymoon in Scotland. Which was entirely pleasant.

Chapter 2

In defense of a stone

My new wife sat astride my lap, naked as pearl deprived of oyster. There was indeed something pearl-like to her skin. A satin shimmer felt with finger as much as eye. A fairy glimmer running across chin, down the valley south of the throat, over the hills of breasts and far away, but not long ago. No, where touch of her went, there was *now*. And still is; and still is.

"It's entirely mad," I observed. "Does it have a name?"

Her cat-like look of petted pleasure gave way to surprise. "Why on earth would I give it a name?"

I shook my head. "I mean the monstrous big castle on the rock outside the ship. You must have noticed. It looks set to fall upon us."

"Oh, that," she said. "Ah, it would never take to a name. The spirit of the oldest ones lie heavy upon it. I suppose we call it "*Àite a 'chruinneachaidh*."

I'd ceased falling for these family traps. "Which means 'Big Castle on a Rock at the Edge of Nowhere'," I declared. Someone stood just outside the door, had done so a full minute. They lurked silent enough; but ears will learn to tell the measure of weight upon a creaking deck. My ears, at least.

Lalena shook her head. "Just 'Place of Gathering'." She glanced to the door as well. "Best we be up, then, or they will be playing pipes to drive us out again." With a sigh and a glimmer, she stood. "Out, man. I must dress."

I stared. "What? You're naked as sheared lamb now. What nicety is offended that I behold you dress?"

She crossed arms before breasts. "My Da's mother taught me so. A proper lady shall proudly undress before her man. But he is not to see her dress for the day."

Almost, I laughed. It seemed a child's play-rule. But she stood so serious, sharing this womanly secret. A rule folded away in the hope-chest passed from mother to daughter in ancient line. Now brought out for the ceremonies of married life. Unfair to think Lalena a child playing tea-party. Behold a grown woman, pondering the bounds and customs of sleeping with her mate. A sacred ritual to be performed in solemn wonder. Therefore did I dress myself, and kiss her brow, her lips, the black-button tips of her breasts, and sigh, and move to the door, rapier out.

No one waited outside the door. Well, they had been there. I disliked this narrow passage to the deck. It held the foreboding shadow of back-alleys where old bricks whisper *murder*. I stooped, grasped something glistening in a puddle of sea-water. A ring of iron keys. I weighed them in my hands, studied wet prints leading up the steps. Clearly, someone took a dip in the sea, prior to lurking at our door, leaving a present of keys. Made no sense. Ergo: family nonsense.

I pictured different sea-clans of the family clambering over the ship-railing. To welcome us, challenge us, or play some unfathomable prank. During a respite from bed, we had stood at the railing, watching the sea-waves. Watching seals dive and surface. Lalena told me of the *selkies*. Seal-people who could take human form as they wished. Cousins from afar, she believed. They hadn't attended the wedding. But they would be curious about us. The family were always curious about family. Gossiping beasts.

Perhaps a selkie or three had clambered aboard to spy upon the newlyweds. It was bother enough keeping the dry-land cousins from knocking, asking if we required food, drink, air. Smirking creatures. One night they'd played bagpipes outside the door. I'd chased them away naked, sword in hand, determined to kill. Wrong of me, I know. I should have spoken maturely: *Yes, good people, Lalena and I are having conjugal relations. We are newlyweds.* Had no one ever married in the damned clan before?

I pictured Lalena dressing below. What mystery there? Just undressing in reverse. The shift first. Under-petticoat. Regular petticoat. Chemise. Stockings. Why not stockings first? Picture Lalena naked before the mirror, posed in stockings. I did so. The image turned me back to the cabin. I stopped myself by main force, taking cold breaths of salt air. My wife deserved her privacy. Probably she applied magic potions to ankle and thigh, recited secret cantrips passed down from Eve.

I stood on deck, stared up at the great stone box of a castle. Sea-gulls circled it, astonished as I. What mad creatures build a fort to defend this waste of cold vapor? My new kinsmen, of course. This castle, our wedding present. We could not sell nor trade it for a home someplace sane. It looked livable as a cave north of hell. It loomed over the sea, the ship and the me, as grand symbol of the present lunacy of my life.

I smelled coffee from the galley. The very aroma of sanity. Even mad vampiric highlanders acknowledge coffee, though they often burn it. Well, they cooked for themselves, and cleaned. No servants on board, nor a single common sailor. I inquired why, first I beheld the Lady of the Clan herself emptying a chamber pot.

"*'Servant and king, each to each',*" said Lalena, shaking the stinking porcelain over the sea-railing. It sounded a quote, perhaps from their *Play of Lost Glory.* "A disgrace should family ever live in servitude to family, save in love."

"A servant need not be kin," I pointed out.

She smiled sadly, letting long teeth show. She leaned close, whispered. "We would want to eat them, dearest." Well, of course. My new family.

Sanity and coffee to the right. To the left glistened the mysterious trail of wet footsteps. I sighed. If I ignored the mystery, it would leap out upon me, while I slept or pissed or drank coffee in peace. I followed the prints to the gang-plank. No one on watch. Well, crew and passengers were mostly vampiric highlanders. They'd smile in delight to find a sea-brigand creeping upon them. Breakfast, served warm. As well, the ship sat at anchor in a cliff-walled harbor beside a rock five-hundred miles north of where the rest of the world lived. A guard was superfluous. Excepting for who left these tracks.

The plank-bridge led to a long wooden dock, waves splashing weak beneath rough timbers. A few boards missing, some slyly loose. The water-prints traveled halfway, then ended. I stopped, peered over the edge. Deep water, not yet sunlit. Cold for sure. Did I see a face staring up just beneath the surface? I jangled the ring of keys in my hand. A string of kelp twined the largest key. I plucked it off, let it drop.

I pictured these keys lying on the sea-floor, till webbed fingers grasped them, delivered them to the door of my cabin. A mad wedding present from watery in-laws, perhaps.

I pictured the same webbed hands reaching up through the boards, pulling me down to the dark cold sea, embracing their beloved new relative as he drowned. I whirled to look behind and beneath, near toppling myself into the water. The sea gulls whirled, laughing at my antics.

I continued, careful of loose boards and webbed hands, and so came safe to shore. I stood before a flat work-area lined with sheds built of ship-timber. A road led in jagged back-and-forth up to the castle. Gulls crying, wind blowing, but no sound of voice. Alone for the first time in weeks. It felt good. I wandered on.

Events kept moving me farther from where I wished to be. By right of duty and vengeance, blood and law I should be in the capital. Important battles were taking place. I had a small fortune to recover from my former valet Stephano. I had accounts to settle with the Magisterium, the Aldermen's Guild. With Green and Dealer. And a debt to collect in coin of heart-beat and life's blood from Alderman Black. That name stood to the fore in my ledger: *payment due.*

But I was outlawed, house burned, accounts closed. Presumed dead. Going back would be a mad game of lurking in shadows, watching my enemies, avoiding the eye of guards and spies. I would do fine, of course. I'd fight in style, and survive astonishing odds, and be declared alive again. And so doubly abhorred. The mad arsonist-killer returned with the spring pox. I'd become a symbol of social change designed by bankers asking the dissatisfied: *would you side with this blood-thirsty animal?*

I slashed air with rapier. I was *spadassin*, not blood-thirsty beast. I know the difference. The knowing did not suffice. I played a good courtier; making speeches of eloquence that astounded those considering my bear-like person. I understood votes and proxies, goads and bribes, faction and finesse. But these were cut and edge, point and guard of *political* fencing. In that fighting art I was no master. Such as Black and Green ruled the field.

The old ones of the family. They were wise to scoff at convention, at restriction. They defied chains of definition. *"We are from where we wish,"* said Flower. *"We go where we wish,"* agreed Light. *"And we are who we wish,"* Brick finished.

Why couldn't everyone live so free? I wondered. It only required one be mad, be pocketless, nameless, and homeless. Here I stood on a mad rock in the sea. It had no name, made no home, and put nothing within my empty pocket. There could be nothing to eat upon it. When ship's stores gave out we'd fish or boil our boots. My vampiric in-laws would gather about the innocent lamb they'd adopted... Best make this a short visit.

I stopped, wiped sweat from brow, stared up the worn steps of the castle. A rusty iron portcullis barred the way. But a side path led to a great door set smooth within dark stone. A *sally port,* they called them, in days of armor suits and battering rams, boiling oil and flaming arrows. Rollicking times, no doubt.

I approached. The path near-buried under gull crap, scraps of sprouting grass and moss. Few feet had passed here in long days. The door stood bound and bolted. It looked solid steel. Unlikely. But then, the damned castle was unlikely. It stood in proud defiance of all probability. I rapped knuckles upon the thing. As well knock polite upon a mountain-side.

I stared a long moment at the ornate lock, weighing the ring of keys. In normal life one finds a strange key in

14

a drawer. Or in the dirt, perhaps inside an old book. For days, even years, one awaits the True Lock for which the mysterious key is destined. It shall open a magic door, or a treasure chest or your prison cell.

But no Lock of Destiny appears. You find the key turns the back door to the cellar. Else you lose it same as you found it, a riddle never solved. Dropped to the dirt, or left in a book for the next reader to find. Such is *mystery* in normal life. Something hinted, never completed.

Of late my life ran *abnormal*. It bore strange coincidences, astonishingly completed. Not moments of sudden luck. Nothing that protected me from hunger or defeat, loss or imprisonment. Mere inexplicable events that shouted cryptic meaning, theatric messages delivered to imply a grand secret destiny. Magical incoherence substituting for wisdom.

I considered tossing these keys to the sea. Pointless. I'd find them on my doorstep again tomorrow. Or in my soup. And was not the castle mine? My wife's, at least. As I was hers. How strange, this belonging of each to each. Key to lock. Both of us still almost strangers. I knew her body, somewhat. Her moods, somewhat. She knew naught of me but my scars, my cock, the easy laugh of a long campaigner. I'd never spoken of the cause I considered my serious work. Nor my fears of living as a beast, eating till I was eaten. Lalena was in nature an aristocrat; by nurture of ancient elite. She would think my interest in the *Commons* absurd folly; and my need to return to the city a betrayal of what we'd vowed, each to each.

A year from now we might be deadly enemies. Why not? How soon infatuation and need turn to contempt and loathing. Where were the friends from my life before? Black, Green, Stephano, Dealer. Foes now. I pictured Lalena as enemy in her turn, declaring hatred hot as she now declared love. She'd hiss, teeth bared in rage, leap for my throat. Would I strike her down? I vowed never to do so. But within me something laughed. I pretend survival is my art. In truth, it is my master.

I watched myself testing keys to lock, clearly looking for answers. A few tries, and the largest turned with a satisfying *click*. The portal opened inwards with an untheatric lack of creak. Within waited dark. Cold musty air wafting out in greeting.

It occurred unto my suspicious mind that if you wished someone to hurry through a dark door, you left the key in some mysterious fashion that enthused a foolish seraph to rush in when wise angels would *think*.

Thinking, I turned to look at the schooner. It floated small and unreal, a portrait of a ship requiring only square frame, the artist's signature. How easy to fetch my wife, a few spare vampirics from the portrait. How warm and comforting to be kept safe by others. As fascinating a concept to my spadassin mind as calling out to strangers in the street for help. I considered this concept in wonder awhile. Then rushed into the dark doorway, rapier at ready.

Chapter 3
The art of continuous breathing

It should be asked: if survival is my art, why the hell charge needlessly ahead expecting attack? My answer: I did not really believe aught waited within this sea-bound stone, save cobweb and dust. Perhaps an old suit of armor. I would crash into it, sending pot-steel toppling in comic clatter.

In point of fact the castle is far from empty. When I rush through that dark door I will be greeted by shadows, a horrible growl and the terrifying assertion *"I don't want to hurt you."* But at the time I judged nothing waited beyond but ghost and shadow. And I disbelieve in ghosts, which left only shadows.

Why then the caution of consideration, forward charge sword drawn? Because in a life of violence I have gained the habit of weighing shadows; even knowing the sinister shade lurking ahead is only my coatrack. One cannot retreat, shout for help every time one passes the coatrack.

And final truth: every key challenge of my life I have survived by rushing forwards. In battle, in duel, in marriage. When one is large and dangerous, a forward rush is excellent strategy. My preferred method of not dying in the war. Let us delay meeting the monster beyond the doorway, and first discuss the art of continuous breathing.

Surviving is my art. In a life of violence this requires mastery of sword and knife, creeping through shadows, striding bold into taverns, charging sudden into danger, running damned fast away. Compare that to Chatterton's, whose art is mere *killing*. Trained from infancy by mad masters to deliver death by sword and knife, hand and foot. Our art-work appears similar. Same tools, equivalent corpses. Yet different goals.

In the war I had a commander determined to see me dead. Any sunrise he might have ordered me hung. But that lacked style; and style is much to officers. Besides, as *Seraph* I made a popular figure among the ranks. Far better than loathed *striker*. The change in how the eyes of passersby met mine went to my head like whiskey to a virgin's buttons. I'd gone from villain to hero, in their measure and my mirror's.

Which explains my later politics. The thirst to be seen as *hero*. What of it? Vanity makes as useful a wind to sail ship to port as any breeze of the soul. To play hero to my mirror is as valid reason to pursue *Just Labor Laws*, as the thirst for righteousness. One rushes to save cats from burning houses, or defies the Magisterium to save the poor from work-houses, with equal satisfaction of self-worth. Dangerous acts both. But my art is surviving danger.

Bah. Shelve politics for later. After we cross the castle-door, perhaps. For now, we discuss *surviving*. I reveled in defying my commander by mastering the glorious art of continuous breathing. Poor man, every bloody mission he handed me I returned bleeding but grinning. At length he wearied of game and grin. He presented me night-orders to infiltrate the French command-post, return with their maps. A death-sentence.

I argued we had maps of our own, no doubt better maps for being English. He insisted *their* foreignish maps would reveal where the French troops were placed. I pointed out we knew the French placements. Over that hill, beyond this river, across a few cow-fields and *voila Le Français*. Exactly as stated on our own paper-models of reality. Alas, he replied, one cannot always trust one's eyes, nor yet what is writ. A wise officer requires *proof.*

Argument spent, I went. I considered cutting his throat for farewell. But that lacked style. Important to seraph as to officer. I vowed to do so on my return, though I had no belief in that return. A vow I kept, self-pride wishes to mention.

The mission summed to certain death, even for the *survival artiste.* I stood at our camp's edge watching the sun set; accepting that I would not see its rise, nor it mine. I put myself at peace, since no other stood by to so do for me. Years later, *I am still in that peace.* To truly surrender one's life is a kind of death, whether one continues to breathe or no. And when sun and soul had set, I rushed forwards to my task.

I crossed this hill, swam that river, slipped past cows and pickets to survey the French camp from the perimeter of the outlier tents. Lines and rows of dreary canvas set beside a ruined farmhouse. Lights here and there. Far fewer men moving about than I expected. There reigned a ghostly silence mixed with river-mist and camp-smoke. This quiet worried me. A huge bonfire burned towards the center. Perhaps they roasted a captured spy. Or waited to so do. I shivered in wet clothes and autumn wind. A mild roasting appealed.

I needed new clothes to walk in safety. I chose a tent, shut eyes to tune them to dark then entered, knife at point. *Rushed* in, I point out. Critical that I take who I met before they sounded alarm. I found naught but a cot where a figure lay silent.

Palm to their mouth, knife across throat. Quick clean slice. Scarce a quiver from the man. A liquid gasp from the cut, but no struggle. God grant me as easy a death. You as well. But something felt off. No one passes so easy. I took hand away, said my 'sorry's, searched for a uniform.

Fresh pants, too small but my high boots and his long jacket helped. I could not read insignia. Something higher than private, if not major-general. And really it is not sense to walk about dressed as major-general. Amusing, I admit.

Exiting I noticed a leather satchel. If it held maps I was a lucky man. But no, it contained scalpels, thread, scissors, bottles and pill-boxes. I examined my uniform again. Well, I was the regiment doctor now. That would do. I left the tent, deciding to make my way towards the great fire.

The silence of the camp unnerved more than swarms of guards shouting of spies. On a sudden a figure staggered towards me, waving lantern, sending shadows dancing. Before I struck, I decided he was drunk, needing help to walk. No, not drunk. Sick. He gasped each breath, stank of fever-sweat and vomit. He considered me in the light of his shaking lamp. I held knife behind me, waiting upon his consideration.

"*Por fin* I find you, *Messier Medecin.*" He slurred French with the accents of Spain and fading life. "Bon Dios. More are dead than alive."

Ah. I understood then. Fever took the camp. Typhus or cholera. Both, why not. The man I killed, the camp doctor on his cot? No doubt he lay dying as I cut his throat. But they would be moving position of the command post from this plague-pit. I had little time. I studied this man by his own light. A priest's robe. "Come," he said, tugging my arm. "I will bring you to those who yet live."

I felt no compunction in killing a priest. But why do so? He aided my cover. And it stank of poor style. So we walked, slow for his staggers, his retching. He reached out a hand and I felt the devouring fire within. He'd be dead by dawn.

"I told *El Commandante* this ground was miasmic," complained the priest. "Too near the river. Night-mist infects, no? He would not listen. When the fever spread he ordered a fire-pit. *Blasphemia.* In they tossed the Captain without ensuring soul departed body. He lay in the flames screaming, just screaming. A vision of *Le Enfer*. The *Commandante* ordered him shot. While others yet worked to pull him forth. Many ran from camp, from the screams. Ah, Dios mio, c'est triste."

"*Tres triste*," I agreed. Where officers were, would be the maps. "Where is the *Commandante* now?"

"Preparing," he coughed, then collapsed. I caught him, caught the lamp, held both up. What now? A tent beside us. No sounds within. I sighed and carried the dying man within.

A few empty mats. One with blanket-rolled body, no doubt dead or deep in fever. I lay the priest down, covered him warm. I wondered if aught lay in the medical bag I carried. Opium to aid his passing? Idiocy. My knife would work as well, and faster.

"Where is the *Commandante* now?" I repeated. "What is he preparing?"

The priest sighed. "Water?" he croaked. "Thirsty."

I looked about. A canteen, empty. A wine bottle, empty. "God take mam for a blower," I sighed. It's what my father used to say. I have no idea what it meant.

"Are you colonial?" asked the priest. "That's an English colonial's curse." He chuckled a cough. "A priest knows his swearing."

23

I drew knife. He lay eyes closed, laboring to breathe. But it might not matter. Colonials sided as much with the French as the damned English King. Best learn all I could first. Though the camp lay in confusion, the commander would still have guards. I grabbed the canteen, left the lamp, went in search of water. It made passable cover for scouting. And the poor priest burned cruelly as the captain in the fire. I felt a tug of duty for the uniform of healer, though it belonged to another.

A larger tent down the path. I poked my head in. Cots and mats, a still body in one. A table piled with papers. A pitcher upon the table. I tiptoed forwards, *not* rushing. The figure in the cot stirred.

"Water," I said, showing my canteen.

"Yes, please," answered the man. "So thirsty, but cannot stand."

I groaned, feeling fevered myself. No doubt I'd breathed in the plague mist already. I'd lie raving before dawn. But the water-pitcher stood full. He'd lain burning helpless, in sight of drink? Typical of '*le vie*'. I poured the pitcher into the canteen, brought it to the man. A young face stared up, grayed to old age by the fading life within. I poured drink through lips cracked as dirt in summer drought.

"Merci," he whispered. I felt a sense of pride. Absurd. What was I doing? I rummaged the medical bag. Ah, a bottle of pills. The light too low to read the label. Did it matter? Probably not even to the doctors. They bandaged you when you bled, bled you when you sweated, gave you pills when you purged. Purged you when you ached. Physics to the dogs then. I shook out two pills, put them to the dying lips, ordered him to chew. He did. Smiled.

"*Trop tarde, Messieur Doctor.* Can you fetch the priest?"

I considered. Nodded. "Rest," I told him. Left the tent, returned to the previous tent. Within the lamp-light lay the priest. But the other bed showed only blankets. The man I'd seen before was gone. I frowned, debating whether to enter or retreat. A hand clasped my shoulder, pistol pressed into my back. Settling the question.

"Identify yourself, *messieur*," demanded a voice.

"*J'suis le medecin, vous fou*," I said. "I am the doctor, idiot."

"A strange boy-doctor with English accent and colonial curses," considered the other. Well, he was no fool. No hint of illness in the hand grasping me. Yet he had not killed. He was suspicious, not certain.

"I bring water for the priest," I spat, waving the canteen. "And then I must drag him to the dying man across. If you are going to shoot, do so."

The words had the ring of truth. Well, they were truth. He released my shoulder. "Excellent. To it, then, youngster," and pushed me into the tent. I near tripped, did not. Nor did I draw knife. I knelt beside the priest, gave him water. It gurgled down his fevered throat. I gave him two pills, wondering what they did. He chewed.

25

"Better," he whispered. He smiled. I smiled. How could any still doubt my guise of healer?

"Can you make it to the tent next us?" I asked. "A young fellow requests absolution."

The priest sighed, nodded. He knew his duty. Cruelly, I helped him rise. Leaning on me, we exited the tent. I held knife in the same hand I grasped the medicine bag. I searched for the soldier with a gun, spotted a likely shadow watching. Well, he had not yet shouted '*spy in the camp.*'

Priest and I made slow journey to the second tent, where I sat him beside the dying soldier. Both began whispering, confession and absolution wheezing out their dying throats. I sliced the tent-back, slipped out. The two were far on their journey elsewhere, uncaring what theatre yet occurred in the world left behind.

I crept through night-mist round the tent. The pistol-carrier crouched by the front, eavesdropping to confession. What a suspicious man. My turn to come behind on a sudden. But I had no questions of identity, for him, for me. I held my hand over his mouth till his trembling ceased, till he ceased.

I put the pistol in the medicine bag, dragged the body back to the first tent, laid it down, covered it. Took up bag and lamp, made my way through the camp. Twice I encountered soldiers who pled for aide. I gave them water and pills, ordered them to rest. When I reached the great fire I stopped, gagging at the stench of burning

26

men. From out the flames stared faces, skulls burned black, opened jaws screaming spark and smoke.

A man stood at the edge, running back and forth, waving two pistols at the flames. He glowed with madness, sure as the fire sent out waves of heat, as the ground sweated fever-mist. I considered killing him. But he showed no interest for my approach. His flame-lit face stared at the great fire in horror and worship.

"Do you see any move?" he asked. The man's face shone bright with fire, wet with tears.

I considered the pit of living flames and dead forms. Within, all was motion, light, disintegration. And yet those blackened eyes, twisted limbs seemed fixed, unable to pass the door of fire into the peace of ash.

I put a hand upon his shoulder. "No, *mon ami*. They are all dead there. Go and rest."

He shook the hand away, did not turn from the flames. "Not so! I hear the Captain screaming. He is alive, burning." The man danced so close to the edge of the pit he near tumbled in. The heat was unbearable. It would soon set his guns to fire. Set his clothes aflame.

I felt an evil urge to push him into the fire. Perhaps he desired this of me. I did not, I passed on and around, towards the ruined farmhouse.

Ahead, three French officers loaded a wagon. One greeted the lamp-lit vision of healer with relief, begging for pills. The second ignored my presence, hurriedly piling map-boxes into the cart. The third studied me, frowning. Fresh bright blood shone on my doctor's jacket. Not entirely out of order. He started to speak when from the fire-pit came screams, the clap of pistols. All three turned. I did not, I used the distraction to cut the throat of the first, backstab the second. From the medicine bag I pulled the pistol, shot the last.

He died frowning. I had come as healer and brought death? It sickened me. As if I had shoved the madman into the hell-pit. I took the officer's pistol, went back to the flames. There in the dance of fire I saw the form of a man writhe, twist. If I say he lifted blackening hands in ecstasy of conflagration, you must suppose the rippling air deceived my vision. But I shot cleanly, and he sighed, surrendering himself to the flames.

I went back to the wagon. I took the maps, freed a horse and spurred away. Past guards not questioning my departure, only envying it. I rode in a daze, brain overcome by flame, by whispers, by swamp-mist rot. Still, I kept mind enough to remove the French coat before reaching our picket line.

So. My art is survival. In battle and marriage I prefer to rush forwards to what waits. Say what you will, it stands a sound strategy. But enough. Time to rush forwards into my honeymoon castle. Rush through the dark entrance of my wedding-present, monster-haunted castle.

Chapter 4

Wherein the hero dangles in philosophical argument

"I don't want to hurt you," growled a voice from the dark. Growled? It rumbled the words out a throat of bones and rocks.

Wonderful words. I approved. Alas, I also disbelieved. Rather than extending the hand of fellowship, I ducked something that slashed air above me. *Retreat,* I decided, and of course the door slammed shut. A trap. Just as I had warned myself, not really believing. One should lend ear to these wise inner voices. No choice now but charge forwards, slashing the dark with the rapier.

A shadow-blurred form leaped back. It moved quite fast. Fine, so do I. Who had closed the door? They were not behind me now. Just one to face, perhaps. And now my eyes found use for the faint light. I could not make out the shape before me. Two legs? Four? Something big. It crouched in a way that boded... familiar. My mind flashed to the forests of France. Snow drifting from branches, blood dripping from my leg. Dodging between trees, besieged by winter-starved *wolves*. I'd been wounded, on the run. The pack knew so from the blood, else they'd have left me alone. Ah, that was a hard winter for wolf or man. The last I fought in the war. Well, in that war.

The crouch forebode a leap. I dodged, slashed as it passed. The creature howled. Perhaps words. If so, they were curses. It smashed into the closed door.

"Don't want you to hurt me either," I declared, and prepared to run the thing through. Mistake. Save such lines for the after-thrust. Arms from behind grabbed my throat and waist, lifted me in the air and ran with me.

I am a large man. Not many could run with me over their heads. The experience so astonished I almost laughed. I didn't, I dropped the rapier, drew dagger. I caught a brief glimpse of a railing, beyond and below a wide banquet hall. A candelabra wheel, hanging from rafters. I slashed towards the throat of the creature carrying me. Horns poking from the head spoiled the strike. That also astonished. The strike missed, crossed the face of the creature. It screamed, threw me as I might a sack of flour filled by a dishonest baker.

Over the railing, catching sight of the floor beneath. A long table, chair-lined. Here I might boast how I flipped in the air as an acrobat, caught the chandelier in dexterous ease. But I was never so poor at my work, that I need claim a lucky fall as intent. No, the creature threw me blindly, and I crashed blindly; into a great wooden wheel of candles hanging over the hall. I grabbed without thought. Then swung back and forth astonished, while the creature bellowed, pawing its wounded face.

A forwards swing, a backwards swing, holding tight to the chandelier. It tilted till the frame creaked, candles toppled. I looked up. Ropes held it to a pulley among the rafters. A path of retreat, if I pulled myself up. Or I might drop down upon the table below. For the moment, hanging in comic safety seemed wise.

I turned to consider my attacker. He stood at the hall railing, watching my clock-pendulum self. A large... personage, wrapped and double-wrapped in muscles till the shape of man blurred to a wall of stony flesh. Horned. Two horns, half-circles rising up in bucolic threat. Nostrils flaring in anger, and yes I am trying to describe a bull-headed man without using the literary designation. Why? For God's sake I am married to a vampiric madwoman. At my wedding I danced with a *lamia*. Nor was a snake-woman the strangest guest of the party, not by far. And yet, I hesitate to name these things outright. Even hanging from a chandelier, a man strives to keep some dignity.

Fine. I faced a Minotaur. A thing of myth and muscle, and I'd slashed his face. I waited for him to bellow, an angered bull. No doubt he'd hoof-stamp the floor. Perhaps he'd charge in rage through the railing, smash himself on the table below. But no, he stood panting, wiped blood from his face. He studied that hand now red-stained, and then pointed it at me.

"Ordinary man, of ordinary blood," he declared. A voice high and boyish, out a chest designed for low thunder. "Creature of blades and lies, pacing your dull life through the mud-steps of the crowd, soul-dead and dull.

You have no spark of magic, no touch of fire in the cold grate of your mortal, metal being. I will crush you, not as equal, but as a man who has reached revelation may kick aside a mad dog."

"Fool," snarled a second. "Again you make the animal the lesser thing. The man the higher." Swinging like a clock pendulum, I studied the second. Here came the creature that attacked me at the door. He bled from a wound turning the fur of his shoulder wet black. Yes, fur. He spoke well, for someone with the muzzle of a wolf.

The Minotaur threw back his head at the words, gave the bellow of a yearling ox.

"I am the true man here. I am the one reaching integration of animal soul and human mind." He thumped his muscle-massed chest, then pointed at me. "This creature is the lesser. An ignoble clay-thing unworthy to join proud family."

That again? Really, if they object to my marriage then dare say so at the wedding. *'If any beast knows reason this spadassin and vampiress shall not wed...* How small-souled, to object on the honeymoon.

I surveyed the hall as I swung forwards, swung backwards. Stone and rafters lit by narrow windows, unglazed. Wooden shutters hanging in disrepair. Tatters of banners upon the walls; stone hearth wide enough to roast an ox; an idea that currently appealed. The table below ran long and wide, and at its head a throne. In which lounged a woman, smiling at me. She wore red silk dress, low top revealing swellings of two pert breasts... I counted. Below the expected bust, two more, smaller breast-swellings, silk-wrapped. Below those, in line along the stomach, a third, last, smaller set.

She wore long scarlet hair as a cape, and wide green eyes, and did not in the least remind me of Elspeth. Not just because El had only two breasts and lacked ears poking up as a fox's hiding in the grass. No, this creature lounged as no servant-girl would allow herself to be caught. Knees pulled up, revealing bare feet, the usual number of toes.

She smiled up at me, biting lip to hold in laughter. My pendulum self slowed. The two at the railing watched, heads turning left, turning right to follow. The silence became awkward. I reviewed the conversation, realized I was expected to respond with some argument. Ah, welcome to the Family.

My mind returned to the forests of France. I'd slain one wolf, wounded another. Limped to a ruined farm-house, no door left to shut. A frozen corpse upon the floor; old man blue-white in death, a musket wound to his head. A chair, a table. I could use this to bar the entrance, or break them to pieces for firewood. The cold decided. I smashed the wood against stone hearth, built a fire, rested. At some point I realized I shared the firelight with two green eyes.

I could have shouted, waved rapier. I did not. The creature rested, licking wounds in the fire-warmth. I tended my own hurts, took out rations. I'd have shared but the creature fed upon the corpse. I did not hinder it. Better to have one's remains devoured by proud life, than lie a blackening horror.

In the morning, the wolf and I eyed one another in cautious respect, then departed to face the daily challenge: eat, and not be eaten. That was a meeting of respect. For all their fur and claws, those watching me now were not of such clean nature. No. They'd attacked, not to feed but for idiot purpose of family philosophy. Failing to kill, they now used words to pose. How very human.

"I was told, he who makes a beast of himself escapes the pain of being a man," I informed the hall. I tested my grip, preparing to pull myself onto the chandelier.

"Then you were told a lie," snarled the Wolf-man. "He who has only one nature, is least in nature. Whether dog or worm or man. It is those who rise above their design who are highest."

I searched for a reply. Something from Voltaire? But in the stance of Wolf and Minotaur I spied a familiar anticipation, seen when those before you watch their friends come up behind. I checked below. The fox-girl sat, still biting lip. Something lurked behind her chair. I checked the opposite railing of the hall. Someone in the shadows… well, it was Cousin Chatterton. He gave me a puzzled look. Not to express surprise I hung upon a chandelier above animal-men. No, he was wondering where he was, and what was my name? But he had rapier out, and stood in shadows in a way that forebode. He pointed up to the rafters…

Ah. Now I heard the scrabbling, the faint panting. More animal-men, preparing ambush from the beams lacing the heights of the hall. Would they stoop to using crossbows? The vampiric Blood Clan foreswore swords and knives. An admirable custom, granting ordinary clay a bit of chance. To be fair, the vampirics lacked interest in the tedium of mastering blade-work, being naturally able to shred a man with their hands and teeth. One could hope these beast-people frowned upon bolt or arrow, much more a musket.

Best drop to the table below. But the fox-girl's smile said she expected that move. One figure behind her chair. Another by the stairs, keeping still. Yes, an ambush waited. As above, so below.

So I hung between enemy floor and enemy ceiling, discussing the nature of man. I could think of nothing from the classics. Other words came. Strange words that of late sounded in my head, though only heard once in a tattered puppet-show.

"So proud a thing, to be us." I recalled.

The beast-men stared. I took a breath, pulled myself up upon the wheel. More of Brick's speech came to mind. I recited as I climbed. The stone hall echoed the words, lent them a quality of theatre.

"From sweet jealousy of love, we turned envious of excellence in craft and power. We gave our hearts to knowledge, not to wisdom. Pride turned to rivalry; rivalry turned to fear. Alliances were made with dark creatures and mad things, folks of air and fire and blood."

Now I stood upon the chandelier-wheel, grasping the centering rope. There came threatening creaks. More candles toppled to clatter below. Falling angels, I thought. More words of the family play came toppling from memory.

"The clans withdrew to cave and forest, mountain-top and sea-depth, each seeking some final mastery. Few returned. Those that did wore faces we no longer knew."

The Wolf-man howled. The Minotaur put hand to bloody face as though struck. The fox-girl jumped from her throne, put hands to hips in fetching anger.

"You dare," she hissed.

"Dare?" I asked. "You attempt to murder me. Failing, you bore me with philosophical babble while you bleed, waiting another chance to kill. I've shared food and fire with real wolves. You don't measure up, darlin'. Not you, not your furry friends. Just human clay, using words to justify what an animal would not." I considered, then added: "*Bitch.*"

I began to climb the rope to the rafters. Swiftly done. The hall echoed with curses and growls. Well, I had insulted them. I should have spoken diplomatically, appealed to pride in family. Hell with that. They'd tried to murder me. Well, I thought they had. Some room for

36

doubt. Perhaps they'd only wanted to intimidate. Alas, I was the *Seraph*. Not a person to intimidate.

The rafters ran close to the ceiling, requiring my tall self to crouch in humility. I faced a complex path of beams above the castle hall. A figure approached, four-legged. Red eyes shone, white teeth grinned. I grasped my dagger, regretted the loss of the rapier. I should carry a second. Absurd requirement for honeymoon.

Something scrabbled behind me. I did not turn to see. I ran forwards to an intersection of beams. The beast before me retreated. I followed a side beam and then turned. The nearer creature continued its approach. A second backed awkwardly, searching for a path to come up behind me again. I considered the beams, moved towards a new intersection that would give me further choices. Again the creatures maneuvered to attack from front and behind.

I could not help but laugh. This was game, not battle.

Then the Wolf-man howled. The Minotaur squeaked; comic sound from bull's chest. I did not turn to see why. The creatures on the beams would have attacked. So I missed Chatterton's leap to the chandelier, his easy climb to join us in the rafters.

Drat the fellow. He could be more me than I. And forever with that vague, dreamy expression. Now he perched in a rafter-maze with monsters as casual as a cat on a garden fence. Face expressing puzzlement to recall why he'd made the effort.

A third creature came sprinting down a beam, leaped for my throat. I could neither duck nor dodge. I met it with dagger, letting the beast's rush knock me onto my back. Feet up, hands up, I continued its flight. A claw raked my shoulder. No, it was *hand*. Fingernails, not true claws. Fortunate or I'd lose flesh instead of cloth. I cursed, it screamed. I heard a thump against wall, then a second thump upon the floor.

I stood, drew my last knife, seeking my balance. Another creature menaced along the beam. Hissing, grinning, waiting for its fellow to come from behind. But Chatterton leaped between beams, found his footing beside me. Now we stood back to back, facing creatures suddenly unsure.

At last I had time to study what I fought. The one before me seemed demonic mix of cat and man. It hunched on four legs, but the forelegs ended with hands. The face presented was not sane. A low flat forehead, a mouth of white icicle teeth; eyes of sly murder.

"Can these things talk?" I asked the man at my back.

The creature hissed to insist it could.

"Not really," said Chatterton. "They understand a bit. We call them *aberrations*. Those of the Moon Clan seek to master animal form and spirit. This is what happens when form and spirit master them."

"Ah," I said. "What about the thing with tentacles?"

"What thing, which tentacles?" He sounded surprised. Ha. I lived to startle the man.

"Just came up through the floor. Green. Slimy. Gives off a rotten-fish glow. Six, seven squid arms."

The fox-girl screamed. "Holding the fox-girl," I added.

"Well that's not good," said Cousin Chatterton. "What is it doing?"

I took quick glances between the hall floor and the cat-creature. But it seemed fascinated by the squid-thing below us. I considered attacking, held off. I returned eyes to the newcomer.

"It's giving a speech, I believe." This sounded mad, yet I felt sure. "Yes. It's waving its tentacles about and making long sentences in that bubbling popping sound. A language of the family?"

Chatterton sighed. "Well, such a beastie could only be an Abomination."

"I thought these cat-things were." The creature before me hissed again. It did not care for the association.

"Ach, no," corrected Chatterton. "The creatures here with us are just Aberrations. Family that lost their humanity, or never found it. Yon beastie below is an Abomination."

I nodded as though that made sense. The *Abomination* made an important rhetorical point, pontificating its popping-burble words, waving the fox-girl. The *Aberration* hissed, insisting it had its own opinions. Chatterton explained.

"Long past, some tomnoddies of the sea-clans tried to ally with the creatures. Failed. The things are too eldritch, too separate from this world. But they gained the idea they were invited to join the family. So they appear at times, declaim a while in their frog-words. Tear someone to pieces in dramatic gesture and then disappear into the floor again. Don't be asking what they mean by it. They are too mad, even for the family."

The fox-girl struggled, but remained bound in snake coils. The Wolf-man had leaped the railing in impressive show, but now circled the Abomination carefully beyond reach of the tentacles. He snapped wolf-jaws in dramatic pretense. The Minotaur struggled with trophies on the wall, tugging at an axe fixed to stone. He broke it free, rushed for the stairs.

Now another beast-figure rushed forwards, waving a torch. The Abomination turned frog-eyes towards it, still popping and burbling in a fury of exposition. Tentacles shot out, grabbed torch and beast, smashed them against the floor. The fox-girl cried out. The Wolf-man snapped jaws uselessly.

"Right," I said, and charged the cat-aberration thing before me. It shrieked, backed away. I moved to a different intersection of beams, prepared myself.

"Seriously?" drawled Chatterton.

"Quite," I admitted. "Watch my back?"

"Done and done," he drawled. "Luck."

I jumped.

Chapter 5
Declamation and descent

While falling towards the Abomination feet-first and dagger-down, I would like to take a moment to explain the basics of my political beliefs.

I remain convinced the essence of the squid-creature's frog-croaks were also political, making appeals to common truths between Abominations and Humanity, no doubt quoting chthonic greats of the past. I say this because he clearly did not care whether he was understood. No, he beheld an audience, and his eldritch heart felt moved to deliver *The Message of the Cause*, as would an angel from On High. Or a Seraph five cups down. The Abomination and I differed in all details of being but this: we shared the duty to Proclaim Truth. And let him hear, who has ears to hear.

One assumes Abominations have ears. It would be a strange species that could speak but not hear. Besides my own, I mean. In any case, the monster waved the fox-girl in the air exactly as I wave cup in expostulation, sweeping along with the major points. Ignorant of the words, I recognized both motion and emotion.

So, to my politics. I was born in the States. The 'Colonies', as those beyond its borders smile to say. Enemies and friends alike mocked my New England origin. Yet I left at seven. My family were wealthy Tories, and suffered a frequent fate at revolution's start. They

41

sent me off to *Londonish*, they stayed to be burned alive in their home.

I lived in Londonish with two great-aunts, who argued my road to manhood. Path of Hard Knocks, or Path of Knowledge? They compromised. By day I was put to work in a tavern; by nights I was taught French, Greek, the basics of human history and art. I enjoyed French but preferred the tavern, as it was loud with music and violence. At thirteen I first killed. Still a high-voiced virgin; but I faced a grown man and smiled at his fear. An understanding passed between us, close as lovers. We realized he would shortly lie cold, soon to rot. I would live, yawn, remembering him vaguely while I peed.

A groom for some rich family, he swaggered fine for a fighter. But he grasped knife as if to cut boot-leather. I sliced his throat butter-neat, and felt no more remorse to watch him bleed than a woodsman sitting on a sap-fresh stump.

The family for whom he worked took offense. He'd died in their livery; clearly an affront. Though I acted in self-defense, they had me arrested, whipped. My aunts washed hands of me; I was sent to the war as boot-black to junior officers. A humble position, but I had tasted pride in my potential. Stronger than drink. Camp-fire fights soon gave me reputation. A genteel Commander gave me position.

"God or Satan made you for a striker," said the Commander. "I don't really care which." Wise ambiguity.

A striker's job is to bully frightened men to face toward
the fight and not away. A striker wanders camp-fires
silencing grumblers, challenging insubordination. Chasing
down deserters. Hellish work, yet divinity made me for it.
For I believe in duty. We should all face towards the battle,
not away.

Granted, by the time I plunge towards an
expostulating Abomination I no longer know any man's
battle but my own. I must be my own striker then. By
God or Devil, the bullying of self is much the same.

But all that is biography, not belief. The same steps
might lead to *King's Man* easy as *Supporter of the Commons.*
Life forces us into parts; but what story we make of it
remains to our inner theatre. In war, I saw my role as
machine-part. And the worth of the role in the faces of
those *machined.* Grown men and proud veterans avoided
my eye, stepped from my path. I had turned from person
to thing.

Anger and terror run much alike through heart and
spine. War, dueling, night-fighting; I've never felt the
death-fear that groom knew. Still I have trembled, dry-
mouthed, palms damp. Raging against the loathing I spied
when I entered tent or tavern, searching for friend's eyes.

From that, it was a simple step to despise every last
wheel of the machine, greater and lesser. King, Lord,
Alderman, Magister, Priest, Judge, General, Commander
and Captain, down to the beggars in the alleys. Wheels,
all. We were men and women surrendering our common

humanity to the grand Mill of Civilization. And gaining nothing from the grinding, but lives worth less than a dog's.

Some-when in the war I met Green and Black, abandoning my family name to become Gray. A jest I no longer recall. Drunk, no doubt. We held long bouts toasting the world to come; by which we did not mean the afterlife. Merely life after war, the current George and the changing of the century. Checking behind us first, for what King's ears pricked.

The squid-creature below is raising the fox-girl high, as a street-preacher does his bible. He prepares to dash her upon the stones in dramatic conclusion. Before that I shall have landed heels-first upon his head. I dislike dropping from heights far more than facing foe with blade. With edge and point it is a matter of skill. But with a fall there always comes a dice-throw. Someday I shall twist a knee, break an ankle; and the Seraph's spadassin days will be over. His life too, like as not.

Politics. Green and I championed the idea of the Nova Carta, a guarantee that all men and even some women shall have a voice in the kingdom. No more poor-houses, no debtor-prisons, no press gangs. No herding of families from farm cottage into ditches, from ditches to work-houses, from work-houses to graves or the holds of ships.

Black sympathized, acting Devil's Advocate. At some point Green and I realized Black was no rhetorical opponent. No, he'd accepted employ with Satan to destroy the coming Eden. Ah, and we stood so close to regaining the Garden. Workers and farmers across the kingdom stood united for the promise of the New Charter. City guilds marched in approval. Bankers at banquets toasted the prosperity that came with an *empowered working-class*. Vicars in parish churches explained the holy purpose of *Freedom*, rolling their r's royally. Crowds in streets and taverns read hand-bill copies of the Charter aloud, as news of victory fresh from the battle-front.

And then the Cause went to hell, I went to jail, Green joined Black, the New Charter became a radical French pox thought to poison children in their cribs. Crowds denounced it, priests reviled it, bankers shifted funds to ensure it remained forever enshrined as a folly of Jacobin madmen.

The frog-eyes note my downwards plunge. The creature stops mid-burble, waves a tentacle towards me as though I am the very subject of his sermon. Perhaps I am. Then my boots strike his head, which crunches with sound and sense of a leap into a barrel of cock-roaches.

The dagger pierces a frog eye while I roll past. But feet remained trapped in the creature's slime, as a bird in the fowler's lime. A tentacle grasps me, twists, I struggle to retrieve the dagger. The fox-girl screams in rage and fear. The Wolf-man circles, snapping jaws in dramatic safety. But past him lunges a deer-headed being wielding

45

an ancient wall-ornament of a spear. The newcomer dodges the snake-riot of tentacles, plunges the shaft deep into the burbling maw.

The Abomination convulses, shivers, stills. I am dropped next to the fox-girl, who rolls towards me, grasping my person as a rock in stormy seas. Truly I am not. Her silk dress is torn, revealing a fascinating surplus of teats. Those smaller, extra breasts astound; I stare like a boy.

"My god," she moans. "You saved me. You saved me. You saved me."

At this moment the hall door is flung open, slamming each half against stone. My wife strides in, stops at the stair-top to behold the entire idiot tableau. I struggle to stand, the fox-girl still clinging to my side moaning her ecstasy of gratitude.

I meet Lalena's eyes. Sky-blue buttons turned night pools. Eyebrows so thin and blond one only guesses their position. Arched in surprise? Or frowning in a V? Her teeth show sharp and prominent. She wears red kilt and circlet, sign of rank for the Lady of the clan. The long strands of her hair wave wind-blown, though no breeze dares the hall. I struggle to peel the fox-girl from my side. She clings tighter. The task will require salt or boiling water.

The deer-man pokes the frog-corpse with the spear, though it rapidly puddles to foul dissolution, passing a month of rot in a minute. I consider him. He has a perfect stag's head, eyes set to side so that he must turn slightly to consider me. The small antlers and thin wrists imply a yearling.

"Sir Stag, I owe you my thanks," I say. Best move the proceedings into formal mode. Beside him stands a shaggy-haired man, bare-chested. Fresh wound upon the shoulder. I realize with a start it is the Wolf-man. Changed in form. Well, I knew some of the family could so transform. Cousin Coils, for one. The Man-wolf surveys the decaying Abomination, the moaning fox-girl, the victorious stag; then turns and walks away. His stride displays the dejection of defeat. He knows he fooled none with heroic jaw-snapping.

Behind remains the Minotaur, still horned, animal-faced. He holds an axe, and stares in consideration whether our fight continues past tentacled interruption. He begins to speak, stops, turns to Lalena still standing at the stair-head.

The body of a cat-thing lands with a wet crunch upon the stone floor. He jumps, waving axe. A second aberration leaps down, flees mewling into shadows. Last comes Cousin Chatterton, landing cat-neat at the table-head, rapier at ready. The Minotaur steps back, places axe upon the floor. Wise of him.

Again I attempt to peel away the limpet of a fox-girl. "You saved me," she moans.

"Shut up," I say. Her eyes fly open. Green as spring fields of clover. I prefer the blue of Lalena's; eyes of day-sky given in tribute to night's child.

"What?"

"I didn't save you, you brainless chit. The fellow with the antlers did. Now get the hell off me."

She unfolds from my person realizing she clasped a serpent, instead of her hero's hand. "What?" she tries again.

"And put some clothes on," I add, pushing her away. She gasps, tugs tatters together, staggering backwards through the decay of the Abomination.

"Doe," says the deer-man.

"What?" I ask.

"Doe," she repeats, and shivers, and suddenly in the puddling Abomination stands a girl in leather jerkin and riding breaches. She twirls the spear to show she can, then grins. She has hair straight as Lalena, black not blond. The same wide lips, strong chin. Cousins for sure.

Lalena. I turn in desperation to my new wife. I want her to see I am not the least interested in these females. Bah to extra teats. Away with hair like a scarlet sheet on the shoulders of a spring-fresh whore. Did she witness how I rejected the fox-creature's thrust of body into mine? And this forest-creature version of herself? Nothing to me.

But my wife is standing with a hand to mouth, shaking. My heart sinks. Lalena feels betrayed. She is a

48

mad thing, dangerous as a tiger, delicate as a lily. There can come no words to sooth her heart's anguish. A sound breaks forth from between the masking hands. It rings through the weird castle hall like a bell, a horn-sound, a mad fairy song.

Well, my new wife is laughing at me. I consider this awhile, and decide it *may* be for the best.

Chapter 6
In the court of bones and roses

I stand at a country gate, gazing at the house of my parents. The town of Maidenhead waits down the road, beyond a bend of woods. Counting windows I might tell which room is mine; perhaps even spy my young self looking out, wondering at strangers by the gate.

"Where are we?" asks Lalena.

It becomes a metaphysical question. A few weeks of married life and I grow used to certain things. My wife enters my dreams easily as walking into a garden. Not that my dreams are usually gardens.

"In bed, I suppose, wrapped about each other." A wonderful thought, that beyond the seeming world is a bed, where past all pain and sorrow you lie in peace; held tight, tight by one who loves.

"You snore," observes my wife. She turns face to sun, as she does in dream. And in life, of late. A long-dead wizard wedding-gifted us a tomb of sunshine. Since then she dares walk by day, vampiric though she is. Brave of her. Sun's light is a fire to dare, in life or dream.

"Well, you fidget," I retort. "You toss and turn and strike me about the head."

"Do I really?" she asks. The accusation fascinates her. Who knows how they sleep till they lay with another? And I am first that ever lay myself beside her. A holy honor, if a deadly risk.

My parent's house is taken by mist. The fog carries the smell of battle and powder. A rumble of thunder, too cruel to be Heaven's. The dream falls fast to bloody fields and cannon-fire. I grab Lalena's hand, hurry us down the road. But ahead I spy a farm house where a girl and a dog toss a blue ball with white stripes. I stop in horror. Anywhere but there. I pull Lalena off the road into the trees. We flee through sparse forest, sunlight greening to old copper as it filters through the canopy of leaves.

I run now with boy's feet, shoeless and nimble. Why did I ever exchange these wonderful limbs for the clod-feet of a man? I leap fallen trees, dodge beneath brambles, sly and quick as wind, as rabbit, as thought. Beside me runs a girl, seven at most. Her long hair follows as a solemn flag, refusing every chance to tangle. I stop, struck by the vision of my wife at seven. She halts, examines me.

"You look a savage native," she declares, prim as the pout of a preacher's maiden aunt.

I consider my person. Shirtless, shoeless, rough cotton pants. Shoulder-long hair, darker in childhood than man-hood. Skin brown as if I bathed daily in summer sun and coffee. I recall my grandfather was a Mohican. Ran wild in leather pants through these same trees, or so claimed Mother.

Lalena stands a pale elf-child, strands of yellow wire for hair. Eyes button-round, two blue puddles reflecting

October sky. I can think of nothing to babble but what I feel.

"I hope we have a daughter."

She goggles open-mouthed, then whirls round about. Hiding her face, her feelings. What an idiot girlish thing to do. I consider pulling her hair. Yes, I think I will. I do it. Give those over-serious locks a hard tug. She shrieks. I run. She chases after.

* * *

Sunrise began with a funeral. In a life of violence, I am not used to buryings. It is a housekeeping task I've left to others. In war I stood to the back of services, daydreaming of beer, of women, of all things the shut of a casket declared *done.* In peace-time I declined the funerals of those I slew. Attendance would be cruel *faux-pas.* My parents perished as I sailed from home. All my adult family had been Elspeth and Stephano. I was denied her funeral. But I shall attend his; by and by.

We gathered at dawn in the great hall, where stood a half-dozen in the silver-blue tartan of the Moon Clan. Standing apart from their cousins of the Blood Tartan, who numbered full dozen. I watched for trouble, spied no hostile eyes. The clans stood at peace; for the nonce.

There remained no particle of the Abomination; only chill wafting from the stones where it died. But the dead beast-man lay upon the table. I recalled him rushing the tentacles with a torch. A brave end. Then, he'd had the look of an ape. Now in death he lay an old man. Such

52

little difference between the old and the ape-like. For both the ears stand out, hair becomes a fringe of mane. The back hunches, teeth yellow, eyes sink deep. The hands folded upon chest looked wrinkled paws. Arthritic, perhaps.

Beside him lay the two cat-like *aberrations*. Furred bodies, low foreheads, faint chins. A plentitude of teeth. Neither men nor beasts, I decided. Nor yet some halfway creature between. The aberrations were less than human. It did not bring them closer to true animal.

No matter to the family. I stood a silent outsider, watching grief touch faces of either clan. A tremor, a grimace, a quick gasp. Tears in eyes, shakes of the head. I had forgotten the holy words. *Peers we were each to each, and cared nothing for princes waiting at the door. The least of our blood was royalty in the measure of our love. We feuded and laughed, each of us all the world to each.*

The cousins wrapped the dead in sail-cloths, placed them upon a bier. Quiet procession then wound through the hall, up far stairs. Those of the Blood Tartan and the Moon sharing alike their sacred burden. Candles marked our path through the castle, bright lonely stars leading I-didn't-know-where. Chatterton followed after, playing soft dirge upon pipes.

I recalled the old sailor Light, describing Chatterton's empty village. Hollow houses, fresh graves. How many of his own had Chatterton wrapped in sheets, placed into earth? Not a thing to ask, nor ever want to know.

At the forefront Lalena marched solemn and sad. I considered hurrying to her side, taking her hand. Best not. She walked in formal mode, the Lady of her clan. Beside her strode the Fox-Girl in blue-tartan, silver circlet binding red hair. She tilted her head up at times, clearing away tears. Behind the two came the Doe; lacking tears but walking so lost the Minotaur must take her arm at times, lead her gently on. Moving, that kindness from such rough creature.

We traveled dark hallways to doors opened wide for dawn and sea-wind. Through a courtyard, a final gate leading past castle walls. I expected to tumble into the sea. But no, we came to a garden of roses and headstones. I stared astonished. Beyond ran a long narrow valley, of grass and trees worthy of some dale a thousand miles south.

No sight of the sea, though its waves surrounded us, besieged us, shouting to the wind beyond castle wall and valley slope. Here waited a fresh grave. I wondered who dug it. Billy River and Horse Mat, perhaps. They'd handled the schooner as master sailors. No doubt they also served the clan as sextons, blacksmiths, lawyers, architects and chemists. The family were mad, but the least of the blood could astonish with mastery of some craft, of language or art so arcane as to merit the label 'magic'.

The dead were given to the earth. *Returned*, as the saying goes, we being but clay. No one mourned the old man by particular name, this being family. He was old Uncle Ape; he was Aiseag Mac Tier; he was Wise-eyes. To the Minotaur he was Friend; to the Doe he was Father;

The Fox-Girl lay down a loaf of bread, a bottle of wine, and said farewell. Then the two cat-things were laid with Ape, respectfully. Only then did I see the remaining aberration appear. It slunk from behind a headstone, slouched on paw and hand to stand beside the Fox-Girl. It pressed its face into her side, as if to hide.

The Fox-Girl laid one hand upon the creatures back. Another upon the sheeted forms of its kind. She whispered words I did not hear. Words not meant for me. She wore dignity and sorrow sure as her circlet. I felt ashamed to measure her figure, counting the curves of breasts.

At last she stood, and began to recite, and those about whispered along, save I, outsider. Strange words overcoming the sea-wind shouting beyond the sheltered valley. Kin to the play-speech of Flower and Brick. Perhaps some part interrupted by gun-shot.

The candle-flame folk, shadows of passing clouds.
Wind's children, carrying song, whirling dust, wandering on.
Too real for naming, too free for taming,
We are the seal cries, the wild geese laughter.
No beginning, no ending, safe in the heart of hereafter.

Last came a reading from Common Prayer, more afterthought than ceremony. The Minotaur and Billy River set to filling the grave; the family turned back to the castle.

We entered the great hall. Worry wrinkled the eyes of the Moon Clan. I spied the young man-Wolf considering exits, the positioning of red tartans. The Minotaur did the same. Pointless. They were outnumbered. And having seen them fight I doubted even an equal number could best the Blood Clan. Their darting eyes implied they thought the same.

"Sit," said Lady Lilly-Ann Elena Mac Sanglair. Well, there was room at table for a clan and a half. All sat. Save Chatterton, who remained a nonchalant threat leaning against a pillar, studying dust in a sunbeam.

Family business, I decided, and seized the seat next Lalena before Billy River could claim it. He rolled eyes, snarled incisors and claimed Mattie-Horse's seat.

"Now, cousins," said Lady Lilly-Ann Elena Mac Sanglair, placing hands upon the spot where the dead had lain. "What do you here? Why did you attempt the murder of my lord?"

The Beast Clan looked to the Fox-girl. Tears and dignity were put aside. The mindless smile of amusement returned. Ah, but I saw farther now. She was no fool, but feigned as needed. A sound strategy with those busy counting breast-tips. Not with Lalena.

Fox-girl tossed head in dismissal of all questions. "This is the Place of Gathering. We have as much right here as any." She turned, gave me a polite leer. "And though your *consort* would make a fine bear, he is no cousin to any."

Lalena merely stared; but with eyes quick turning from blue pools to black pits. The Fox-girl flinched not. These two were much alike, beyond hair and certain numeric details. She shook her scarlet-haired head. "We broke neither rule nor faith, nor can any say we gave insult to your clan."

The man-Wolf spoke. "We did not mean to threaten your… consort. He rushed upon us sword drawn. We would have only restrained him, mere mad outsider though he is."

Lalena grinned; and her teeth showed a length and point I do not like to see in bed. "Oh, you did not find my man so easy to best? I see bandages upon your chest, Cousin Howl. And poor Cousin Bellow. Your new-scarred face! While three of your clan, blood of our blood, lie cold outside when they would have been warm within."

The Minotaur, who could only be Cousin Bellow, clenched fists. The man-Wolf half-stood. His teeth extending outwards, re-sculpted by rage or nature to become fanged muzzle. The Doe kept human semblance, but braced herself to leap from chair. A faint scrabble

57

from the rafters, told me the last *aberration* prepared to drop upon us.

Dramatic show. The Blood clan only smiled. Grinned even, teeth lengthening, eyes darkening. This fast threatened slaughter. I considered my rush through the door, sword drawn. It was true. For those within I would seem the aggressor. So I stood, drew sword, laid it upon the table. An ominous act that made for silence.

So proud a thing, to be us. These were formal creatures seeking a way to keep honor, yet avoid a feud that might spill blood across the next century. A spadassin understands the search for words that will sheath weapons. Part of the job, if you can believe.

"I accept it as misunderstanding between us," I declared. "And I offer what sympathy a mad outsider may, for the loss of your own. Truly I have only a last question. Who left the keys to this castle outside my door?"

The beast-people and vampiric cousins shared blank looks. I drew the black ring from my coat pocket, tossed them down upon the table. They jangled in a way to cause flinches, the rattling chains of a ghost.

Ah, but they offered a change of subject from the ledger-books of honor. Cousin Bellow relaxed his fists, Cousin Howl's face regained human semblance. Billie River took the keys, jingled them in wonder.

"The very keys of the castle," he declared. "Thrown into the sea by Great many-grand-uncle Fulgurous himself, long years back. With a curse upon blood spilled twixt family in this very hall. 'Tis a rebuke to raising of blade or tooth between us."

"A gift of the sea people, perhaps," declared Doe. A voice to make one shiver, warm as sunbeam through forest trees.

"The old ones playing us for pawns again," sighed Mattie Horse.

I took my seat once more. "Did they send the monster with snakes for arms?" I asked.

All the table stared, weighing the presence of my ignorance. *Who was this fellow again?* they wondered. I felt an urge to grin for a mindless *consort*. I did not, I have my dignity. I folded hands and waited an answer.

"Ach, no one sends the Abominations," explained Billy River. "The creatures are naither ally nor kin, not even to the Sea Clans. No, the mad creatures gained the fool idea of joining the family, or perhaps they think they are already proper brothers. They pop out of the floor a'times, bubbling their frog-babble blither."

"Shame none showed to your wedding," sorrowed Mattie Horse.

"Alack that we missed it ourselves," added the Fox-Girl. "From the clan of the Moon Tartan, I extend full congratulations upon your recent nuptials." She smiled prettily.

"Hmm," said Lalena. "You were here, not there. Which returns to the question. What do you in this hall long forbidden to family?"

An uncomfortable silence descended upon the beast-folk. At length their leader shrugged. "The forbidding, I do not deny. But one intruder may ask the same of the next. What do you here, cousins?"

Lalena brought fist down upon the table. And though it was a hand to nestle neat within a tea-cup, the heavy table jumped. "You and all the gossiping aunts between Sun and Moon know full well that title and deed were given to myself and my lord, fine gift for our marriage. You sit now in the hall of the Mac Sanglair. Do not dare name us intruders."

Fox-girl flushed. Her eyes grew greener, madder. The long pointed ears twitched. She stood, placing hands upon table. The fingers fast crinkled and furred. I stared fascinated. What must it feel, to shift back and forth from human to beast, led by mood and moon? She leaned forwards, *growled*.

"You know well as I, these were long the common halls and walls of all the family. Till Fulgurous himself banished every clan equally for the blood-gaming he beheld when he came sudden on a dark Revel."

She pointed at the stairs. "'Twas your own many-great uncle Sinclair himself who stood upon those stones, axe in hand, swinging the head of my poor grand-upon-grand father of the Mac Tiers. While all about the stones of this hall pooled the blood of family. All fled his anger, and all suffered his curse. There is no title to be given past that pronouncing, Mac Sanglair. Not by your Raven Uncle, wise though he may be. The clans have no master now. A thing the children of the cold brides had best be thankful for."

"Tedious," sighed Lalena. Her turn to stand, place hands upon the table, lean forwards. The two stood so, reflections of defiance. "My many-great uncle Sinclair was yours as well. The old Mac Tier who lost his fool head dripped blood as much mine as yours. I enter this hall with deed and title given by Fulgurous's heir. Granted me before a Revel of the clans." Her calm voice grew sharp and harsh as winter wind. "Now the keys themselves come unto my lord, and you *dare* question the right?"

Fox-girl's ears twitched. Still, she did not flinch away. Nor yet did Lalena. She spoke loud words to echo on old stone.

"I claim this hall as right of gift. And if you wish, we confirm our right by yesterday's blood and battle."

"Or today's," added Mattie Horse, grinning.

Now Billie River stood. His blond locks looked much the same as Lalena's. As his half-brother's hair reminded of Cousin Howl's. As Doe's hair resembled Mattie-Horse's. I wondered how much I resembled what family I'd left across the sea. How strange it must seem, to spy bits of oneself in others. Like staring into a

61

shattered mirror, spying noses and chins, eyes and grins of oneself at different times, laid out in pieces.

"Cousins, let us keep our heads," said Billy River. Then added "and not look to swing those of others." Some smiles at that. Billy was a personable man, if vampiric. "The stones of this hall are cursed with kin's blood. It cannot be chance that brings us here with title and key." He turned to the Fox-Girl. "Lady Vixen, you know why we are here. To inspect the gift given the clan. Speak now honest. What do you here?"

Lalena frowned at this usurpation, but stayed quiet.

Fox-girl 'Lady Vixen' exchanged looks with the man-Wolf Cousin Howl, and the Doe. There came silent agreement. Vixen sighed, sat again.

"The Mac Tiers have gone mad, as the Blade clan before." As one, all turned eyes to Chatterton. He leaned against pillar, considering the motes in a sunbeam. If he heard he did not mark the hearing. No, he put hand to chin, tilted head as if deciding names for the dust-motes. Beautiful names that would immortalize the motes forever, so they remained fresh in memory a thousand years hence.

Vixen continued. "Our laird is driving all from clan and land who cannot shift to beast and back. Upon our lands lived many not even of the family blood. We shared in peace." She considered. "In the main at peace. No more. The Laird takes their lands, harries them away."

"Ach, all the lairds are doing that," said Mattie Horse. "Driving out the old peoples, emptying the little crofts and villages from Sky to the bottom of Erin. Bringing in sheep. That's just English money, not family madness."

"What does the family care of English money?" demanded Vixen.

"Right plenty," laughed Mattie Horse. "We are not the old ones to live pocketless, wander roofless, feasting on cloud shadow and cups of starlight. The Mac Sanglair keep lands and sheep, bank accounts, titles to sound business." He looked for a flagon of beer to toast this sensible habit. Alas, this was sober conference. No beer. He sighed for the flaws in existence and the duty of solemn conference. Then thought to add, "But we keep honor as well. We do not harry poor plain-folk. Still less our own blood."

Vixen lay head in hands upon the table. There came a long silence.

"One knows the madness when one sees it," she told these shielding hands. "There is no arguing. The Mac Tier are lost. My father the Laird is mad. My sister Sionnach who should be lady of the clan, has fled the southern city. We stole a ship meant to cart away a village. Persuaded sea-cousins to guide it. We hoped for refuge here. The Laird himself will be coming for us."

Mattie Horse sat up from his slouch, cheered at news of coming beer. Approaching drink, anyway. "Ah, and will he now?"

Lalena turned, growled at him. "Can you not listen, you brainless nit? This hall is cursed for kin's blood spilt. We cannot be having clan-war within these walls."

Billy River nodded. "Fulgurous himself would return from dust, like as not, and cast us all to the sea, castle-keys shoved down throats, up asses."

Mattie Horse shrugged. "Why then, 'tis simple enough. We slaughter 'em outside on the steps. The old lightning rod cannot object to that."

There followed a chorus in Gaelic from Lalena and all at the table. Mattie raised hands in mock surrender. "Well enow! Talk in peace to mad old Mac Tier. No doubt he will hear sweet reason."

"Likely not," sighed Lalena. "But we need not deal with him today." She rose, prepared to speak some words of welcome, of conclusion. We never heard. Instead, thundering booms echoed through the hall. A knocking upon the great castle door. Vixen leaped up. So also, Lady Doe. Cousin Howl snarled. Mattie Horse smiled, hearing full tankards come to call.

Chapter 7
A Meeting of Wind's Children

The family were not ones for sitting quiet. The creatures must forever be slouching, stretching, jumping up, walking about, kicking walls, opening cabinets, studying shadows, sitting again. Tapping fingers, tamping pipes, lighting candles, puffing pipes, extinguishing candles. Stillness did not suit their restless blood. The morning's solemn conference had required *effort*.

By the second dread knock, all stood. The Doe produced her Abomination-slaying wall-ornament. The Minotaur pulled an axe from beneath the table. And yes, I had noted its presence. Pointless to hide a weapon, then feel for its comfort.

"Bide still, all," commanded the lady of the Clan. I stared, admiring. What a creature of parts was my wife. And though the whole always summed to mad vampiric Lalena, yet the separate pieces astonished. I first met her a naked creature crouched on my burning roof, lovelorn and blood-spattered, mad as the moon. Now she stood calm queen in besieged castle. Ah, but that was all the Family. I shall never explain them better than to say: each lived as playwrights of separate roles they scripted, enacted and forgot; all for the exclusive audience of their kin.

"*We are who we wish.*" So the boy Brick solemnly informed me. No greater declaration of power ever came from general, from king, from emperor, from pope. Minor roles, those.

"Cousin Chat, if you please," said Lalena. "Cousin Doe. Lady Mac Tier. And you as well, Master Gray. Let us see who waits at our door. All others keep here, and keep cool heads. We spill no blood but what we must."

Master Gray. Ordered to maneuvers. How soon the wheel of the world turns. And just last night *I* was on top. I nodded, but leaned to young *Master* Howl as I passed. "Too many entrances hereabouts. Keep eye to balcony and the far door. Were I them, I'd send others round about."

He looked surprised I should address him. Then nodded, turning different directions. He had a wide chest and thick mane of hair, but beneath that paraphernalia of manhood I spied a boy. Fifteen at most.

I weighed our forces. Twelve vampirics and half a dozen shape-shifters. An aberration in the rafters. One Chatterton, one Seraph. Excellent, we could crush a platoon, if not a full regiment. But faces in the hall showed fear. This Laird Mac Tier of the Moon Tartan cast a dark shadow across the family. It would not be without reason.

Seven vampirics besides Mattie, Billy and Lalena. Three women, four men. I knew names, acknowledged greetings, but they were not creatures quick to befriend. More cold, more vampiric. More Gaelic, perhaps. Could they fight? Almost certainly. I considered ordering some to the upper hall.

I was the soldier here. I have led men. To die at times. More often to live. Proud I am of that last. But long ago I grew to hate command of any but myself. In war I declined promotion beyond Captain. Higher, one's motto can no longer be *'go but come back'*.

Silent, I observed my bride march to the great castle door, take battle stand. Again I longed to take her hand, push her behind me. But no; unforgivable to the pride of the clan's lady. So I moved beside her, rapier ready. One soldier beside another. Close enough I caught her faint tremble. But she closed eyes, took breath, shook head. Every last strand of hair shivered, straightened to Euclidian perfection. Then with cold glance left, calm glance right, she signaled. *Unbar, and let wide the doors of war.*

Mattie to the left, Billy to the right, the wings of the door swung wide. Beyond the portal waited the iron bars of the ancient portcullis. Raised high, alas. The vampiric Sanglairs have no instinct to bar doors before bed.

Thus we faced morning light and an old man. Tall, taller than I, bearded and blind. Eyes of egg-shell white. Sea-weed tangle of a beard trailing down bronze armor, verdigris-stained. Greeves and cuisses too, dull green as anchors dropped to sea a century past.

Behind this ancient stood two dozen others. Men and women of different age, size, dress. Some naked and dripping fresh from out the sea-waves. Others stood clad in skins of seal, or rags of old sailcloth. A woman in ragged sailor's clothes held a basket of unearthly flowers. Clearly a gift. She took a step forward, but the old giant held his metal-clad arm to bar her approach.

"Taras, wisest of eyes, tell what you see." A low wind-voice to bring shivers. Deep sounding, a voice calling up from where water is only shadow and black, far below where a man can dive. At least, and return again to light.

A youth of either sex tiptoed to the fore. Flat-chested, long-haired, delicate face; the eyes round in fear or wonder to behold us. I exchanged looks with Lalena. She gave me a nod to say, 'at ease'. I pointed my rapier to the ground but did not sheath it. The youth spoke.

"I see three of the red tartan, Father. Two men, hearts to our hearts, faces like to the Mac Mur, with teeth white and long, sharp as the angler-fish. The third a woman young and blond. She wears a scarlet circlet. She might be Aunt Lorelai with legs, long hair wondrously combed."

The old man considered. He sniffed. "Blood, I smell," he commented. "Family. Who else then?"

"Two of the Mac Tier, father. They wear the blue and silver of the Moon Tartan. One with silver circlet about hair dark as deeps in winter water. Surely a lady of her tribe. Hair red as anemone. She wears ears long and sharp as spear-points." Taras considered. "She has many breasts."

Vixen sighed.

Eyes-to-the-blind continued. "The other Mac Tier stands proud with the head of a stag-"

"*Doe,*" corrected Doe.

"Of a female deer, and she bears a spear. She is young, not so womanly as the other females."

Doe sighed.

The youth turned gaze to me. A solemn look, unblinking as kitten or fish. I felt urge to make a comic face; constrained myself.

"Here is a man near tall as you, grandfather. Scarred as the bull-walrus. He carries sword thin as the ray's tail. He taps point to ground impatient for battle. Hair wild as kelp in storm current. Eyes blue, nose-broke."

I ceased tapping the rapier. I hadn't noticed I did that. A habit? If so, rather menacing. I refrained from combing down hair. The blind man sniffed. "The mad outsider of whom the family speaks." *Me,* mad? Ha. He took deep breath, nodded, prepared to speak. But the sea-youth had not finished.

"Behind these wait a crowd of ghosts, grandfather."

The old man blinked pearled eyes. I turned. Behind waited... the grand castle hall, the figures of the Mac Tier and Mac Sanglair standing at the long empty table. No ghosts but tattered wall-hangings, dust-motes dancing in sun-beams through narrow windows. I exchanged looks with Billy River, who shrugged. Mattie Horse didn't even turn. He merely laughed. The speaker continued, fascinated by the reality revealed to him alone.

"I spy men and women with faces of family. They wear grave-shrouds for dresses, festive lace torn. Father, some carry wounds, some bear weapons, all seem sorrow-burdened. One stands upon the stairs swinging his own head by the hair. The eyes of the head are wide, the mouth opens to shout words I do not hear. Grandfather, now all the crowd raises cups and tankards in toasts to our coming." He stopped, shivered. "The cups pour dust and spiders, the tankards spill old blood, black and foul."

"No more, then," said the old man, reaching out a hand to the youth. "Peace." He turned blind eyes upon the living before him. "The family hear, sea-change comes to the Mac Sanglair, so that they do not fear the sun. If so, it is the first good wind for family in long years."

Vixen prepared to speak, but Lalena held hand up. The Mac Tier frowned but kept quiet. Lalena's right to speak first, castle threshold being hers.

"Change comes to all, Laird Mac Mur. We of the red clan never feared the sun, no more than those of your blood worried to sit warm and dry by fire's side. Are we not all of the true family? *We are who we wish.* But if it pleases you, know that of late we choose to take our fair share of sun's light. It cannot lessen the share of others."

Took a breath. "Cousins, be welcome in the Hall of Gathering."

70

* * *

The folk of the family were most truly themselves when gathered together. Not a rule for others peoples. In that difference lies a key to Lalena's race. In the company of their kindred, they preferred faces to masks.

For us of ordinary clay, reality runs screaming in the opposite direction. Baptisms, balls, feast days, weddings or wakes; these are ceremonies of stilted speech, cautious moves, polite nods, practiced laughs. With riot and resentment ever threatening to pour forth from the too-filled cup, the over-accumulation of memory.

Not that her family did not quarrel and fight, mock and deceive. They merely wore their real faces while doing so. As the play of the family went: *We tumbled and tangled hearts and bodies, furious in our love. We feuded and laughed, each of us all the world to each.*

I stood ignored, observing the delight the folk took in one another; the shy glances, the sly threats, the incomprehensible jests, interminable circling and embracing and standing back affronted. Proud-grinning Mac Sanglair, sea-deep Mac Mur, and mercurial Mac Tier... Watching, I knew myself a creature of clay sitting to table with porcelain princes. And by God, I have never felt so before, not in the presence of two Georges, three Cardinals, a gaggle of princelings and a dreary host of lord and ladyships.

Chatterton to the rafters again, playing the chanter from his pipes. Astride a beam, long legs dangling, piping

71

soft melody down upon us like summer rain. Beside him perched the aberration, singing in time if not in words. A kind of mumbled purr of a song, thrumming down. In its song I caught sorrow for its lost kin, and joy in the gathering it beheld below. I understood that it wished to remain distant, because it knew itself separate, and yet it was happy, for it shared in the presence of family. Chatterton and it were much alike. Creatures apart, but not alone.

The Sea Clan Mac Mur came varied as the Mac Tier. Some near-tall as the old blind-man, others child-sized with features of adult mien. Some showed scaled patterns to skin, others flushed fair and pink, else dark as old sea-timber. Many wore webbing between fingers, as gloves for solemn service. Eyes large and dark, ears small and round. Yet one caught in those faces the common features of the family. As well, in quickness of move, sureness of step. Several bore swords, others knives. I judged them dangerous. Fair enough. I judged me dangerous.

The sea-folk gifted the table with foods and flowers, fish and oysters, green-bottled wines with no faintest touch of sea to the taste. The quiet *vampiress* Rowena fetched baskets of apples and pears from the unlikely valley beyond the castle, placed these before us with a laugh that shook the hall. First I'd heard her voice. I'd thought her a solemn silent governess to Lalena. She kept habit of eyeing me in warning: *harm not the child or I eat you.*

Now she threw cap back, set hair free, and tugged a merman in scaled loincloth to swim the music. For swim they did; and if they looked beings of different worlds, the graceful match of their steps revealed two hearts set to a shared beat.

The Moon Clan lit a great fire in the hearth, therein set spits of mutton and chicken to send wafts of salted, peppered paradise through the hall. Weary of ship's rations, I forgave their violent introduction. Mattie and Billy climbed stairs, returned with the prisoner of a great harpsichord. They bore it easy as an empty travel trunk. The blonder sat to the keys attempting Bach; the darker set to tune the ancient works within. Which by rights should make a clatter of dead notes and shouts. But I listened in amaze as they wove melody from the struggle. In impossible harmony to Chatterton's rafter-piping.

Then came sound so subtle it took seconds to realize it already chilled the spine. There at the stairway-top stood the Minotaur, violin to his ox's chin. He stood in his barn-animal oaf's stance and pulled from out catgut and wood an angelic reply to mortal anguish, a celebration of each day's joy. I stared open-mouthed. It could not be, that such meaning could come out such a brute.

When a choir of mer-folk began to sing, I shivered, and sheathed sword in surrender. I could not glare on guard in presence of such joy and beauty. I found a pewter cup last washed a century past, and poured the

73

wine of the sea-people. Then I the *mad outsider* toasted their coming. My tongue feared the bitter tang of saltwater, found something closer to French hills than Atlantic waters. Burgundy, perhaps. Sea-wrack prize, else just wise purchase.

There came dancing, came feasting. Music and laughter, loud tales in different tongues. Soft song in layered harmony. Couples twirling, skirts swirling, partners laughing, toasts echoing. Lalena bustling up and down, kilt rippling with legs half-seized by the music. I recalled our wedding dance. Ha, I'd supposed her a clumsy girl, bearing woman's breasts and buttocks like sacks of flour. Then we'd danced. I found in my arms a woman in full command of body and tempo. I sought her eyes now to say, let us wander away alone and continue our dance...

Alas, tonight she served Duty. To her clan, not her mate. She seized my hand neither for dance nor bed, but diplomacy. To smile by her side, pleasant consort nodding greeting to each separate newcomer. I sighed, acquiesced. It offered chance to relax, quaff wine, study people more interesting than Aldermen with tariff proposals, guild-elders proposing incomprehensible alliances; whiskey-drenched dukes poking a finger into my chest, explaining war and women.

A figure passed along the upper balcony. Light of feet; I caught no step. Hood covering hair, face turned away. But head tilted down. In thought, perhaps, else considering the dance below. A small hand finger-traced the balcony-railing as they passed. A woman, I decided. In strange cloak, disguising exact shape. Mac Tier? Did more lurk within the castle? Or more family. Perhaps entire clans would arrive, down from the sky, up from the earth. Out the very flames of the hearth. I look to Lalena to ask. She engaged in fevered Gaelic with the Laird of the Mac Mur, with the Vixen interposing impassioned interjection. Polyglot show-offs.

No eye but mine noted the newcomer pass into halls beyond. So I gave a nod to all ignored by all, refilled my cup and followed after.

Chapter 8
What wolves won't do

We retraced the candled path of the funeral march.
The guiding tapers now guttering low. I took out rapier,
and with exact slash murdered each wick I passed. It
made pleasant practice. Besides, I abhor the wasting of
light. *Snick,* a flame died to the left. *Snack,* a flame
perished to the right. The figure ahead took no notice.
Pity. Imagine walking down a night-shadowed hall,
realizing some trailing presence extinguished each candle
with the twitch of blade. Frightening. Not that I wished
to frighten. But after days playing the dull outsider, I felt
rebellious. My turn to strike a pose. Perhaps I'd utter
something cryptic. Who to say my blood held less magic
than a race of shape-shifting, sea-dwelling, vampiric
dream-walking masters of music, art and artifice?

Alas, the figure sensed my intent, stubbornly refused
a glance back. I sighed, drained the wine-cup, reached to
place it upon an ancient throne. In the seat hovered two
eyes, emerald windows to bright hell. I cursed, dropped
cup, leaped back.

The thing blinked once, slow. Not a bit alarmed.
Well, it was a great cat. No aberration lost between forms,
but the real thing. At least in appearance. Sitting pert, tail
curled about feet, considering me. It gave the cup a sniff,
shook head to say *shame.* For what? Excess of wine, or the
lack thereof?

We considered one another. The creature sat so very dignified. At length I felt my silent stare *gauche*. "Good sir," I said, bowing low, "whether we be in-laws or mere man and beast, I bid your whiskers welcome to my castle." Fine words to a cat on a throne. I considered, added more. "As no doubt you bid me welcome to what you consider *your* castle, being, as we so name your kind, a cat."

In answer, the creature shuttered the hell-window eyes, then leaped into candle-snuffed dark. Gone. I took deep breath, attempting to clear my wine-muddled mind. Strong drink, that of the sea-folk. Or France anyway. I looked ahead. The mysterious figure I followed had passed into the courtyard, stood silhouetted by the doorway. I perceived she'd worn no cloak. She'd worn wings, folded close upon her back. Now in open air she opened them, as the awakened sleeper raises arms high to grasp the morning.

Chatterton's angel, I thought. She hadn't wings when we met before. Maybe she was a Mac Tier, shifting in and out of fantastical bird-form, as the mood and moon pleased her. Whatever her nature, I felt sure it was the same creature. The mysterious personage who'd delivered mysterious advice on my mysterious wedding day.

I hurried after, in cheerful desire to achieve *rapprochement* between Chatterton and his obsession. Poor star-crossed creatures. A few cups of wine, I become the romantic. Out the door into cold twilight, I looked about. Of course she was gone. I continued to the courtyard of roses and graves, rapier at ready. Not in fear of angels; but dusk-shadows of a haunted castle stirred round about. The mist rising from old graves looked to be reaching out hands.

Ahead on a slab of black stone sat a figure, wingless. No angel, but man armed with pistol. A flash-pan antique, large and heavy. Perfectly serviceable when pointed to one's head, exactly where the figure placed it. His head, not mine.

Of course he heard me approach. At such time every sight and sound sharpens. Even for a man not sharing his humanity with his wolf. He heard and straightened, prepared to squeeze trigger.

Well, I have attended this play before. Men in war grow weary of waiting to be shot. They determine to get the ceremony over and done. I never found words that persuaded to give dawn another try. I doubt such words have yet been said.

Still, this was young Master Howl. Kin to the folk now rejoicing family bonds in the castle. I recalled the morning's solemn grave-side grief. Vixen, and Lalena and the Doe. Even the aberration now finding consolation in song. Therefore did I flick rapier-tip to the flash pan of the gun. Instead of *bang* and a *cry*, came only *click* and a *snap*. Act of amazing swordsmanship performed, I stepped forward and kicked the thing from his grasp.

Howl leaped for my throat. As I expected. One can picture some virgin to human complexity waiting to be *thanked*. The spadassin knows better. I stepped aside, struck with fist as he passed. Useless, the creature came carved of muscle, bone and rage. He struck back, sent me tumbling.

He stood shivering, face reshaping to muzzle, eyes slanting, ears sharpening to spear-points. Threw back head and howled to shiver every sheep for twenty leagues. That satisfied, he extended hands, re-forming fingers to claws forged in fires of rage.

But by then I had found his pistol, re-cocked it and stood, brushing myself off. Howling is a long silly business. I suspect real wolves save it for the party after the fight. His green-fire eyes stared at the pistol, at me, at the pistol. I considered as well.

One can see the paradox pausing us both. I'd stopped him from shooting himself, so he was going to tear me to pieces, so I was going to shoot him? A deep bell-tone of irony rang into the night.

"You make no sense," Howl declared. His muzzle gave no faintest slur of lupine accent. How was that possible? "You will kill me to prevent me from killing myself?"

Ah, but note he chose to talk, not leap. I recalled he'd wanted to discuss life and meaning in our earlier confrontation. The man was tormented, seeking escape in violence and philosophy. Now he extended both arms.

"Shoot, then, outsider. The family will think it murder. My cousin will renounce you, my clan share pieces of your still-screaming self."

"Hardly murder to shoot someone's knee," I pointed out. Many a black mood has been driven away by a sound dose of agony. Or so I've heard, I've heard. But I did not fire. In truth, I felt the person before me was too much a thing of wonder to damage.

How easy it is to assume magic in book or fireside tale. But to witness the reality shakes mind and soul. I stood before a man turned into the shadow of a wolf. Astonishing as a symphony shouting music down from clouds. This man was an artist, molding form and nature into chimeric dream. I had as little wish to hurt him as fire at the Pieta.

Therefore did I sheath rapier, lay pistol upon convenient headstone. Why? Well, the gun's powder pan had spilled, leaving it a chunk of wood and iron. And rapier makes poor weapon against a creature designed for *corps à corps*. I had a knife close by. Ah, also I was half-drunk.

So I sat upon the tomb of black stone, recalling the dinner-feast I'd attended with others of Howl's family. Flower, and Brick, Lucy Dog of Mystery, and the old sailor Light. Good people all. And then that conversation with Chatterton's angel among the graves of Melrose… I looked about for her now. Only night, only stars, only headstones.

80

"Is there a preference of the family for graveyard settings?" I asked.

The man sighed, shivered, gave himself human face. I wondered did that come simple as smiling, or difficult as backwards somersault? Howl did not sit. He began to pace. When he spoke, it came fast and low, a breathless rush of words.

"Cemeteries, tombs, chapels, churches, castles, ruins, abandoned houses, the roofs of cathedrals, the edges of cliffs, crossroads, bridges, city gates, mountain tops, the tops of trees, the bottoms of mines, the inner caves of the sea. By the light of gibbous moon, witches' bonfire, foxfire or firefly, storm-light, ship's lantern, altar-candle, cottage rush light, else the dungeon's sputtering torch… my people forever seek proper settings for laughter and murder, for dance, for words and shouts and songs."

He paced, easing soul-ache by bleeding words. "You must have seen. We make a host of theatrical flies trapped in amber, contemplating ourselves through eternity. We cannot escape each watching each. Ah, I would be no wolf if I could choose. I'd be a common outsider of dull clay like, like *you*. One who never came within a thousand leagues of my accursed family."

He waved hands to the night sky, brushing at the tangling cobwebs of starlight. Then kicked a gravestone. I kept face solemn, nodding outwardly, within applauding as he strode the stage declaiming against *theatre*. I realized the powder pan had not spilled. No, it never held powder.

81

He'd not meant to kill himself, nor feared I'd shoot him. A performance for the self, the night, the graves.

Perhaps enacted regularly. Perhaps whenever he despaired he sought some place of death, enacted an ending. I recalled a Lieutenant in the war with a habit under fire. He'd put finger to temple in sign of pistol, drop thumb for hammer. The enacting of suicide as anodyne to the pain of life.

Granted the Lieutenant had eventually scoured the brains from his skull with a shotgun. No more enacting but the act itself. I did not wish Howl to follow that path. The world needed creatures of magic. Damnation, would I could take the entire family marching as an army of wonder into Londonish. Teaching guilds and Magisters and Aldermen that the boundaries of life were greater than coin-purse and social title…

"You!" shouted Howl, making me jump, reach for knife. Mere rhetoric, I saw and relaxed. He ceased pacing, pointed at me. "When Vixen was seized by the Abomination, you leaped to her rescue. And you're not even of the blood. While I snapped teeth from safety like a fool. And Doe, Doe! Finished the creature. I'm not a wolf. I'm a child hiding his face when frightened." He ceased pacing, put hands to face. Whispered to the night-roses, "And I am always frightened."

"Of what?" I asked. One couldn't help but wonder. "You could break the average man over your knee without bothering to don your fur coat."

He kicked a stone. "Of life. Of death. Of things."

"Things with tentacles?"

He shook his head. Now he whispered low, foregoing drama. "Of my father. The Laird of the Mac Tier. He grins at me and I shake. He snarls at me and I cower. My own Da." Howl's hands reached up. He forced them down.

Fathers. Not a subject I knew well. I longed for the wine and fire and mutton and women within the castle. I knew *them*. "A sensible opinion," I tried. "Vixen says your father is mad."

Howl looked affronted at this slight to the creature that terrorized him. Naturally. Family is all about love and hate, pride and pique, loyalty and resentment. I was outsider not for lack of supernatural ability, but for shear incomprehension of these people's tangled hearts.

"My Da," he intoned, arms spread wide to proclaim, "is the most frightful man in the world. The most terrifying being born. He is beyond madness and sanity. Not even a Mac Sanglair can stand before him. The Abomination would flee at his coming."

I sighed. Other men's knots are so easy to solve. Particularly those of the young. It's only our own tangles that achieve Gordian status. I considered Master Howl, his fears and strengths as I would a weapon on a shop-bench, guessing mettle and temper.

"What do you know of wolves?" I asked.

83

Howl took hands from face, puzzled at the fool question.

"Know? I know everything. How not? I become a wolf," he declared. He returned to pacing graves. "It came hard at first. The change-fire melting flesh and bone and soul. Now it is effortless. I become winter's wolf. I am white teeth, the night-bright eyes of the hunter. I swim a sea of scents. Speed and strength in leg and heart. My nails are knives. I move through shadows noiseless, seeking blood." He stopped to consider the glory. "*Know* of wolves? I myself am Wolf."

"Yes, but would a wolf attack a six-foot madness of green fire and tentacle?" I inquired, looking about. One hoped talk of Abominations did not draw the creatures. Howl ceased pacing, tilted maned-head in sign my question summed to insect-buzz. I parried the look, riposted.

"You know right well, Master Howl. No wolf would approach such a great uncanny creature. It would turn tail. *Howling*, as it were."

The man's face shifted to muzzle, returned to mouth, rose and fell in waves seeking balance between warring forms. The changing made me queasy. I looked up to the night-sky, not for inspiration but to settle my stomach. I beheld stars shining through a curtain of rippling fairy-glow: the Northern Lights. Behold why the family built a castle in a cold waste of sea. To have this eldritch curtain for private stage prop.

Something passed across the sky. A gull, no doubt. I refuse to join those seeing and seeking angels in clouds, in the smoke of battle or the shadows of death-beds. Granted, I'd followed an angel to sit among these tombstones and roses chatting to a pre-suicide. But that did not count as surrender to superstition. Chatterton's angel was family madness, whether she herself was family or no. I recalled the words she gifted me as wedding present. Words of purpose: to deal with the mad natures of my new in-laws.

She'd advised, *'He who makes a beast of himself, escapes the pain of being a man. And so loses the wisdom'*. Surely she held the Moon Tartan clan in aim for that arrow of insight. Staring at the mad dance of light, it all seemed clear enough.

"You've had things backwards," I informed Howl, as old soldier to new recruit. "Keep your wolf-self for when you want *to live*. When you must perform acts of insane rage and suicidal courage, stay a man."

Which words poured out all the wisdom I had in the cup. I stood, ass sore and cold from sitting on stone. Of course the boy wanted to stay, debate and declaim.

"But Doe…" he protested, gesticulating towards the castle, where no doubt Doe danced mad jigs with vampiric cousins, quaffing sea-wine, singing of her victory. Sensible actions, all. "A deer is a thing of timid spirit. Yet she rushed in when I backed away."

85

I shrugged. "She used a deer's speed to dodge the arms that slew Ape. But she kept human hands to use the spear. Human mind as well, I'd guess. Perhaps she and Bellow don't go so deep into the animal-soul." I shrugged. It was no art I knew. "You should ask her."

I eyed the path back to wine and warmth, wife and dance and sizzling mutton. Could I leave this gloomy creature alone to graves and roses, debating manhood with the stars? I should clap him on the back as camp-mate. We'd share tips on fighting and fornication. I didn't want to. I thought him as an idiot. Fully an idiot as I had been at his age. I had swaggered then with unearned pride. He gloomed now with pointless doubt. Came to the same.

Before I could decide, a bell rang. One long leaden toll from a high corner of the castle. I shivered as the metallic ripple passed through stone and night and my frighted heart. In answer to the tolling, someone screamed high in the opposite tower. A long cry, horror-filled to cup-brim.

Then in answer to bell and cry, the ground trembled. I expected graves to yawn beneath us. I whirled round about, rapier ready. No grave opened. No, they merely shivered, as I shivered. The white mist shrouding the stony ground swirled, forming faces and hands.

"Ah," sighed Howl. "Midnight already?"

Chapter 9

The Essay on Criticism, and other stage props

Let us return to Londonish. In narrative, I mean. I
lurk there now, observing the imposter *Rayne Grayish*
from shadow and disguise, while recalling my honeymoon
on a mad Northern isle. Pleasant recollections.
Occasionally violent, often terrifying. Always interesting.

Yet I recounted only acts and words, places and
faces. I gave the shell, never revealing the heart. Here, I
shall put the truth to words. *I was falling in love with my wife.*
Dueling with beast-men, standing solemn at grave-side,
preparing for battle at the castle door, trapped in the
burial room of a possessed doll… whatever insanity
occurred, half of mind and all of heart was with my bride.
Wondering what she thought now, how hung her wise
hair this moment? What joy or sorrow twisted those red
lips, the shy invisible brows? Above all, was she thinking
of me?

Infatuation is old acquaintance. A fire sparked by
pretty face, the touch of hands, a revelation of ankle or
thigh, just the coy toss of hair... these things enchant till
you stagger drunk with imaginings, bold with desire,
clumsy with lust. Till, till and till. Enough suns rise, the
face beside you stares familiar as the one from your
mirror. Touch becomes repetition, kisses taste sweet-stale
as last week's cake.

I had not loved Lalena when we married. Nor mistook her mad obsession as love for me. She and I met on a dark crossroad of our lives. From that came our clasped hands, joined bodies. Not love nor infatuation put us side-by-side reciting eternal vows. Our marriage: a mad act of sane need.

Yet each night since '*I do*', I lay myself beside her, to awaken amazed that sun should rise, world should spin and this strange inebriation did not fade nor sour. What a thing, to swim up from dreams and turn, finding a face pillowed beside one, a face offering exact answer to every question that once tormented the mind through long nights.

Bah. I was wise to talk of wolf-men and mermaids, abominations and ghosts. Simple to describe. Monsters are striking, so absurd that imagination draws them with a few strokes. But *love*? No description captures the reality. Perhaps love is one of the old ones of the Family, and defies chaining by name and word.

So back to Londonish. The sun has climbed, Highstreet become the expression of *Mankind as River*. Wise carters and drovers take to the side-streets. The stubborn and foolish goad horses onwards, making halting progress. While hands reach from the humanity-river, help themselves to anything loose in the wagon's unguarded contents.

Rayne Grayish stands from the cathedral steps, stretches, scratches privates then strides though the crowd in sudden determination to be elsewhere. I consider. If he is bait, then I risk revealing myself by following. And what can he be but bait?

Well enow. Assume hunters watch for those who follow Rayne Grayish. Find one and follow him, and you march safe in the back of the parade. Granted, I might be spotted by those who follow the hunter as he watches for those who follow Grayish. A tangled yet reasonable risk.

But I study the roofs and windows, alleys and passing humanity. No primary watchers. No secondary watchers. No thuggish faces eyeing round corners, no dull idlers protesting their innocence with a bored yawn whenever I eye them. Puzzling.

Rayne Grayish strides side-streets to quieter boroughs. He keeps a loping step faster than a stomping blacksmith. I could hurry but choose not. Pace of motion is full half a disguise. I might dart into doorway, become someone fleeter of foot. Perhaps the *School-Proctor*. In bag upon my back I carry a red periwig, cheap bifocals, a frock-coat, high collar and copy of Pope's *Essay on Criticism*. I am anxious to become this scholastic bore. I shall stop strangers in the street, read to them of poets and wits, nature and watches.

But if Grayish is guarded by competent hunters, they may note my change of appearance. Then again, they must at length wonder why a blacksmith grows familiar across different streets. I hesitate, wondering where the hell-fire these theoretical hunters hide.

89

Grayish jumps to avoid a puddle of horse piss, putting himself in the path of two burly sailorish creatures. They hold animated discussion with no interest in steering ship's course around obstacles. One thrusts arm out to remove him from the path... Grayish accepts the arm as a gift, pulls so that the sailor flies forwards, splashes face-forwards in the piss-puddle.

The second man reacts on the instant. He strikes down with the short club one sees in dock-side taverns. Sailors call them pins, for no sensible reason. They are clubs, not a bit pin-like. Another man would dodge or back away fumbling for blade. I laugh in delight to see Grayish step *forwards* under the strike. The two men stand face to face as if to kiss, then the sailor collapses with knee to the stomach, strike to throat.

But the first sailor is up, piss-dripping and furious. He draws knife, throwing himself at Grayish's back. Almost I shout warning. But Grayish does not turn, merely steps aside letting the man fly past, landing upon the downed fellow. The two sailors tussle in confusion. Grayish kicks both to submission. Neither is dead nor unconscious; merely aware they hurt and that if they rise the man smiling kindly and mildly will hurt them more.

I am not the only witness; yet by the time the street understands that free entertainment is at hand, Grayish is tipping hat to all, striding on. Well done, Master Grayish!

He whistles to the sky, eyeing a maid emptying pots out a window. She cannot help but return smile, blushing

90

at their lascivious exchange. But Grayish's walk says he will enjoy the day as it comes, and to perdition with other opinion. What an excellent fellow. Should I feel ashamed to declare it?

Not a bit. Modesty was never my forte. *Rayne Grayish* is a fraud, but he is a wonder. And so I wonder will I kill him, or shall he me? A loss to the world either outcome. *C'est la vie.* I wander into an alley, wary of stray dogs and canny assassins. Naught but trash and shadow, stink and silence. Excellent. I swift-change clothes, sighing to hide my rapier beneath trash. Fresh bought and un-blooded. It will be gone on my return, of course. And my coin-purse grows light; I can scarce afford another. But a rapier is too tell-tale to carry in disguise. Improper for a proper school-proctor.

Enter as blacksmith, exit as scholar. And yes, I wiped face of soot. Insulting that you should think to remind me. I hoist Alexander Pope's *Essay on Criticism* beneath my arm. A poetic drollery critics should have flayed. But no, they loved it. *C'est l'art.* The bifocals pinch my nose and blur my sight. To see where I go, I must peek over, under and around them. Exactly as do true wearers of the things. I stoop my back, stride with knees scarce bending. A wooden doll of a scholar, anxious to attend some meeting of pedagogic dust and ostentatious Latin.

The street grows crowded again, though noon-time is past. These are tradesmen sharing the city path. They should be manning their benches and counters, storefronts and booths. Some gathering of the working class occurs. Can Grayish be attending? Well, Gray would do so. So also, his imitator.

Peering over the lenses blocking sight, I deduce our destination. For a moment my pedantic pace falters. A baker behind stumbles into my person, curses his doughy obscenities. Bakers always seem ominous and deadly to me. I reach for rapier but find only a book. And reaching for blade is no part of my scholar's persona. I refrain even from drawing a modest knife. I shrug, put hand to glasses to study him, prepared to smite with Alexander Pope. He snorts flour, darts around. I follow after, comforting myself *I would have won.* I would have smote him to the dirt with my grasp of literary formula.

As I feared, we come to the steps of The Church of All Souls. Elspeth's old house of worship. Fine in that. This stone box filled with holy vapor brought her comfort. Comfort I had been too mutton-headed to know she'd needed.

"I was a house-girl caught up in lords' affairs. Spyings and beddings, and promises of a glorious future, with threats of a dreadful end. I lived in more fear and shame in a week, man, than you did in a year of war." So she'd confessed to me.

Well, her ghost confessed. In a dream, to be honest. Not a testimony to stand in sober court. Yet dreams, ghosts and memories make half my dance companions since she died. I scarce know the quick from the lingering shades.

But if this church had been a place of comfort to Elspeth, not so for me. The cold solemn face stood witness to the final betrayal. The old life of the true Rayne Gray ended here, with my last friend passing me a sleep-poisoned cup. Ah, that was a knife thrust to soul and heart. No wonder I'd moved so effortlessly into the mad dance of the family. I'd been a kind of ghost; a soul with nothing solid left of life or love...

I shake myself. *Bah!* to brooding. Pathetic as Howl. Next I'll be sitting on tombstones, empty gun to head. I take a breath of determination and follow the crowd towards the door of the church.

On the steps stand pamphleteers thrusting tracts and booklets to those entering. Not an organized effort. Multiple armies warring for God and Law seize advantage of the passing crowd. A tall presbyter in black hisses at a thick-set laborer in leather smock. A gangly boy moves smoothly between, stands in my path. His hair bound neatly behind, dark clothes, smart shoes; he might be page-boy for a wealthy house. Out of place in this gathering, in danger of being trampled. He takes from a satchel a booklet, offers it.

I study him over the rims of my faux glasses. Something of *family* in those insistently innocent eyes... It might be a fresh-washed-and-combed Brick. I check ears; round. Not Brick. The crowd shoves about me, anxious

93

to enter the church. I take the offered booklet; then to poke this solemn messenger I give him Pope's *Essay on Criticism*.

I expect him to stutter refusal of the offering. But he accepts with a bow, turns attention to others. I move on, watching for a spy, a knife, a clever eye seeing past disguise.

Within is far too crowded. The inner church is packed, aisles filled. Just as well, I prefer to keep by the entrance. This may yet be trap. It makes no sense except as trap. Surely hunters fill the throng. Yet sniffing for danger I smell only crowd-sweat, mud, perfume, candle-wax, kerosene and dust. I spy none spying me. Grayish's hat marches towards the front. I consider whether he will simply exit the back.

I move towards the wall. An old man, a young woman consider my solemn school-house self. I smile, fumbling with hat, book and glasses. *Harmless*, they decide, and shift to give me space. Through an archway I watch events at the distant front. Figures speak, but crowd-murmur and stone pillar filter words to loud mumble. I see gesticulations, hear echoes of introduction. I watch in surprise as Rayne Grayish steps to the podium.

There come shouts, applause, cat-calls. He smiles, waiting for this to cease. It never quite does. Here is no church service, I realize, but political meeting.

"Was not this Gray ruffian sentenced to hang?" I ask the old man beside me.

The girl next him shakes bonnet, rolls eyes. "His Majesty pardoned the rogue."

The old man looks left, right for royal ears. Then mutters. "The king is mad. All know so."

"But I heard Gray was torn to pieces in his cell." I consider adding '*by vampires*' but refrain.

The old man shrugs. "That was some French family named Jacob or what-like. Rescued him, left some poor body in his cell, carried him to the coast. But he cut their foreign throats, came back to take his punishment like a proper English madman. What could they do but pardon him? God's luck they didn't make him bishop."

I watch Grayish deliver solemn words, expressing dramatic points with push and raise and flourish of hands. Now he shouts. The crowd shouts in return. At this distance it sums to a clearer cacophony. I puzzle, feeling I have witnessed this scene before. In dream? I recall the Abomination. Yes, it waved tentacles in just that conductor's sweep, orchestrating truth and argument. Not understood, nor caring to be understood. *Delivery of the Message,* was all.

The memory of the Abomination recalls to me the castle, and my wife. I lean against cold stone, watch this shadow-man mock my own dramatic gestures, listen to the incomprehensible mumble of his thoughts. I am forced to admit: if he is true shadow of me, he shall drone all the day. He shall have word and breath and stamina and opinion to stand declaiming till the audience sleeps or

95

starves or wanders away converted to the Cause. For God's pity, let us go back to my honeymoon on that mad island. Anything is preferable to this. Even a midnight courtyard fast congregating with ghosts.

Chapter 10
A wedding present proves no tea-set

"Wine, women and fire," I said to Howl. "Let us seek these good things out."

Words needing no expounding. They summed the desires of a man's heart. The fact that ghostly forms gathered about stands secondary to the eternal truth and rightness of the words. Secondary, I say.

Howl, melancholy and morbid, showed no concern for faces swirling in night-mist. He only sighed in resignation. He supposed I encouraged him towards cheer and light. As I did, I did. Cleverly combining this ancient remedy for black humors with my personal desire to flee the castle courtyard. And flee we did, at casual pace.

A wisp of white clad in ghost-kilt and pallor stood up from cold stone and old earth. A great two-handed sword loomed over his shoulder, crucifix-blade for a menacing penitent. The creature held palm out to bar the way. Howl walked on as through a cloud of gnats. I halted, considered circling. I faced the antique beard and mustache, the *moue* of anger. At me. Why me? Howl was the one who'd transpersed him. But the thing tugged the great-sword, raised it as executioner's axe.

I lunged, piercing the very heart of fog. Ghost and I stared a moment at the blade fixed in wispy chest. Then with a mighty heave the spirit swung his fog-blade, achieving the result of a moonbeam attempting murder of a rock. Again we paused, considered our lamentable inability to kill and be killed.

The ghost rolled vaporous eyes. I shrugged. Howl reached through the creature, grabbed my elbow, pulled me on. "Ach, don't be playing with these fellows," he chided. "It encourages the pesky things."

We continued; Howl marching brooding through the wraiths, I preferring to circle. At one point this caught me in tangles of rose bushes. I was not alone. A buxom-looking wisp stood beside me. A young woman, robe-clad, arms raised as though emerging from the flowers.

I tugged my jacket from thorns while she considered me. Then lowered pale fingers, chose a fresh rose. I heard the stem *snap*. I blinked. These wisp-people were more than vapor? In proof, the white hand lifted the blossom. Offered it. Manners made me nod, accepting the gift. I took the flower, placed it within my collar. Fit token for Lalena, red as her lips.

The ghost-girl raised hands again. Closed pale eyes and shivered. I understood she burned in this pyre of roses, and must do so alone. I backed away, circling past all night-forms, seeking Howl.

He stood at the entrance to the castle. Beyond and within waited darkness, black as Stygian coal-cellars. He sniffed. "Some fool has put out the candles," he growled.

I menaced the dark with rapier and stern glare. "Ghosts or evil winds, no doubt. Best walk wary."

We continued on. The hall grew too dark even for my night-wise sight. Howl's eyes glimmered yellow. Must have returned to wolfish form. Very sensible. *The better to see you, my dear.* I walked in the dark beside a werewolf. A suicidal creature who'd tried to bite my throat out, twice in two days. Still, that was past. I tapped before me, rapier reduced to beggar's cane again.

I *supposed* Howl could see in this mirk. Till he stumbled into an ancient stand of armor, set the thing tumbling for a hail of tin pots on stone floor. I felt a certain satisfaction to hear his curses. At least we walked equally blind. Through halls of a haunted castle, granted.

"Damnation," he declared. "We need light. Well, I smell a burning candle. To the side hall. Doe's chamber, I think. Ah, you'd best wait here."

If he could see little better than I, he could still scent a path. I fingered my much-broken nose. What a gift, turning one's face to wolf-muzzle as needed. To wander the night knowing a reality hidden to uninitiates. Adding wolf ears, one could hear each thing creeping and breathing, tiptoeing, lurking. Excellent talent in the forests of war.

I reconsidered. The wolves in France had spied from hiding, hungry, wary and weary. Exactly as the soldiers running through the same forests and fields. No, life's gifts offered no security but to live with one's back to the wall, sword before one; waiting, watching.

So I put my back against the wall, rapier ready, waiting, watching. Howl's steps faded down a side-passage. I considered tiptoeing after him. But I bear more scars from friends in night-battle, than ever the enemy gave me. No, let the werewolf fetch light. I listened for the echo of music. I caught the faint sound of mice scrabbling. A muttering that might be wind, though I felt no motion of air.

The wraiths in the courtyard outside; could they follow? Perhaps they had. I might stand now in a sea of unseen spirits. Equally possible any moment of my life. Perhaps every dull day we slog through a crowd of the things. Why should it matter? Well, because now I had seen those gasping mouths, the egg-shell eyes. My life became strange of late. Who knew marriage could so change a man's world?

I cursed the idiot whim that tempted me to extinguish the candles. Whim, wine, and the desire to impress Chatterton's angel. Where had she gone? Had she led me to Howl for some divine purpose? To pull the boy from dark thoughts? But wings did not an angel make. Devils and sparrows had these appendages. Just as likely she'd sought to lure me into dark thoughts. If so, here I was. In the dark, thinking.

"No light," sighed Howl's voice beside me. I did not leap in alarm, nor strike in panic. A lesser spadassin would have done both. I merely nodded impressed. The man had come upon me soundless as thought. His words did not surprise. Of course we were doomed to clatter in comedy about castle halls, no doubt passing through horrors to freeze the blood, could one see them.

"Then we follow your nose to fire and mutton," I sighed to the unseen. With further consideration and a lick to lips I added, "And that hell-brew of intoxication your sea-cousins bottle."

"Why, this way then" he replied, and stepped away. Feet now loud upon the stones. How helpful. I stifled a shiver and followed, tapping before me with rapier. And now I did feel wind; a faint chill wafting. We made turns that confounded memory. What a warren was my wedding-present castle. I'd need a week to learn it. Which required I survive the week.

"I don't remember these stairs," I remarked, after some while.

"Hmm," replied my guide. He loped up steps as though four-footed. Likely enough he now so stood. I hurried after, disinclined to linger, sensing something wrong. Faint hairs brushed my face, I lashed out, grabbed sticky strands. Cobwebs.

"We can't have come this way," I observed, drawing knife with my free hand.

"No?" Howl replied, unconcerned.

"And I don't recall that smell," I added. Yet I did, from years past. A familiar stench, the very essence of the corpse-well.

"Smell?" The voice asked. Not really bothering to sound like Howl anymore. This tone came higher, lighter, all but breathless.

"I don't remember you being so taciturn, either."

"No?"

"Rayne?" called a distant voice echoing down the halls. Howl, of course.

It struck then. Pushing the rapier aside, wanting to grapple. But my left hand held knife ready; close and low. I stabbed upwards into something soft and wet as rotted fruit. We tumbled back, the thing falling upon me. A cold flabby creature with grappling hands of steel. But the fall drove the knife deeper. The thing gasped. I rolled, pushing it with both feet. The thing released my throat to gibber and thrash. I abandoned the knife, scrambled up, staggered away. It scrabbled after me. I heard no feet. It sounded to be wiggling. If I came to stairs I'd fall, break my neck. Preferable to re-encountering the creature. I crashed into a wall, put back to it, edged along the hall and away.

The handle of a door. I tugged it open, darted in, slammed it shut, pressing body and soul to keep it shut. I studied the wood grain of the door. Thick, age-blackened oak. Excellent. Webs of scratches across the surface, as if a host of weak fingers had sought to scratch their way out. Not quite so excellent.

I studied the scratches, realized I could see. The room behind must hold light. No sound beyond the door, nor within the room, save my panting breath. I readied myself to turn and face horrors. Well, I have faced horrors before. And overcome. Best get this new set faced and done.

Yes, best get this done, I reminded myself. A few more times. Then turned.

Behold a bedroom of faded silk. Heavy curtains, thick rugs, a great four-poster bed shrouded in hangings. All of it... *pink*. Bright light from a lamp on a tea-table glowed bright welcome. In a great pink chair sat a small pink child, clad in pink night-dress. She stared at me unblinking as a doll.

"Flower?" I almost asked. It seemed a smaller version of the tangle-haired waif I'd known in Londonish. But no, here was only family resemblance.

The doll-creature smiled, making a pleasant beginning. Still, I shivered. It disconcerted to encounter pink politeness in this castle of mad dark. No doubt she waited to catch me off guard. Then she'd exude tentacles, leap with razor teeth. I considered attacking first.

She climbed down from the chair, adjusted her dress. Turned head to the side, staring at me. Then curtsied. I blinked, considered what she welcomed. A man bursting into her chamber with mad face, rapier in hand. Gore-splashed from whatever still bled and wiggled outside.

Ah, well. She reminded so of Flower, we could not commence slaughterous. I sheathed sword, bowed to match the curtsy; and perhaps I caught a glance of surprise in the girl's features. If it was a girl. Arms and legs might pass for a child's. But the face seemed the flawless porcelain of a doll or statue. Excepting faint twitches to eyes and lips.

Amenities satisfied, she sat upon the floor at the head of the low table. Patted at a place beside her, where waited a dusty plate, a dusty cup. Now she spoke. A high girl's voice with neither hint nor shimmer of supernatural. For a moment I could not follow the words. Then understood.

"Voulez-vous une tasse de thé?" she inquired, lifting a porcelain pot near big as her head.

I listened for sound beyond the door. Nothing. I would confiscate the lamp, make my way back to the Great Hall. Back to fire and cheer, wine and mutton. If it hadn't all been consumed. A horrible thought. And yet, letting the thing beyond the door bleed awhile seemed good strategy. Therefore did the Seraph sit himself to tea and dust.

"Merci beaucoup," I responded. Difficult to sit at a child's table. Kneeling does not allow for sudden defense. Squatting is uncomfortable. I settled for tailor-fashion. Knees jutting out absurdly, compared to the compact form of the doll-child. An ancient wardrobe against the wall gave a view of my face in yellowed glass. Excellent, I could keep an eye behind as well.

I held out the dusty cup. The doll-child nodded, tipped the tea-pot spout over the rim. She waited a bit, then satisfied that I had a proper amount of conceptual tea, put down the pot.

Had I ever pretended so as a child? Not that I could recall; or believe. I'd gone from the woods of Maidenhead to the taverns of Londonish without attending a single play tea. I felt no loss. My childhood had been, in the main, glorious. I'd won all my fights, mastered Latin, charmed girls old as fourteen. Who needed play tea-parties?

The doll-child now proffered sugar-bowl and cream-pot. The bowl held tracery and lacery of cobweb within; centered with the mummy of some great Pharaoh of the Spiders. I tapped spoon to the web, emptied the fantasy sugar into my cup. But I declined the cream. It spoils the flavor of good tea.

Next came an empty pastry plate. "*Biscuit?*" offered my hostess. I considered the imaginary assortment, deciding on a sugar-cookie rather than the chocolate pastry. Not that either existed. But in the spirit of things I pictured the choices, hesitated, then placed mine beside the cup. Ears caught faint whispering of wind; yet I could see no movement in drapings nor bed curtains.

"Now let us enjoy pleasant conversation," declared the child grandly. *En Anglais*, marked with accent more of time than place. "Clearly you have been at adventures." The creature put china cup to porcelain lips, pretended to sip. "Do please share a bit of the tale."

105

I considered, taking a dusty sip. I knew from bitter experience: success at tea depends upon avoiding the *faux pas* of inappropriate topic. Nothing of politics or betrayals. Or beds. My sentencing to hang? Anti-climactic, I'd escaped. Perhaps the fight with pirate mummers upon a bridge? But no, the Harlequins were probably cousins to this waif. Avoid family quarrels.

I wondered if Lalena had yet noted my absence from her family clatter of clan-politics. By now she must have reached for my hand, touched emptiness instead of love. She'd look about in alarm. *Ha*. Served her right.

"I find myself recently married," I declared. "A strange adventure, that. Can you imagine beginning to learn to know someone only after you have pledged them all your life and heart?"

The doll-child considered this question, taking a bite of her imagined pastry. Shook pale doll locks, as if the business threw her. As it should, she being child. I wiped a bit of imaginary crumb from my lip.

"She and I are two nations deciding our borders. Just preparing for bed takes compromise and diplomacy. We have entirely different sleeping habits. Lalena's vampiric, I'm a spadassin. *She* always slept by day, *I* always slept sword at hand. But doing so now would seem I lack faith that she will not bite my throat away. As she so loves me, she struggles to sleep by night, while I lay me down weaponless." I shook my head. "We both toss and turn."

Granted, that was not all we did in bed. Definitely an inappropriate topic at tea. I reached for another sugar-cookie. Was that rude? They were imaginary, surely then, enough for all. While the doll-child considered my words. At length she leaned close, whispered her thoughts. "You are a rather unusual visitor," she confided.

I sighed. I never sail the tempest of tea without foundering upon some reef of polite conversation. Aldermen's wives, majester's mothers, the occasional duchess and such. They raise and lower eyebrows in semaphore signals: *barbarian on the couch*. Probably I'd violated order and rules again. The business always confounded my colonial soul. *This* pastry only, with *that* delicacy only, in *this* sequence only. *Bah.*

No doubt sitting to tea while spattered with the blood of a night-haunt counted for another *faux pas*. I checked the mirror. The wardrobe glass shone yellow as parchment from long years loyally serving light. It seemed to ripple, water-like. No, like a pond surface beneath which fish-schools swarm. I studied it, pretending to munch another sugar cookie.

Ghost faces pressed against the glass. Well, *that* made little surprise. Only these wraiths hammered shadow fists impotently, sealed safe behind reflection. They stared at me mouthing shouts, moans and warnings. I continued to munch the sugar cookie. It'd leave a white snow frosting on my mustache.

"*Moi*, I have never married," lamented my hostess. A child's imitation of adult ennui. So similar to Flower's grandiose declarations. She stirred the dust of her tea-cup with a blackened moon-sliver of silver spoon. "But I have my gentlemen courtiers. Those that enter from time to time. Quite different from you. So dull! They never want to talk of life and art. They just demand to be let out."

A cut-glass vase centered the table. From it poked a skeleton of a stem. I reached to it, fingered the thorn. It fell to dust. A long time past, that blossom's spring. Time to leave myself. I finished my sugar cookie, drained the tea cup, feeling refreshed. I stood.

"They sound total bores," I sympathized. "But I promise to visit again." I followed that with a bow. "I shall regale you with tales of marriage to curdle the blood and open wide your porcelain eyes. But now I must be off."

The doll-child smiled, sipped tea, shook head. She did not bother to rise. "Oh no, *monsieur*. You cannot leave. We have hours and days and weeks to finish our tea."

The creatures in the mirror covered faces with hands, hiding their eyes but not their despair. I turned towards the door, expecting to find it gone. There would be blank wall, as in a dream just edging into nightmare. But no, the door remained.

"It will not open, *monsieur*," the pink-child assured me. "This is my chamber, you are my guest. Only the master of the castle may dispute my right, and the last long departed to dust and roses. You shall stay, as all my visitors do. But you must go into the mirror only when you grow wearisome. More tea?"

I strode to the door, reached, pulled. Against all expectation of nightmare premonition, the door opened as any door. Neither locked, nor magically sealed. I turned to the girl, showing a politely quizzical look. Inwardly I rejoiced. The doll-girl swore, not at all lady-like. Her turn to make a *faux pas*.

"*Mierde*. How?" She jumped up. Her movement fast, fluid, yet failing full humanity. She was a puppet-creature, animated by something else. Just as well, not to know what.

How indeed? I wondered. A thought occurred. At my belt hung the ring of iron keys, gift from out the sea. The answer, obviously. "I find myself the master of the castle," I explained, jangling these tokens. "A wedding present. Not the usual silverware set."

She crossed arms, stamped foot. Turned away. The faces in the mirror pressed to the glass astonished. I backed towards the door, ready to flee this pink damnation. Gave a last look at the doll-child, lest she follow.

But no, she stood forlorn, arms hanging down, hair hanging down. Gaze to the dusty tea table. She looked so like Lalena, and also Flower. Family for sure. Creatures apart, incomprehensible in their sorrows and joys and mysteries; yet not unappreciable. What a lonely child's mind was this pink cell. I felt for the rose in the tuck of my collar. I stepped to the tea table, placed the stem in the cut crystal vase. There it glowed red as Lalena's lips.

The doll-creature stared wide-eyed; at it, at me, at it. "Oh," she said at last, holding a hand over the bloom to feel its scarlet fire. I gave a final nod. She hesitated, looked to me; then curtsied again. I returned to the dark hall, rapier ready.

Chapter 11
The World is Made of Faces

The door slammed shut behind. Was not me that closed it, I needed the light. Now I stood dark-drowning again. I tugged the handle. Pointless formality, naught budged. It might have been a door painted onto stone. Perhaps it was. And the mad pink bed-chamber beyond? Mere delirium. This castle was the demesne of people who walked in dream as much as life. Who knew which door opened to what reality? Not I.

Doubtless the castle held stairways to airy voids where dreams completed the architecture. Those of the family danced on faery floor, while my heavier race plummeted screaming to the familiar dirt. Yes, and there would be hallways ending at blank walls, confounding dullards to pass. The true-blooded would march into bright chambers, chatting with kindred ghosts and shadows. Here and there would be frames of window my mortal eye judged blank brick. But the Folk would stare beyond, beholding forest and field where fox-cubs and unicorns gamboled.

I had rushed my mortal clay from the right, leaving behind a monster half-gutted. Thus the left way now appealed, whether it led to dream, void or brick wall. Go left, then, man. Else wait here for dawn. I felt drafts. A window must be hereabouts… But no. Linger here and morning light would reveal a white-haired creature huddled into a ball, gibbering of horrors, tea and walls.

I went left, tapping with the blade. Once I struck something that rang a silvery chime; one spine-shivering, eerie note. A great glass gong, I imagined. Or a shield all of crystal, part of a set of magic armor. The sword would be an icicle wonder. I did not investigate. Next I tapped something that snarled, ran with claws skittering stone and wood. It cursed at me in chitters.

At some turn of hall I began to suspect someone walked beside me. I wondered, doubted, at last reached conclusion. Yes. Someone walked beside me. Not the conclusion I wished. But the admission made the presence obvious. As if acknowledging '*you exist*' thereby summoned them from the night-sea of possibilities. Now I felt a flow of air, heard a sigh of breath, the faint click of heel on stone. One more companion on the dark road.

"In all truth," I sighed to my mysterious companion, "either this castle is vast as the Great Cathedral or I wander in circles."

The unseen personage sniffed, then spoke.

"Truth?" he intoned. "Nowadays, one *declares* truths. We carry them in our mouths as squirrels with nuts. Else we print them. A clatter of paper and ink, and behold! A captured Truth. Matters naught whether hard truth or simple fact. The paper weighs the same. A boy waves the boulder 'Life is hard' above his head. While a grown man struggles to lift the sand-grain fact that his mirror shows a fool."

Ah, I knew this voice, this academic declamation. Lalena's uncle, the Birdman. The very patriarch who gifted us this castle. No doubt he held thumbs behind lapels of his frock coat now, instructing dust and dark to their edification. I shuddered. I knew that next he would inform of how things were done right, in *his day*.

"But in my day, sir, reality ran as intended. Truth bore weight and mass. An absolute law of conservation required one expend units of energy in proportion to the weight of fact affirmed. '*Two plus two equals four*'? A pebble of a fact for a child to pond-toss, learning from the ripples. As we grew we learned to lift heavier affirmations. At manhood we hefted '*Life is hard*' upon our shoulders, and set off down the road. Nothing was more comic than to pass some adolescent attempting to shift the mountain-boulder '*We can know nothing*.'"

I stopped. I halted there and then in open rebellion against lunatics expounding their particular mania to the unseen moon. Then, there unto forever I swore eternal loyalty to the race of dull humanity who talked of beer and crops and weather, using small words, simple sentences.

"Speaking of knowledge and nothingness, do you know the way back to the Great Hall?" I demanded.

"No idea," admitted the Birdman. "I am forever getting lost in this labyrinth. They say the pattern shifts like thought, so that one can never know it."

"Of course," I spat. "A maze of monsters. And we trapped blind within."

"Hardly trapped," scoffed the man. "Dawn's gaze shall peek through various windows within the hour. Until then we are free to walk as we wish. Company me, if you would be kind." With that his footsteps continued onwards.

My holy oath of rebellion required I cross arms and stand an iron pillar in the dark. I renounced this idiot vow, hurried after the *click, click* of boot-heels. If he did not know his path, the man walked with suspicious confidence. Soon he halted, there came a creek of hinges and a weak wash of light.

"You've seen over-much dark of the family," said the Birdman. "I would not have you think us a cabal of mere madmen and monsters. There is great potential for joy, for love, for light in the hearts of those whose lives you have joined. This is the gallery. Here, one can see a bit of their promise."

I stepped through the door, wary of the next ambush. Found myself in a wide long hall. I breathed air cold and clear, free of castle dust and decay. One side held glazed windows stretching from floor to ceiling. I rushed towards this light as a starved man would charge a banquet table.

Through thick, rippling panels of glass I beheld the small valley beyond the walls. Past that, a line of dark sea. We must be high up in the castle. Sun not yet visible; but the promise of dawn gave the room illumination, so that when I turned I gasped.

For a long while I wandered the gallery gazing, wondering. Sometime laughing. Other-times I circled wary of what I beheld, careful to examine all angles. Just once I reached a hand out, daring to touch a face. A face I knew right well, and had begun to love. At some point I turned to the Birdman to express my amaze, even my joy. As per the tradition of mysterious companions, he had vanished.

* * *

"You've no idea," I told Mattie Horse. We sat to table in the Great Hall while I sipped hot coffee, chewed cold mutton. "It's a treasure-chamber. Paintings and statues, sculptures and etchings, creations of gold, silver and bronze; of glass, of wood, of paper. Faces, mostly. At least the faces were what you noticed. Each showed a real person, you felt. Not just random shape of eye or nose or mouth. Not just an ideal. These were people you knew lived once, breathed once."

Mattie Horse yawned, scratched, rolled eyes to show he lived now, breathed now. I considered him turned to glorious statue, perhaps of bronze. He'd appear far more noble as a representation of himself than he ever would being himself. The idea made me laugh, which made him scowl.

I shook with relief, with laughter, with hunger. Knew I babbled. Didn't care. "There was an old stone creature, all wrinkles and sags and little-lady bones but she was beautiful. Laughing." I tried not to talk mouth full, but I had returned to the Hall famished for food, drink and sanity. "Laughing at Time. I don't mean *'at times'*, I mean she was laughing at years and decades. *That* kind of time."

Lalena perched on the arm of my chair, hand brushing my hair back and forth, forth and back. I can't recall anyone ever doing that before. I felt like a cat, petted. Excellent feeling. I'd always wondered what it felt like to be a cat. Contrasting to my babble, she wore her silent mood. I knew better than to draw her out. She knew better than to fuss upon my return. See how fast we learned?

"Surely all the faces were of your family," I informed them. Sip, chew. "I saw bits and pieces of all you lot, your cousins and clans. How can there be such a resemblance across such diverse peoples? It goes past noses and chins. But a copper shield had Vixen's face. Ha, they'd given her snakes for hair but that was her down to the sly." I didn't mention the statue so resembling Lalena. Marble pale as her skin, almost.

I struggled to eat, drink and describe wonders all. Tangled the struggle. I thrummed dizzy with hunger, with exhaustion, with elation to be free of the dark halls.

116

"There was a great winged woman carved out of black stone. It was Chatterton's angel, down to the sarcastic eyebrows. She must be family after all." I looked for cousin Chat in the rafters. Gone. Dawn had chivied the revelers to beds and blankets. About us lay the battle-debris of bottles, plates and ghost-smoke smell of vanquished feast. Or had the feast proved the victor?

Billie River lay across the far end of the table, a girl in seal-skin curled beside him. Master Bellow slumped in the throne at the table-head, someone's scarf draped across his ox's face. It puffed out, in, out with his tidal snores. Howl and Doe traded earnest whispers at mid-table. Howl raising hands to express '*well what about*'? Doe tipping head, expressing '*on the other hand*'.

I sipped coffee so hot it blistered tongue, burned gullet. Excellent, exactly as coffee should. "Say, who is Fulgurous, anyway?" I asked.

Lalena's hand ceased petting. Mattie Horse twitched. Farther down the table Doe and Howl turned to study the innocent who wandered into their dark forest. Finally Mattie Horse shrugged, snatched for some of my breakfast as salary for reply.

"Ach, he is the bug-bear of the family. Long ago he'd pop up a'times, ensure all behaved in accord with the rules. As if anyone knew what the blazes these rules were. The old ones were always for keeping things unsaid."

Mattie reached out, seized a bottle still splashing in the bottom. Sea-folk wine. I prepared to rescue it. Too

117

late, he saw my intent, put it to lips, consumed, curse him. Then continued.

"Fulgurous is recalled for a wee problem with temper. Ah, the Rivalry drove him to fury. When he came upon the clans blood-dueling here in the Gathering Place itself, bodies of our kindred cast like emptied cups, why he banished the whole family from his cold stone Eden. He could do it, too. Was the last master of all the clans. They say he could toss lightning about easy as hay-stalks."

Mattie grinned to say *he doubted such*. The lady of the clan began tapping fingers on the chair. I pushed my head against her arm in hope she'd pet some more, but no. Mattie sipped sea-wine, continued.

"The banishing were little loss, most thought. The world is wide for gathering, whether to duel or dance. But the madness spread like pox when summer heat ripples air. The folly took entire clans. The Blades, the Harlequins, the Scribes. Ah, the clan of the Dawn. You couldn't fathom their minds or hearts anymore. Couldn't find them in dream or valley, road or revel. Other tribes hid, or grew so strange we'd not know their faces if we met by the fireside. Some say that madness was Fulgurous's curse. But such was never the way of those old ones. No, they preferred to let man or clan follow a path over the cliff; and then show up at the funeral with nose high to say '*told ye so*'."

Lalena hissed something fast and angry, in Gaelic. Doubtless some Gael variation of '*Shut your fool mouth.*'

Mattie Horse shrugged. "Ha, the old grump's dust and ash centuries past." This affirmation did not keep him from glancing about. No antique busybodies threatened. Mattie finished *my* sea-wine, wiped lips. "My Da's da said he looked as a man with face all black-burnt by fire and smoke."

I considered, recalled. "Kind of bent-shouldered? As if at some bench-work all night, every night for years? Angry amber eyes, and holding a hammer?"

Mattie bent forwards coughing sea-wine. Served him right. Lalena stood, whispering curse or prayer. Farther down, Doe and Howl stared owl-eyed. I laughed. Astonishing the family was always a moment to cherish. But I raised hands to reveal them empty of omen, holding only knife and mutton.

"Relax, good people. Just a statue in the corner of the gallery. Lifelike enough. Sitting in a heavy chair." I tried to recall. "Leaning forwards, as if about to stand." In fury, I recalled but did not add. The artist had caught a king or judge rising in rage. Eyes glowing an angry amber by dawn's rays. Best not mention this.

Mattie shook head. Lalena shook head. Doe, Howl: shook heads. Fretting silence followed. Mutterings between cousins. No business of mine, I decided. Nor worry of mine. I finished breakfast, digestion not a bit spoiled by ancient family bug-bears. I felt full and sleepy. Dawn light through the high windows turned all the night's deadly shadows to comfortable friends.

119

"Just a statue," I repeated. "Painted wood. No more alive than the rest of the stone and lumber."

Mattie Horse sighed into the empty bottle. With a great patience he sealed the cork, placed this bottled breath upon the table. Considered this captured lament in solemn meditation. "None of the family would be so daft, Master Gray. Make a statue of Fulgurous? Man, it's not thinkable."

I rose. Family politics, art and legend were for family. I turned to Lalena.

"This castle fast bests me. I require a guide to my bed. My wide, warm bed." I reached hand out to her. She smiled. She would have reached to clasp mine in return, but for the sudden knocking upon the castle doors.

Chapter 12
On the Biting of Thumbs

Polite of them to knock, but they did not wait upon our welcome. No, the wings of the castle door slammed open with a boom echoing for cannon-fire. The revealed entrance showed no happy sea-folk bearing gifts. Instead there stood a wolf.

A wolf of sorts. It had the form correct. The hunched, muscled shoulders. Black-lined eyes of wary violence. Long graceful legs, the fur thick about throat. An ivory-toothed trap for jaws, red tongue hanging for a banner.

But no real wolf loomed so large. It filled the castle doorway, casting shadow into the hall; casting fear. It knew it so, and grinned. Behind stood a troop of similar sorts. Wolves and bears, a great boar near high as the wolf. A tiger-man who walked upright, a great two-handed blade strapped to back. Impressive, for all that a sword is simply not a tiger's weapon.

In strode the wolf. Approaching, he changed. With every step he dropped some part of *Beast*, donned some feature of *Man*. Half across the hall he reared up on two legs. By the time he stopped before Lalena, he stood a man caped in wolf-skin, rough cut for kilt.

As wolf he stirred spine and gut to fear. So too as man. Tall as I, broader of chest, with narrow waste. Scars across face, across hands, across neck. A fighter for sure.

Howl's boast of his father came to mind: *the most frightful man in the world, the most terrifying being born.* I studied him, and in return he ignored me. I took no offense. I delight in being ignored by those I may need to kill.

He bowed to the lady of Clan Mac Sanglair. Rough, yet not entirely mocking. "Shall we speak first?" he asked. Voice of a gentleman-wolf, low and rasping.

Lalena tilted head back. Face pale, eyes black. Teeth white and long. But a minute before, her tell-tale hair had hinted pleasant possibilities of bed-room tangle. Now each strand lined itself with neighbor, forming an ordered warp of blond.

Laughter from the railing above. I turned to see. Yes, more in the gallery about the hall. Entered my castle without notice? Annoying. Past time to post pickets. Behind me I heard Bellow stumble to rise, cursing. The sea-girl remained curled on the table, snoring oblivious. Doe, Howl and Billy River stood back to back. Around them circled various clan-cousins. At another time these fool creatures would be embracing, wet-eyed with affection as they recalled past dances, common great aunts. Now they traded glares, claws out, pride and rivalry to the fore. The Tiger began an ostentatious cleaning of his claws.

I considered drawing, confronting. Standing with my in-laws. But no. My wife is an excellent dancer. These were her kindred. Let her set the tempo.

"Greetings, Laird of the Mac Tier" said Lalena. She considered, added politely, "If you wish, *you* may speak." At which grant of permission the Wolf-intruder grinned. At which words, I laughed. That earned me a surprised look from some of the newcomers. Not a glance from the Wolf.

"I seek my stray lambs," he said, waving a hand towards Doe and Howl. "I also require their foxy little leader." He looked about the hall in thought. "But perhaps I shall bide awhile. Is this not the Hall of Gathering? And we are all family, are we not?" At last he tossed my beggar-self the crumb of a glance. His eye measured my soul, breeding, manners and potential threat. The measure found naught. He shrugged. "All that matter, 'tis to say."

I looked to Howl and Doe. Howl stared in fright at his Da, face rippling to muzzle, returning to human, back and forth fast as the panting of one running for his life. But there was anger there as well. I marked it. Part of a spadassin's job. The man's huge shoulders and arms tensed, impatient. They wanted to strike, for all the fear deviling the mind above. A good sign. The Doe threw back graceful head, took some form of deer. Stood ready so, to fight or flee.

Billy River stood beside them both, in pose of stillness, head tilted, watching all. Had I come across him so in a crowded tavern I'd draw knife not waiting upon ceremony. That man stood ready to kill.

123

More of the Mac Tier entered the hall. Clever, to come in waves. Let the first establish position, access danger, engage opposition in talk. In these newcomers I beheld normal-seeming men and women, some in kilt, some in dress. But closer exam remarked on animal ears, tilts to eyes, sculpt of teeth that mortal clay never shaped.

Ah, they were a wonder. To describe their march through the castle door challenges words to capture the truth of grace and confidence, of mocking threat and solemn step. Each Mac Tier walked clad in dream of animal shadow, animal spirit, animal form. Pity that most showed the same sharp point of tooth, slant of eye. Twitching predators, sidling sly. Did none ever seek a peaceful form? A man with art to reshape his being to rabbit or goat would be no less a man; nor any less a miracle than wolf or tiger. And he might well be the wiser for it. There is plenteous wisdom in rabbit-kind. And the average goat? A mad genius.

Ten invaders at least in the gallery above, some thirty now in the hall. We made eight defenders; with some fifteen farther within the castle-maze. Not counting any sea-folk remaining. If any did, I wondered would they side, or flee. I watched the Mac Tier take positions by the farther doors. Their chief had gauged our numbers, knowing the main of the vampiric clan slept the day. Ah, they had thought this out.

Seemingly he thought it safe to defy Lalena. Seemingly, Lalena paid no heed. She but smiled upon the

Mac Tier chieftain, if perhaps overlong. When at last she replied it came in tone of flat courtesy. A paper greeting, cursive ink writ red.

"Indeed this is the Hall of Gathering, Laird of the Mac Tier, and all your blood is welcome." Which point of subtle knife forced a grin from the man. Lalena continued, "But know, this holding is now in the keeping of the Mac Sanglair. If all are welcome, none enter but we first open the door."

Mac Tier shook head sadly. It sorrowed him to disagree. "The sun is up, milady, and you should lie fast in dark and dream. Go, and sleep. With your wits night-freshened you shall recall these walls stand banned to all our blood, equally and forever. No sweet uncle may make of it a present for a favored child. When the dragon cast keys to the sea, an end was made to any here except in defiance of his dead fire."

Why this speech? Every motion of the man shouted hunger to become wolf, rending flesh and ripping throats. Surely the curse of the hall itself held him back, for all his disdain of dead fire. Yet he provoked Lalena… Romeo and Juliet came to mind: two houses at war, each forbidden to make the *first* strike.

Do you bite your thumb at us, sir?

Is the law of our side, if I say aye?

No.

No, sir, I do not bite my thumb at you, sir, but I bite my thumb, sir.

"I am sorry to hear you speak so, cousin," sighed Lalena. "Billy River, go and fetch Mistress Fox. Explain her father awaits in the hall."

This acquiescence surprised the Mac Tier as much as Billy River. The blond vampiric hesitated, then nodded, shoved past the tiger-man. But Laird Mac Tier held long arm out to bar the way.

"I would not see the hall overcrowded, young Aibne Mathew," he advised. "Fetch none but the Vixen. All others I shall count as foe, and treat as such."

Blond Billy River stood before the man. Face now pale as corpse in snow; but not with fear. It startled me, grown used to his cheerful ease. That was cold rage or I was a rabbit. Billie did not bother with the trash of traded glares, threatening smiles. He turned night-blackened eyes to his clan's lady, waiting her decision. I shivered, fresh realizing how casual I'd become with creatures more deadly than those of war, night-alley and nightmare. I saw the wiser of the Mac Tier eye the castle door. Not their Laird; he but turned to Lalena.

Again the lady of the clan spoke, in words of chill peace. "Certainly that is for the best. Billy River, by the honor of the Mac Sanglair see you neither wake any, nor give word to any. Go only to Vixen; return only with Vixen."

These meek words erupted a shout from Laird Mac Tier. "A keeper of peace has come to the Mac Sanglair!"

126

He stamped a foot. "There's hope for an honest world yet. Nephew Stripes, I would have you behold some of the wonder of your family's heritage. Do ye company Cousin Billy."

The Tiger-man made a sound; whether growl, laugh or both. He hurried to match Billy River, who neither turned nor slowed. The two exited, stage left.

I recalled Vixen's childish grin as I'd hung from the chandelier. Her solemn grief kneeling before the grave of her kindred. A creature of parts, making no whole I would ever fathom. As were all the family. But one did not need comprehend to appreciate. Surrender that mad fox-child to this posturing, posing, slavering, mocking, bullying beast? Never.

I opened mouth to call Billy River back, readying words to argue and defy. Again I hesitated. How could Lalena stand so cool before such affront? Because she had duty to her people. What right did outsider have to interfere? The Laird of the Mac Tier came to collect his own. Who knew these creatures well enow to say it were not best to yield?

Not I. Was it possible to truly know any in this family? Perhaps not, whispered my heart's despair. Behold the reason they eschewed exact naming. They were actors. I'd sat in my theatre seat giving my heart to the stage's *Lonely Vampire Princess*. How well she'd delivered her lines, depicting at times the moon-mad maiden, then the queenly statue, and my favorite role, the love-besotted wife. I knew all these parts. But the actress depicting them, bereft of costume and script? Why, I might not know her if we met on the street.

Despairing, I appealed to Lalena's hair. But every last strand hung straight, in sign of cool and ordered thought. She would act here in accord with reason, with policy. Surrendering her cousins to this beast. My role merely to glower at stage's edge, the outsider disapproving for lack of comprehension.

But I looked twice, as soldier must. And noted how a ripple stirred Lalena's locks, regular as heart-beat. Behold the wave of a wind belonging to my wife alone. Her face gone salt-white as Billy River's, with same cause. Eyes black as holes to the outer dark where demons beg not be cast. I shivered to see it, and I smiled, and do not confess in shame. For I am a killer, if a kindly one. And I knew that my new wife stood enraged as I had never beheld her. That was storm-wind rippling her hair. Again I laughed.

"Your pet finds our family amusing, milady," noted the Laird Mac Tier. He rummaged among bottles and debris, shaking head at memories of feasts past. He found a bottle I'd overlooked, sighed in satisfaction. "Past time you ate him. We've brought you fresh drink in the ship, as present for our honored sept Sanglair."

Dead silence in the hall. I exchanged looks with Mattie Horse, who had maneuvered to stand by Master Bellow. The cut I'd given the ox-man ran a livid slant across his face. His fists clenched, grasped, clenched, in fear or anger. Mattie Horse shook his head at me, but what he meant I could not say. *Bide patient*, surely. The Laird Mac Tier poured himself a casual cup, center of all attention. Even with this lordly bore of self-assurance, it must be *family theatre*. But he only held cup, did not drink. Ah, he was not so sure as he pretended.

"What mean you, Cousin?" asked Lalena, voice soft. "What drink do you bring?"

The Laird of the Mac Tier sloshed the sea-wine in circles, sniffed the bouquet. "Times change, milady. For proof of which we stand pleasantly conversing where once lightening forbade." Sniff of wine, delivery of line. "The coming age is a prize for those with strength to seize and hold. We of the family, such as the Mac Tier and the Sanglair, have that strength."

I looked about for Green and Black to leap from shadows, periwigs set, speech-notes readied. Then Dealer would descend *deus ex machina* from the rafters, speaking of the glorious future of Art. Even the Abomination would rise up from the stones, prepared to offer eldritch rebuttal. Then we would all pound fists, paws and tentacles upon the table debating Rousseau, Luther and *The Wealth of Nations*.

The Mac Tier tipped his full wine-cup upon the floor, deciding the drink not worth joining his gullet. I decided to kill him then. He continued unaware of this sentence of death, studying the puddle of spilt red.

129

"*Ach*, we clear the common clay from our lands. As they do as well, the kinless fools. Two-legged sheep have grown worthless these past years. In place of their dirty crofts and faces I bring in four-legged mutton. A laird can profit upon such. And we build mills, for why should I send my wool to another man's profit?"

He stamped careful foot into the wasted wine. It splashed a bloody way. I recalled the kin-strife for which the family was castle-banned. Surely he recalled it as well, for he snarled, held back by restraint he cursed. This brute still feared the shadow of Fulgurous. Only for that *dead fire* did he talk and declaim now, instead of kill.

Talked. "I would bring together all our kindred we judge of worth. Mac Tier and Sanglair, Scalen and Mac Mur, clans of mountains and woods, even those fool Decourseys. Reunited we shall be strong and clean again, the madness lifted from our hearts. We shall form a nation that no longer wanders the world, but owns it."

Lalena nodded, repeated her question. "What gift is in your ship, cousin?"

The Laird Mac Tier grinned. "Drink for the Sanglair, as I said. Some of the human cattle I'd have elsewise kicked towards colonies or the cities."

"Ah," said Lalena. She spoke soft. "Ah," she said again, as if she could think of naught else to say. The Mac Tier tensed, shifted balance. He knew his proud cousins. Knew he'd insulted. If he did not dare attack first, he sought to goad the Mac Sanglair to so do. And so avoid

130

the wrath of ancient curse. And if Lalena held meek peace? Why, to such as him that counted for victory.

The family might be mystery, but for the moment I knew this man. To his son Howl, he ranked Most Fearsome Creature in Existence. To me, he summed to every market duelist and tavern bully I'd kicked and sliced to perdition. I saw he would kill as he pleased, once Lalena attacked. More, *I saw what he intended if she did not.*

Ah, I knew the man. But did I know my wife? I felt her anger, as heat from fire. If she yielded to rage we would die. Gloriously, no doubt, but still. Should I go to her? Calm her with words and whispers? No need. The lady stood cold stone. Like to the one in the Gallery of Faces. Only her face shewed now more stone than that I'd touched.

The Mac Tier and the surrounding cousins watched, and she did not reply; nor leap for throats. She merely stood quietly. Hair rippling, the banner of an army told *hold position.* Ah, that settled it. I turned slightly, looking sadly at the rafters; hand drawing knife. The great beast-man sighed, put cup down in disappointment. He shook head for the sorrows of the world. I gazed up where late the sweet aberration sang, knowing the coming bit of music before fiddle-bow ever touched string.

The Laird Mac Tier dared not shed blood in this hall? Not quite. He could not shed *family* blood. One bottle upon the shelf stood proudly *vin ordinaire.* Mine. And so he smiled, nodded, and leaped to spill it.

131

Chapter 13
On the Love of Death and Kindred

He was man when he leapt. He was wolf when he
landed. I'd not have credited the tale had another's eyes
seen, another tongue told. A mere blink to transform
body and mind? These creatures had not mastered the
spirit of animals, but the magic of dreams. I considered
that truth as I stepped aside, master of my feet.

Ah, that caught him unaware. He'd thought the
rabbit sleeping. He crashed where I'd stood, and now my
turn to leap. Had he been no larger than real wolf, this
would have failed, but he stood near great as a horse.
Excellent. Who has never wanted to ride a wolf?

Upon his back, knees kept me in place surely as upon
any battle-frighted horse. One hand grasped the thick fur
about his throat. Firmly astride, I slashed knife behind the
right front leg, seeking sinew. He howled, near buckled.
The strength of those shoulders terrified. He lashed his
head about, and if he had struck my arm he'd have
broken bone, sure as his muzzle were iron club.

I targeted an ear, it being in my face. It fell to the
scythe and the creature leaped full five ells in the air, near
putting me in the chandeliers again. We came down and
the knife cut him across the right eye. By accident, I
confess. Almost was *my* eye.

I could not tell what the rest of the hall thought,
though I heard sound and shout enough. We whirled to

perform all a night's dancing in a minute. Unable to reach me with those massive jaws, the wolf now sought to shake me off. One has horses try the same. Amidst the scream and smoke of war, I add.

Next it tried rolling the monkey from his back. A dangerous move for wolf and ape alike. He crushed me but drove my knife deep beside the spine. Agony brought him upright once more, trembling and bleeding. The Laird of the Mac Tier decided he'd be man again. The creature began to shift bone and muscle till I pressed knife hard to throat.

I whispered in the remaining ear. "Stay wolf, Mac Tier. I will kill you else."

At that he shivered, stayed beast. I kept low above his shoulders, Knife-blade within thick fur I hoped hid jugular. Fool. If he'd thought as a man, he'd have dashed among his own, tumbling and mixing till they ripped me to pieces. But as with Howl, the form of wolf made him think as wolf.

So he thrashed, snapping jaws useless as Howl against the Abomination. I cast a quick gaze upon the room. Not yet in open battle? Excellent. The entertainment of me riding the wild wolf, full consumed all eyes and minds. I'd liked to have seen it myself.

I had knife ready to kill. If killing were to be done, best done quick. But likely that act would end with all the Moon Tartan falling upon me, then the Mac Sanglair

134

falling upon them. War and death would half-spoil my honeymoon. Could I bargain with this creature?

It trembled, wounded and enraged, growling, snapping the air. Foam of rage dripping from muzzle. Clear enough. No bargain. Not with *it*. But perhaps with the son.

"Master Howl," I called out. "Have you a stick? Here's a dog in need of beating."

No answer. Well, let him consider his answer. As likely come to his da's aid as mine. No doubt Howl loved this bullying beast, as he hated and feared. But if I do not know wolves or wives, a spadassin know what moves a man to *violence*. I counted that Howl hated most, the fear he felt for his father.

Snarl from the wolf beneath the monkey. Words within the beastly growl. "I will kill you for this."

"You were going to kill me anyway, you tedious fool," I noted. My concern no longer with him, but his kin. Some of the folk of the Moon Tartan now circled warily, ready to aid their chieftain. A Jackal-headed man looked ready to leap. I shook my head, pressed knife into the Wolf-Laird's throat till the beast gave a growl perilously near whimper. The approaching people of the Moon Tartan slowed, faces shifting in and out of humanity. A dream throng, where nothing need be what it was the second before.

The Jackal-head spat. "Fulgurous's curse shall fall upon the Sanglair, if you dare strike our laird," he declared.

And now at last Lalena gave over being statue, and turned living flesh, moving quick as thought. No, quicker. Thought is often rather slow. Whereas she suddenly stood before the man-beast, lifting him by throat. He gurgled, flailed arms. Then she threw him over the crowd to land with crash by the hearth. Her hair whipped in twists of fury. No restraint now, only the blood-lust of the children of the *cold brides*.

She turned upon the crowd, putting hands to dress. She prepared to rip it away. *'Do you know how awful it feels to stand in clothes dripping with blood?'* Lalena once asked. When we courted, so to speak. She turned eyes upon the crowd, and they stumbled back, because those eyes shone as windows to a madhouse in Hell. Mouth wide open, a furnace of white teeth burning with red delight. The Mac Tier cursed, retreated, shivered to animal form. They knew right well what their cousin's mad fury foretold.

But then Lalena stopped herself, shook herself. She looked about the hall, fresh seeing where she stood. Not in night's dark, but in a beam of morning sun through narrow windows. She faced kindred, not foes; faces like to hers, hearts like to hers. And so my *warm bride* took deep breath and settled her hair. An act of self-command astonishing as turning oneself to beast or butterfly. I longed to go to her then, tell the clans to dance their

136

quarrel in other seas. Leave us to continue our honeymoon, our time of introduction of self to self, body to body.

When at last she spoke, it came in tones firm and sane, the lady of clan Mac Sanglair, daughter of a magic and perilous folk.

"My man is not our blood, else your dog had never dared bite. No curse nor ban applies should Master Gray now cut the cur's throat in return. Your laird's life is ours to spill or spare."

Excellent words. I jabbed knife in wolf-flesh, giving emphasis to their expression. The wolf growled, snapped, but could not dispute the point. So to speak.

In dramatic thunder, a chair smashed down upon the table. The audience jumped, turned. For they were audience, make no mistake. Here was no battle twixt proper armies set in ordered rows for homicide. No, this was family quarrel and entertainment. Each individual present sought to savor the full tangle of hate and rivalry; yes and love and admiration, that set them to shouts, shoves and wary glances.

I alone stood outside the tangled concerns of their hearts. For which reason their eyes judged me more a puzzle than any Abomination up from the floor.

And who broke property of my castle? Ah, Master Howl, who now seized a great chair-leg of oak for a club. He hefted this, weighing whether the tool would serve. His face made no shift toward beast-hood to hide the determination of a man. Bludgeon in hand, he strode on two legs confident as his father had marched on four. He pushed cousins aside, tossing his great mane of black hair, a match to that I yet grasped.

Young Master Howl stood before his father, studying the bloody beast and the bloody lunatic upon its back, and then nodded as if to say '*well then*'. I took this for sign he meant to deal with family concerns, no business of mine. As outsider, it were impolite to remain further *en scène*.

Therefore did I leap from the wolf's back, as surprised to be alive as ever I stood after battle. I staggered, all but fell, strength spent. Trembled bruised and bleeding. When had I taken this rip across the thigh? A glancing slash of fang, no doubt. A straight bite would have taken the leg. It burned. Perhaps I'd turn mad dog now. I had a vision of myself upon all fours like Nebuchadnezzar, growling and barking, chasing the Mac Tier about the Gathering Hall. I laughed, and then beheld a crowd of beast-people eyeing me. Backing frighted as if I were, well, a mad dog.

I looked to the wolf, who stood no better. He dripped from a slashed eye, a missing ear. Throat and back hacked and bloody, right leg lame. Not the proud creature whose shadow had late frightened the hall. Still he turned open jaws to me, promising death. I winked one eye, as I still had two. In reply he gathered himself to leap and rend. I sought footing, knife before me.

But Howl's club came down with a horrid yet pleasing *thump*. The beast staggered, shaking head in pain and surprise. Howl gave no time to recover. He leaped beside the beast, struck again. The wolf snapped jaws, seized the club with its teeth. At which moment of safety Howl kicked the beast's wounded leg. The creature yelped, fell away, now backing towards the wall.

"Face me with teeth, coward," snarled his father's jaws.

"You always frighted the wolf in me," observed Howl, voice mild. "And the boy. But this role of *man* takes a different view."

"Weakling," hissed the beast. "You lack the -," but Howl struck again. Whatever he lacked, it was neither club nor arm. Further words came not, only thumps and whimpers, some groans. At length the wolf collapsed into man, lying face up upon the ground, panting.

Such a look of fury in young Howl's face. More frightening that any fang-lined beast-muzzle. He raised the club for a killing blow, while his father stared up. "You haven't the liver," he whispered.

I made what move I could, but it was Cousin Bellow who leaped in time to halt the killing strike. I doubt many had strength of arm to match Howl's fury. But Bellow stayed the act, whispering fast and low. None but Howl heard the words, but all the hall took their meaning. *Do not kill your father.*

Only then did Howl's features flee into beast-shadows. Which mattered little beside Bellow, seemingly locked into the head of a bull. And yet a master musician. I determined to know Master Bellow better when time allowed. He contained much of the paradox of the family. At length Howl took a breath, stared down at '*the most fearsome being ever*', then tossed aside the club. He wiped tears from eyes. Trembled, as a man will do after long battle.

Doe came then, and stood between the two. She reached hand up to Bellow, hand up to Howl, and the three shared touch and a long beating of hearts. And all the hall sighed.

And if I admit I stood in my wedding-present castle, fresh from victory over a monster yet felt downcast? It will go hard but I sound a fool. But victory or not, I saw I waited a beggar outside a palace of wonder, staring in, never to enter. As their story went: *The least of our blood was royalty in the measure of our love. All others, plaything people.*

Awkward whispers through the Hall of Gathering. The Laird of the Mac Tier laughed weakly up, a gutter-drunk mocking passersby, till Doe kicked him quiet. No one stayed the act. But some of the blue-silver kilts stooped, carried their wounded chieftain to the great table. They lay him down not far from the still-quiet sea-girl, curled in a cloak of seal-skin. A sound sleeper, obviously. Her dark, puckish face held a look of concentration. Being family, she might well run in dreams now across fairy hills, beholding wonders far surpassing a man riding a wolf-horse.

A few of the blue tartan poked their laird's wounds, discussing what to bind, what to sew. I considered reaching past and cutting his throat. I hesitated; it would raise objections and stain the table. Most of the Mac Tier stared at Howl or Lalena, else turned eye each to each, wondering what came next?

What came was clatter and alarum at the inner doors, flying open. The Tiger-man rushed through, fur standing straight in fear or anger. A dark liquid dripped across his chest, too black to be blood. Human blood, at least. Seemingly he'd lost his great sword, and half his reason.

"Flee!" he shouted. "Run for your lives!"

Not a soul ran. This interested them.

The Tiger-man stood panting, staring at the crowd of Mac Tier and Mac Sanglair. He raised arms to air, tried again. "Flee!" he shouted.

"Why?" asked someone.

The Tiger-man stamped a foot. "All the horrors of the castle fall upon us!"

The Jackal-head sat by the hearth, nursing bruises. He groaned. "Ah, what of 'em?" he asked.

The Tiger-man rolled great green eyes, in terror or pique. He looked to the dark doorway as if for prompting. On cue, a blood-chilling scream sounded. Another. Then came a mad laugh. Silence for a bit, then a cough, a low stuttering groan.

141

The Tiger man nodded. "Do ye hark to that? Monsters! Aberrations! Abominations! An army of ghosts led by Fulgurous himself! Run for the ship!"

At that some did eye the castle exit. But most hesitated. If this demonic army waited to take the stage, the majority desired to first enjoy the sight. As well, there rang a certain falsity to the cat-man's delivery. The scream, the moan and the mad laugh tolled thin as a tin bell.

He crossed his arms, entirely vexed. His high ears folded back to emphasize annoyance. "They ate poor cousin William's head clean away," he declared. "Bit it. Clean off." His stare defied anyone to deny this horror. Another scream from the doorway.

Most blinked at that. Mattie Horse cursed, hurried past the Tiger-man to seek his brother's head. But the Tiger considered the room, absent a large looming figure, a mocking voice that should have spoken, seizing attention.

"Where is the Laird?" he demanded. And then sighted the beaten body upon the table. The Tiger-man blinked those green eyes, then turned them upon Howl, who stood beside his father's unstill form.

"Your work, young Mac Tier?"

"Why this 'young'?" sighed Howl. "You aren't a year older than I, Bram, you posturing cat."

Bram the Tiger shrugged to say '*that may be*', brushed at his fur. A most feline gesture. He peered at the wounded Laird of the Mac Tier, shook his head. Turned towards me, considered my bloodied person awhile, at last turned towards the dark doorway to the inner halls. He shrugged to the moaning ghosts offstage, unsure what line to next deliver.

Lalena stamped gentle lady-foot. "Where is Billy River, Bram Mac Tier? And answer truthful, else I give you this very night to my roses."

The Tiger-man bowed head in meckish surrender. "Keeping his word, Lady Mac Sanglair. He fetches young Vixen, with no move to rouse the least of your own." Grin. "But there was never such restraint put upon *me*."

On cue, through the opened door marched some ten Mac Sanglair, kilts red, incisors white. They lacked the individual wonder of the beast men. But more than matched the Moon Tartan in air of quiet violence. Their cousins in animal form stood as children in costume.

"You betray your own, Bram Mac Tier," declared the Jackal-head. Some of the Moon Tartan growled agreement. They shifted together, taking position to match the Sanglair.

The Tiger-man threw back his head, laughing. A victory, by family standards. He'd seized attention, angered and frighted all he loved. Behind him, more entered the hall. Ah, the sea-folk. These did not disdain spear and sword, knife and club. I wondered how well they fought on land. Then I wondered how well I fought beneath waves.

143

I had a vision of fencing beneath the sea. Blood would twist red ribbons through green water. Hmm, but saber or rapier would move far too slow. Even a foil would be hindered. Point of blade then, or short-knife...

Thus sea-dreaming, I did not mark the Laird of the Mac Tier rise up, draw dagger from belt. Nor did the rest, their attention focused upon the newcomers. Not even Howl, who stood close where his father lay. Only the seal-girl sharing the table marked the resurrection. Ha; she hadn't been a bit asleep, not through invasion, declamation and wolf-ride. Canny creatures, your mermaids. She leaped now upon Mac Tier's arm, gnawing with teeth. He growled, tossed her high and hard with a scream to the stones.

Howl turned, face reshaping to muzzle of wolf-fangs. A long second Father and son stared, each to each, a stare in which they exchanged all they had to say of love and hate, courage and fear, madness and humanity. Then Howl lunged forward and bit through his father's throat.

The silence of old stones and held breath filled the hall of Gathering.

Then, "Did I not say?" whispered Vixen from the balcony above, into the silence below. "The love of death has come to the Mac Tier."

Chapter 14
Of Keys in Storms

"Honeymoon," I whispered into Lalena's ear. "Bed."
I traveled a finger across her temple, down the white,
white path of her neck.

She closed eyes, shivered and whispered low *"go
away."* The rest of the conference table grinned, frowned,
or glanced away as prurience or politeness so moved their
souls. I tried again, tracing the curve of my bride's ear
with a whisper of breath. "Bed," I muttered. "Us."

Again that shiver, again that denial of desire. "Rayne
Gray, can you not leave a body in peace?"

I leaned back in my chair. Fine. I didn't want to go to
bed anyway. I considered my wife with cold eyes, recalling
how only days past she'd been a mad thing for coupling.
She'd craved my touch. Also my blood, somewhat.
Though no serious attempts to drink it since the wedding
night. A few nips, no more. But now? Ha. I might lay
myself beside her naked, a scratch across my jugular
perfuming the bedroom with salt red seduction. And
she'd lie a'back to pillows, peering at bills of lading, letters
of credit, muttering of excise taxes. Else turn to me and
ask my opinion of some lunatic tribe of relatives I had no
knowledge of, no interest in.

"Let us say it clear," declared the Laird of the Mac
Mur. The sea-people, if you grow lost among the names.
And really, why not just designate each tribe by their

medium of life and love? The Beast-clan, the Sea-clan, the Blood-clan, and all the other mad collections. Scales and Harlequins and Clockmakers. I wondered about that last. But names are only of use when designating peoples with no more separation among the globe's crowds than a label. For the family, such need counted naught.

"Let us say it clear," declared the Laird of the Sea-people. "Shall Ranulf Howl Mac Tier take his father's place as Laird? The Moon Tartan are become a danger to themselves, and to all the family. They must have a leader. Someone of strength who can repair the evils done by the former laird."

"You would see the son who slew the father, become chief of the Mac Tier?" asked Lalena. "How shall that stay any thirst for violence?"

The Sea-clan Chieftain sighed. "Hardly the first laird to do so. And what young Howl did deserves no shaming. The Old Wolf came here bent on murder."

"You speak ill of the dead," interrupted the Jackal-Head. "You insult those who saw in him exactly the strength you say now is needed. You speak of madness. But the curse of kin-strife and death-love is rife through all the clans. And all the races of mankind besides. We Mac Tier do but make ourselves strong, that we might oppose the madness within and without."

"You came with a prison-hold of common-blooded crofters," spat Billy River. "You treated the creatures like cattle, and sought to buy our favor with their blood."

146

"You are Sanglair!" shouted the Jackal-Head. "Children of the cold brides. You drink life. If you now declare yourselves tea-totaling milk-sops, you canna complain we served what once you favored for feasting."

That went too far. Lalena stood from her chair at table's head. She did so in slow and measured move, as if drawing sword before the sound to charge.

"Take great care, Jacque Mac Tier. If you say our clan ever treated commoners as kine, or drove folk from their homes, or took innocent folk as food —"

Some of the Sanglair turned gazes casually aside -

" then you insult the Mac Sanglair before their faces."

"Before their teeth," offered Mattie Horse.

"Or between?" suggested Billy River.

Jacque Mac Tier retreated not. "See, milady? Your folk threaten. To bite, to slay. I do but note, yours is a more feared and warlike clan than mine. Ever ready to throat-bite upon slight or dispute. Yet you speak as though the Mac Tier were pox-infected with a special love of violence."

Silence followed. The man had guided the exchange to make the point he wished. This Jacque was wily. I wondered whether one must learn to be subtle, when the vagaries of magic and nature gave one a face symbolizing *scavenger* and *hypocrite*. Again I reminded myself. These were family, playing parts; and always more than the sum of the parts.

147

I suddenly felt dull. Common clay, good for waving sharp metal about. Useful for family quarrels, the occasional wolf-ride. I needed a louder touch of magic than mere *Seraph spadassin*. Would I could learn the art of turning to beast. If only Howl's change-fire could burn my common blood. Who to say not?

The thought pleased. I'd been bitten. It ached for a burn. Perhaps the magic passed twixt creatures like the froth of mad dogs. In the morning Lalena would wake, turn sleepy eyes to behold beside her a great lazy... *lion*. Wonderful. She'd shriek... I considered. No, not my wife. She'd smile, and blink, and clasp arms about her clever man. Fascinating possibilities abounded. She'd need be careful I restrained my beastly self from biting *her*.

How to direct oneself towards a lion? I wondered. Surely it followed the rules of disguise. More than mere costuming. One might wear the skin of a lion, and yet be an ass. No, the Mac Tier must throw mind and heart into the part, as stage-board stompers become king or god, fool or lady-in-waiting, how-so-ever script demanded. Perhaps I need only think as a lion would.

I knew as much of real lions as real lions knew of me. A mutual ignorance, exchangeable with supposition. Lions were hairy, fierce and fast. And Lordly. I was already fierce and fast. Modestly hairy. How nice to be *lordly* to complete the triumph. A kingly mane, gracile tail for scepter. I wondered what use one found for tails. Did

Vixen or Bellow have them? I had not noticed such before. Probably not then.

The room's silence caught my ears. I realized all the conference stared at me. I shook daydreams from my head, strove to remember what last words troubled the table. Nothing. Had they even been speaking English? I turned to my wife.

"We discuss Fulgurous," sighed Lalena. "You saw him. Kin have slain kin in his hall, a thing that he may object to. And the objections of Fulgurous are lightning and dragon-fire. Should we flee?"

"How would an outsider judge?" asked Jacque. He spoke in no disdain, but genuine inquiry. A valid question. What did I know of these people's mad ghosts and ancient curses? I spread hands to show them empty of answers.

"I saw a statue," I reminded. "Or your fearsome ancestor sitting to feign stone. A silly thing to do, and entirely within the keeping of your dramatic blood-line."

My colonial honesty was not received with grace.

"Best not mock Fulgurous, Master Gray," intoned the Laird of the Sea-clan. "Not when we await his fire to fall upon our heads."

"If he pretends to be stone in a hall of statues, why then he mocks me," I pointed out. Mattie Horse voted for my view with a grin. The man suffered no fear of God, Devil nor ancestral lightning. I nodded my *leonine* head in return.

149

"And if he objects to that ravening beast of the Mac Tier being given just due, then he mocks again." I said these words with certain pride. Lordly, even. The table received this lion-like defiance by stirring restless, staring about for dragons.

"Perhaps it were best we continue this discussion entirely between family," said the Jackal-head. The Laird of the Sea-Folk concurred. So also Lady Vixen. Even Lalena bit her lip, holding back words.

Excellent. I had no place here, but to assure the crofters brought as vampiric gift, were not forgot. Soon as bandaged, I'd gone to the Mac Tier schooner at anchor. With Chatterton and Billy River, Howl and Vixen. We informed the crew that the Mac Tier were no longer a pack of beasts, but a tribe of men again. Quick men or cold, was the crew's choice.

Within the hold waited some two dozen men, women and children. Frightened, weary, despairing. Much coaxing required before they dared climb up into light. Ah, but they trusted Lady Vixen. That told me much, for all the sluttish grins she favored for a mask. She saw them to quarters in the valley beyond the castle. Promising most solemn, they would neither be eaten nor shipped across ocean. The very crimes against the commons I'd set myself to fight before wandering north, before wandering away…

I felt the old fury squeeze my heart again. At what I raged, I pretended not to know, no mirror being at hand.

Instead I gazed about at these strange creatures, players of parts. What solace there is to have family and tribe. Whether loved and hated, you are watched and answered. You bear meaning to other hearts, share in the stage-play of their lives. But common folk held no lines in the world's script. Mere bodies for a battle-scene, parts for a mill-machine.

I could sit no longer. I had no place at these interminable conferences. I stood, nodded to all. "It is for you to settle your clan-quarrels. Great grand-fathers' intentions have naught to do with me."

Complete silence, and faces of shock. At what did everyone gaze? At me, clearly. Why not? I spoke. But now came an air of attention not granted before. A touch of awe I'd missed. At last they realized I was the famous *Seraph*. Before linking with Lalena, I had been used to stares of admiration. I considered making a bow. Alas, it was not the Seraph's person they admired, but his belt.

I considered my belt. The sight returned me to the Channel, years past. We were fresh soldiers on a troop ship running from storm, hoping to get safe to war. Two masts, and the tips of both wrapped in blue flame. Sailors prayed, soldiers cursed; much the same words. The ring of iron keys jangling at my belt now burned that same ungentle blue, twined in pale storm-fire.

"As I said," I continued. "Naught to do with me. I leave you lot to it." And I departed the family conference.

151

Chapter 15
Night Reflections

Lalena and I sit at table after a long night of love. I wear uniform of war, clean and pressed. She seeks to make me smile with country-wife costume. I do smile, thinking it plain by itself. But upon her it becomes a master-work of joy and desire. We sit in morning sunlight shining upon us for the smile of God.

I sip tea, she sips tea. Far from the dark of the mad castle, its whisper of curse and mystery. How much better to be here in sun and country air. Through the farm-house window I watch a girl play. *Flower,* I think happily. She seems younger. Why should she not. The folk are who they want to be. So also, the dog Lucy who barks happily, catching the blue ball, white-starred.

All is sunlight and peace, a gentle contentment after long strife. We have come through war and storm to this bright morning. I sip tea, Lalena sips tea. The farmhouse is familiar. I have been here before. The memory is a shadow I can't quite touch.

Then a step at the doorway sends a chill through my heart. I know who I will turn and see. Too late I remember. This farmhouse, this kitchen, this dream is no place to be. Not with Lalena, not Flower, not the dog Lucy. I turn to the door and there stands the Striker. Huge bear of a man, yet moving with the grace of a dancer. Scarred and courtly, he nods for a solemn visitor on business he regrets.

"Get out!" I shout to Lalena. "Run!"

She sips her tea, puzzled, staring between the Striker and her mate. She smiles, means to greet this new version of myself. But he lunges, puts war-saber through her heart..

I scream, stand, catch her as she chokes on blood not for drink. Her eyes blink, unsure why she beholds the world fade. The red lips struggle to grant last words. I lay her down and draw sword, facing the Striker. I lunge, he parries, ripostes impossibly fast. Doubt overcomes me, facing myself.

The man stands so *assured,* so at ease. He's a master craftsman considering a minor challenge, tip of tongue stuck to side. I feint a thrust and he expects it, being me. Slashes towards my face, causing my retreat. I slip on Lalena's blood and he is upon me *corps a corps,* hand at my throat. I struggle. This man is monstrous, a thinking wall. Holding me with one hand, he takes knife and slashes my forehead. Then tosses me across the kitchen. He turns, leaves.

I struggle to rise, put hand to forehead. The wound prints in blood on my hand, and I stare at the letter 'C' a striker carves upon those who abandon their duty.

* * *

"That was quite awful," observed Lalena. She sat up in bed, feeling her chest where dream-thrust slew.

I rose, hand still at my forehead, covering shame. I stumbled to the mirror. In the faint dawn light I saw the red C upon my forehead. I touched finger to it. No blood. More like a flush of fever, drawing the letter.

I stared at the man before me. "Coward?" I asked. Not a label I take from many. Well, from none, actually. God's sake yesterday I rode a giant wolf. And yet... *A striker sends a man to face his duty.* Else face a mirror showing this red letter 'C'.

Lalena appeared in the mirror, naked as I. She wrapped an arm about me, not in pity but companionship. "You'll be going south then."

I gaped at her reflection. "How can you know so much?"

She laughed, low and sad. "Ah, man. I sleep in your bed, in your arms, breathing your breath, taking you within me. Walking in your dreams as you in mine, as you in me. You suppose I don't know you want to go fight your bankers?"

I denied it, idiot that I am. "I don't. I want to stay with my mad bride and ravening in-laws in our haunted castle. Who would not?" Her mirrored head tilted, expressing disbelief. My reflection tried again. "I would stay with my soft warm wife in our soft warm bed." I stretched out a hand, watched its reflection trace her arm's reflection. Her mirrored self sighed, in time to mine. Well, she knew better. I surrendered.

154

"But I have a duty," I admitted. There. It was said. Finally. It was release great as the *click* of key to my former shackles. "Those crofters. They expected to be eaten. They are fortunate they were not. The poor are food nowadays. Devoured by nobles and banks and mills and work-houses..."

I watched my fists clench. How dramatic. I became like family. I released them. Studied how my wife's right breast pressed to my side. Her hair ran straight past face and neck, framed the tit as velvet curtain would precious art.

"Are you supposed to be seen in mirrors?" I asked, placing an arm about her, reflecting her arm about me. The red C upon my forehead faded, if the pain remained. *Dream stigmata*, I thought. I become a citizen of dream and mirror. Perhaps I have always been. How shall a man know, till he awakes?

"Ach," she sniffed. "Grand-dam couldn't abide a mirror. But my Da fussed hours with his beard. And he was near the blood-drinking night-beast as she." Lalena leaned mirror-head to my mirror-shoulder. Fetching picture we made. We stood awhile and considered ourselves.

What a thing is woman's body and man's, stood together not in copulation but mere communion. We were two persons mated. Had my parents ever seen themselves so? And their parents, and all couples before, a line of reflection leading back to rough Adam, mad Eve, glimpsed far in the distance of the mirror-window.

She began running a hand up and down my chest, tracing scars, writing secrets. My body took notice, desiring the secrets' solution. She spoke of ships and politics, tracing far different words across my skin with idle finger.

"Howl will be taking the schooner south soon, to make peace with his folk, return his father's clay to his land. Either the Mac Tier accepts him as the new Laird, or they rip his throat away. But if all goes well and he holds his present temper, who knows but sanity returns to the Moon Tartan."

I recalled Howl sitting in the graveyard, empty pistol to head. But did not say. He had come to my rescue, or at least to his father's defeat. He possessed strength. Sanity as well, if he could trace it through the tangle of mouth and muzzle, boy and man. I traced a mirror-finger-tip along Lalena's jaw, up past the cheekbone towards the ear.

"Well, then," I sighed. 'Perhaps it were best I go with him, and then on south back to the city." My wife closed eyes; either in sorrow of my decision, or the pleasure brought by my hand now tracing down her neck.

"I must stay here," she declared. "This old rock must be held awhile, to show all that we Sanglair have strength and right to so do." She shivered, watching the reflection of my hand hold her breast as she the castle. A

156

metaphor, as it were. "If you go, walk doubly beware, Rayne. Stop that. No, and no and listen. You have caught the eye of family. An outsider has won the respect of the Sanglair, and now the Mac Tier? 'Tis not thought possible."

She gazed at my reflection standing in arousal. Trembled. My mirrored hand traveled down her pale stomach, the blond beard below. She struggled to declaim further in points of conference, with wise and wifely advice. But I smiled to mirror-see her prim locks grow tangled as high grass in summer wind. Mirror-nipples stood, and the red cat of a tongue-tip poked from mouth, glistened dark lips. She took a breath sounding close to gasp.

"The old ones dance about you. Now this sign of Fulgurous. My folk will seek to measure themselves gainst, against the upstart. The Rivalry. Ah, no. And the Harlequins. They will attempt some vengeance upon your vanquishing of their, of their, on that bridge… ". Her voice trailed off to guttural moan, deep and warm.

We gave over speaking reflection to reflection. We turned to face the thing itself, no more image of the thing. Clasped together, we staggered back to bed as one transformed beast, a mad creature devouring itself in joy, in desire, in a fever of arms and legs and teeth. Perhaps this conjoined beast was the original mankind; and when we walked separate we were lesser, unnatural beings. If so, now with touch and thrust, kiss and gasp the parts regained the lost glory of the whole.

So we lay, and loved, seeking every last crumb of touch and desire. Final course served for the feast of honeymoon's end.

Chapter 16
And There the Lion's Ruddy Eyes

And so at length I returned to the City. To kill a
man, affirm social justice, place flowers upon a grave and
recover a fortune stolen by my former valet. Sensible
goals each, yet somehow my first day of return I found
myself yawning at the back of a political meeting
watching an impostor deliver an incomprehensible speech
to angry tradesmen. Excepting he wore my face, name
and manners, it held naught to do with me or mine.

I studied my double in the distance, considering
whether his face was truly my face, or merely the idea of
mine. Seemingly life had used my nose for hammering
rocks. Quite right, it had. But did any creature possess
such bushy eyebrows? I looked taller than I felt. *Grayish*
loomed a bear of a man; but with hair the very lion's
mane I'd coveted by daydream's light.

Tempting to put an end to the farce. Why not rush
to the fore shouting *"Ha! Behold the real Seraph."* There
would be shouts, confusion. He and I would duel; and the
true Rayne Gray would by reality's rule be the man
standing at the end, mild-smiling at adventure and the
cooling corpse.

But this crowd was not the family dancing their
practiced minuet of quarrel and affection. Confusion and
blood would lead to riot. In such packed quarters, made
murder in a box. No, best front him in an alley, some

159

tavern used to strife. Not at his political prayers then, but when alone and full of bread.

I wondered what words *Rayne Grayish* proclaimed. Green and Black must lurk behind this show. Had they set the mummer to recite affirmations of banking law? More likely used him as foil, spouting mad calls to revolution and a new currency of cats.

And yet, was there not a smell of *family* in this mad act of imitation? *Mimickery*. The weaponry of Lalena's Harlequin cousins. The in-laws again. Who knew that marriage could so complicate a man's life? A year before, as confident bachelor I would have gaped astonished to see myself, and yet not be that self. Today it was mere puzzle to measure and solve, else leave aside.

I turned to Alexander Pope for advice. But no, the pages I opened were not *Essay on Criticism*. I now held the book exchanged with the prim young puritan. No tract on God and Man. A book of poems.

And there the lion's ruddy eyes
Shall flow with tears of gold:
And pitying the tender cries,
And walking round the fold.

I leafed the pages, confounded. Visions of tigers, of furnaces, of gardens and angels, lions and chimney-sweeps... I held a copy of William Blake. I opened to the front, found Dealer's florid inscription. "*From a connoisseur, to a raconteur*". My own lost copy.

When had I held the book last? That night we'd come through this church, the night my pirate-valet Stephano betrayed me with the kiss of a drugged whiskey-flask. *Run*, I'd told Flower.

The boy outside the church today who exchanged books. Had he not girl's face in boy's clothes? Hair combed and tailed neat behind. Knee-breeches for a page, gormless eyes for disguise. *Flower* or I was a Frenchman. I searched the forest of adults. She might hide among them now, as a fox in tall grass. Then again, act of incomprehensible purpose performed, she might have wandered dockside, singing of mermaids to the stray cats.

Flower and Brick led me here *that* night; not through the church door but up from the catacombs. The certainty came I should seek that path again. At least, if I wanted to follow a mad bread-crumb trail of family theatre. Why on earth should I?

I gave long consideration to *Grayish,* still speechifying. I am fond of my face and the self that wears it. Damned fine fellow, the real Rayne Gray. But that mimic-creature in the distance... annoyed. He reflected my moves and thoughts in parody bordering contempt. He loomed, he grinned, he burned for a pyre of scars and cheerful violence. Now he raised hands to pull the Sword of Chemosh down from the heavens. *Tedious fool,* I thought. One need not hear his words to see he mistook anger for sincerity.

161

Whether a trap set by my enemies, or mockery performed by mad in-laws; of a sudden *Grayish* bored. Let us see what mad path Flower swept today.

I pushed through the crowd towards back-offices of the church, thence down a corridor to basement stairs. A sense of dream touched the air, cold wafts from dark memories. When last I passed this way I climbed upwards from despair and defeat, not knowing worse yet waited. Home burned, Elspeth dead, Stephano her murderer and my betrayer. Green aligned with Black. Dealer coveting my house, my Elspeth. Black crowing victory. Crowds shouting idiot support, idiot condemnation. Final judgement of *death* by a court of blank faces, former friends all.

This book I held: all that remained of my old life. A happy life. I am not a brooding man. I wake each day smiling, knowing fair dice should have sent me empty-pocketed from this world long ago. By Pascal's reckoning I laid me down to eternal sleep on some radish-field of France, some alley of the city docks. So I will treasure each day of my old life, for all it ended in flame and betrayal. Elspeth, Stephano, and I: we made a family true as any mad clan of Lalena's. And as doomed by inner rot. *Bah.* I brood, declaiming I never brood.

I crossed basement shadows. No rapier at hand, but knife. I edged past barrels, found the wooden door leading to the stone-and-bone tunnels that underlie Londonish. Months past, I had come up this path, led by

162

the boy Brick. A ragged tatterdemalion, tangled dandelion-haired with ears elf-pointed. He'd held lantern before him as a child Diogenes, eyes wondering wide at the honest world. I opened the door, beheld the steps still lit by lamp light below. As if I returned after a moment's pause.

It's all very well to laud the strategy of rushing forwards into life, love and danger. But sometimes it sums to fatalistic idiocy. For once I hesitated, understanding that here the path of my life divided. I had returned to Londonish. Why not return to *sanity*? Sound out allies, re-establish my position in the city. Take revenge, rebuild my house, my accounts, my self-satisfied life. Find another red-haired colleen in want of rescue. The mad dance of the last few months need only be left off, and it must fade as any dream dawn-caught.

Surely it was Flower who gave me this book, recalling me to that night, these steps. To descend them risked surrendering again to the moonlight theatre of Lalena's mad family, leaving aside a world I comprehended. A world with boundaries and tasks set by my mind and will, not the moon-music of *old ones* and quarreling clans.

I studied the ring upon my left hand. Plain gold band, placed by Lilly-Ann Elena Mac Sanglair in vow to vow, word to word. My wife. A mad creature, whether in sober conference or warm bed. She bore the matching circle to mine. Did she also now stop, consider whether

163

with a twist she might fling the past months into a drawer, safe-kept for fond memory?

Lalena. Her life had changed surely as mine. The world's wheel had shifted beneath her, as for me. From night-haunt of blood and longing, she had fallen into ordered mind and daylight's law; as I had plunged into her family's lunatic mystery. Did she regret? Feel her wedding band as gold shackle?

What did she do now, leagues of land and sea to north? Not brooding on the past. We were neither of us for walking backwards down life's road. No. This day Lalena enjoyed sunshine's smile on castle tasks. Supplies to inventory, a garden to plant, sheep and hens to tend. Fascinating domestic pursuits for a vampiric queen. Ha. She'd be racing about with a broom chivying ghosts and dust. At such labor she would bind the Euclidian lines of her hair. I was sure of it, could hear the strands struggle to escape. But at night, at night in our room alone, jail-bonnet unlocked, drudge's dress dropped… How hung her tell-tale hair then?

Did she think of me? If so, how? With frown or sigh or trail of tears? A fond fading smile, perhaps. And alone in bed she'd sigh with comfort, freed of the sweaty oaf who'd lately seized half the blankets and all her person. Her hair, her holy hair. If I could but see how waved that flag, I would know where things now stood between us. I recalled the dream-vision of her at seven, and how I'd tugged those locks. My hand reached out to do so again… I laughed, and decided, and continued down the steps.

At the bottom waited Brick, lamp raised, eyes wide in wonder at light and shadow, dust and stone. He stood not a mustard-seed changed than when I climbed these steps months past. The idea came that he had remained here, smiling, waiting my return. Lamp never fading, kitten eyes never blinking. But no, I'd seen him in Melrose. *We are where we want to be,* boasted the old ones of the family.

When with precocious Flower, Brick played the gormless foil. I considered him now by himself, for himself. The reciter of poetic lines unsuited to street-waifs. The child-actor blinking at the audience, hiding behind louder performers. The light he held now cast his form to wall, and that shadow wavered on the stones as flame might, a casting of power, a portent of presence. Dancing, for all the lamp held steady. I shivered. *The old ones,* the family called them. Living nameless, and homeless, and pocketless. Free as winter geese, to wander with the wind. Unfathomable as the void between stars. *We are who we wish to be.* Understand: no greater claim of power ever was uttered by devil, by angel, by man.

We considered one another. Then Brick nodded polite, turned and strode down the hall. I hesitated, sighed dust, followed after. Ah, but I loathed these catacombs. Alas, the family cherished such stage-prop scenery.

"That was Flower at the church door," I declared, walking beside him.

165

He gifted me a puzzled look. "Who?"

"Your sister. Skinny as sticks. Tangled hair, moons for eyes. Speaks in lordly whisper."

Brick shook head, confounded at idea of such an entity. At last brightened. "Oh. *Her*. Ach, she's not Flower now-a-day. She calls her name *The Demoiselle*. Dresses in pants, combs hair back, ties it down. Colognes her silly self. Shoes. Ha."

I made a mental note. *Demoiselle*. "Are you still Brick?"

He shrugged disinterested, but a lynx-ear twitched. The old ones disliked names. They wore them and dropped them, so keeping themselves unbound by words. *We take no names, save as crowns of summer laurel.* Brick glanced left, glanced right to ensure only the dead listened, and no sisters.

"After your wedding," he confided, "she fell to moping. Found a red dress and boots. Stuffed old cloth in the front for a bosom. Ha. Washed her hair straight as pins, colored it yellow as the plague-flag pissed-on."

I pictured that. The child dressed as... Lalena? The sight would astound. "Why on earth would she do that?"

Brick snickered. "The silly thing contemplated wandering up to Scotland, catching a seraph's eye with what her infatuation-flamed brain-pan supposed must appeal."

"But why?"

Brick stopped. He reached the lamp up to my face, verifying some dark truth he'd suspected within the windows of my soul. I blinked, while he sighed at the verification, muttered a bit of Gaelic. We continued on.

"Light was scandalized," Brick confided to the lamp. "He told her to cease such foolishness. You were married man and that put end on it. She disappeared, came back as *The Demoiselle*. Remember to say '*The*' or she sulks. Here you are."

'Here' was a circle of dim light, empty of all but dust, dirt, bone-filled sconces, stink of decay, roots and rats. Oppressive air weighted with the world above us. I studied the view ahead. Just beyond the border of lamp-shine, a figure lurked, leaning casual against a wall,

"You'll be having to follow him next," asserted my guide. "Not I. He's a farther clan of family than I care to company. I shall meet you later." He turned and began retracing the way we came.

"Who is it?" I demanded. "What have I to do with this fellow?"

"Naught, overmuch," replied Brick. "But you asked him for advice when we passed before." The light fast diminished. "It pleases him now to help as you so asked. And polite of you to so let him."

Me? I hadn't asked a soul for advice. I considered the person ahead. But the light diminished as Brick withdrew. "I need the lamp," I pointed out.

"He doesn't," replied Brick, and was gone.

167

I considered running after the light. Not in panic. Merely in manly haste. But that lacked a seraph's style. Best march forwards. No need to rush. Knife at hand, of course. The figure had stood some twenty steps beyond. I took the first ten steps, during which I considered each time of late I'd stumbled blind in the dark. Damnation but this grew daily habit. I must begin carrying a candle, a tinder-box. A bag of torches. At the eleventh step I halted.

"How do you not need a lamp?" I demanded of the dark. Magical eyes, no doubt. Or tentacles for toes. Then again, he needs no lamp, who *has no eyes*.

Question's answer came in sparks of mating flint and steel. A glimmer of candle, then a flow of gold from a lantern. *Fiat lux* complete, he placed the lamp upon the ground, then leaned back to slouch shoulder to the wall. A person in no hurry at all.

I studied the figure by the fresh light. Hat slanted over eyes, arms crossed over chest. A most proper street-lounging pose. He wore antique breeches, silk-stockings, long coat with cuffs wide enough to shelter cats and cannon. Brass buttons shone. I knew when I approached he would tip hat back, catch my eye with a grin, call me *gov'no*r and offer a horse or a woman. Perhaps a watch, the chain so fresh-clipped it still ticked by the winding of the real owner.

I approached, he tipped hat back. Behold a face built of scar and grin, ragged beard, dark eyes lamp-shining. The hat sported a proud turkey-cock feather. That hat thrummed with significance, like a bell just struck... Ah. I recalled. When Flower and Brick led me this path months before. In a moment of dramatic idiocy I'd plucked a skull from the catacomb wall, asked it advice. Not my usual behavior, I point out. Hamlet's an ass. But spend a few hours with the old ones and you find yourself shouting soliloquies to the sun, filling pockets with moonlight, lifting burning coals to the stars in joyous-if-agonized brotherhood. To the family, asking a rotting skull advice made mere social trifle.

They'd given it my hat. I had not asked, *why do you give a skull my hat?* Previously they'd given me the same hat. Though I'd had it before, from an associate in an alley. Later it had been taken and worn by a girl half, half, by a, ah never mind. That hat passed around, and there was end on it. Why this sinister return? I had not asked advice of a hat, but of a skull. Not that I expected advice of the skull, any more than a hat. One asks such things of the mind inside the skull inside the hat.

The man straightened at the stage-cue of my approach, combined courtly bow and doff of the One True Hat. At the low-point of the bend he retrieved the lamp. Then turned and proceeded down the hall. I followed, cautious for what might come behind, what yet lay ahead. He wore rapier on right side. Showy sort of

169

hilt. Duelist, no doubt. Were I him, I'd not fence with such flags for cuffs.

"Right," I declared, and moved up beside him. He gave a nod, then gestured onwards with the lamp.

"Do you have a name?" I asked. For sometimes people do possess these things.

He looked at me and grinned. "Anger." Voice a low note on a flute, a thing of wind. Not the rough gravel-sound one expected of a ruffian lounging in under-street caves.

Anger. Had I caught that right? He looked a cheerful sort, for a deadly sin.

"And where does Anger lead?" I asked.

That got a laugh. It rolled into the dark before us, beyond the lamp-lit circle we walked. The dark didn't know what to think of it.

"We go to Decoursey," said the man. "Old fellow. Wishes your acquaintance to make. Alas, constrained."

I hesitated, near halting. The Decourseys were the Harlequin clan. Mad jesters, bad japesters, pirates despised as vampiric Mac Sanglair were feared. I'd slaughtered several the night I proposed to Lalena. Shot their leader in the knee, if you ask. Then she'd kicked a tune of snapping notes upon his bones. A wonderful night, all things considered.

In hindsight I see that shared adventure gave her the courage to accept my offer of marriage. And gave me the courage not to run when she accepted. Strange, the things that push and prod us, lead and drive and harry us, towards daring to even begin to decide to love.

Chapter 17

In which the hero pauses to recall light and domesticity

I do not spend life wandering haunted castles, murderer's alleys and bone-filled tombs, encountering monsters and maidens, mad-men and in-laws. It may seem otherwise. This narrative depicts an endless night-path down which I stumble, slashing and philosophizing.

Illusion. I never magically jumped from Londonish to the mad castle, and then back. And in either location, there passed entire hours without riding wolves, wandering haunted tombs. There were meals to eat, pots to empty, windows to gaze from in worry and laughter, wondering where in the world my life led.

Sailing to our island, Lalena and I kept to our narrow cabin, finding time for more than mere touch and desire, pant and completion. No, there followed long hours pillowed together, explaining our lives, our hearts. She told of dull childhood days behind light-smothering curtains, learning to knit, to embroider, to play harpsichord and piccolo. To sit straight, walk straight, speak grave straight sentences. And mad nights she wandered hillsides naked to wind and moon, her body thirsting till she pounded fists at tree-trunks in rage for what she did not know, and feared to find.

I talked more, but told less. I described battles and duels, comic adventures where I played heroic fool. Making her laugh. My love for Lalena began with her laugh. I already worshiped her wise hair. But I did not speak of sorrows, of regrets, of my own thirsting rage. Such does not come easy for me. Bah. A weakling's plaint. Revealing our hearts to another, is done with ease by none.

But the loss of my life with Elspeth, with Stephano, all the friends I'd taken for welcoming doors in storm… I confessed to my bride that I could not put it to words. Not yet. I'd had a home; and lost it. With her I'd gained something new, something mad and beyond present understanding. I needed to live this new life awhile before I put anything clear to words. She kissed me kindly, content with that. I suppose there are more ways to travel blind, than stumbling dark halls. Marriage must be such a path. One doesn't see where it shall lead; but moves forwards in hope the end is light.

And on the mad island itself came hours when I sat happily dull with a book, or dueled cup to cup with Mattie Horse. Fenced mad tales with Billy River, setting Vixen to giggle and Bellow to laugh. Howl to sigh, of course. Our last day Lalena and I wandered our wedding-present castle, exploring, laughing, holding hands. Strange, after weeks of joining together, exploring our bodies we could still turn sudden shy. Then she'd whirl about, else stare at the ground. While I stuttered, tripping on tongue and shadow.

And then to argue about my coat! It was a French officer's coat, I bought in cheap market of Edinburgh.

With her money, she having married a pauper. But I'd had just such a coat in my house. Ashes now, unless some canny looter sported it in taverns. We'd proudly worn such in the war, trophy for right damage done to enemy officers. I'd won several but they were of a rule too small. This from Edinburgh fit fine.

My bride explained we were in the North where folk preferred the French or Satan before the English. They would not smile at such a trophy. I explained how deeply I disinclined to care. She pointed out the poorly knit rips, the suspicious stains. All the better for a trophy, I countered. We didn't speak for an hour. Our first quarrel. Not the last.

Before I took ship south again, I visited the crofters settling to the valley beyond the castle. I spent a long day with them sharing beer, listening to tales of the clearances of the poor from the domains of the rich. I told of the New Charter. They knew of it, but it held no hope. They saw such as a struggle for English city-workmen, not Celt countrymen. I wanted to argue. But they smiled with faces weary with the words of politics. The reality near crushed their lives already.

So I settled for sharing what advice I had for dealing with the mad clans. Pointless. Long neighbors to the Mac Tier, they advised me back in sarcastic riposte. I left with their blessing, their eyes pitying me as a mad sheep, honeymooning a wolf.

I will not speak of when Lalena and I embraced, and then I turned and boarded the schooner. Not yet. I speak now of dull daily things, to remind I do not always walk haunted dark. More often I've stood in sunlight and yawned. But if our parting was in sunlight, it was a thing of solemn tear, heart-hid fear. Words not said. She believed I would learn to smile at her remembered face, declining to return. I dreaded that world and wind would not let me return.

That ship south to the shores of the Mac Tier went slow, crowded and conversational. We labored to encourage Howl to see himself a fit chieftain for his tribe. He'd fallen into the melancholy-well again, staring at walls, the ghosts of fathers. I confided to Chatterton the business with a gun. Little use, that. Chatterton was not a man trained in comforting others, save the final comfort. He kept busy staring out to sea, seeing wings and eyes and a girl's face in racks of clouds. Sometimes I saw them too.

But leaning over ship's railing, watching waves and gulls, the cloud-mountains marching... Chatterton told of his life in the lost clan of Blades. How he'd come to be the last standing in a valley of dead. How he'd slain this sly aunt, and cleverly defeated that beloved uncle.

The telling made me edge away, hand checking for knife. I have lived war and duel, but nothing so clearly and finally murderous as Chatterton's. I'll share his words another time, when the narrative threatens tedium. Now I seek to remember things of ordinary life, to insist that much of my tale is entirely dull.

True, the tale now follows a creature named Anger through damned grave-tunnels. But shortly after, Flower (correction: *The Demoiselle*) and I visit a bank. In gray day's light and the bustle of clerks. We will stand in line before a counter, impatient for someone to attend. What is more prosaic than that? And earlier we stopped at a coffee-house, argued with a servant concerning the cream, which was clotted.

So then. That said, let us return to striding through the dark and the dead, understanding this is only interlude between moments of sunlight, tedium and sanity. It isn't always thus.

Chapter 18
The Knight of Dust and Light

Anger and I traveled the underworld. Above existed conceptual crowds, life and light, bells and birds choiring down from smoky sky, carts and dogs battling for the streets. Below, existence limited itself to two men in a circle of lamp-shine. We pushed aside curtains of stench: rot, shit, mold, mist rising from warm pools of sewage, bitter chemical smells of oil and acid. A closed reality of faint music: single notes from a drip of gutter-runoff; tinkling trills of water-spill playing no melody known. Deep church-organ muttering of wind wandering lost. The steps of someone following.

Slow soft steps, keeping beyond our light. But stone tunnels carry sound, even breath. Anger halted, turned. Good. I'd half-decided my guide led me on, knowing enemy tiptoed behind. I have a doubting heart, I confess. No, I boast. All men, all beasts, all flies should frown in suspicion at steps in the dark. The stars themselves should so frown. Who knows but they do.

We halted; the steps halted. Waiting for us to continue. A familiar game in forest or city.

"Bah," growled Anger. "These snake-holes are more trafficked than the streets above. Best we go on. You watch behind, and I ahead."

Properly guarding the rear meant keeping only half an eye on Anger. Not that I did not trust him. As it happens I did not trust him but it was not personal. His gentleman-ruffian appearance made for refreshing honesty. Was he the specter of the man whose skull I'd plucked from the wall months before? Absurd. In the world above I'd dismiss the suggestion with a sigh, a quote from Spinoza, a reminder we stood at the dawn of the 19th century not the 10th. In sanity's sunshine I'd declare Anger just another mad member of Lalena's tribe, mimicking a street-ruffian of past era.

But we were not on the sidewalk in Spinoza's analytical sun, nor even Voltaire's tavern table. In these catacombs analytics did not rule, but *Hermes Trismegistus*. As William Blake might say, in such place one sees by a different metaphysics. Ghost my guide was, then.

We approached faint light that absorbed our speck of lamp-shine. Air become near breathable. We stopped, stood in the entrance to a wide chamber, high-roofed and solemn. One single sun-beam slanted yellow upon a statue centering the room. Dust-motes twined within the beam. They caught the eye, as if pattern hid in the steps of their dance. This light descended upon a broken-winged angel sitting in thought, hand to chin. Eyes bound with dirty cloth. Well, I knew that statue, this chamber. I'd slept here, feasted here, months before when the sunlit world above hunted me as near to death as any other sleeper among the graves.

I returned now rested, healed. Married, even. Clean clothes, coins in pocket for beggars and beer. I held title to a castle on a rock in stormy ocean. I'd become an initiate into a strange world of shape-changers, dream-wanderers, a noble elite of wandering poets. Married, I repeat. My old view of reality, lost with my previous life. A strangeness had been unleashed into the world. I had as well. I remembered the very key's *click*, opening my shackles.

And yet for all the life-changes, I stood no closer to bringing down Alderman Black and his cabal of pirate-merchants than when I lay here in rags and hunger. No, I'd wandered still farther from my goal. While I pleasured in vampiric concourse, chatting with possessed dolls and melancholy wolves, befriending mermaids and mad in-laws, Black had put mind and hand to practical action. The building of ships and mills, the bribing of Aldermen, the consolidation of the ownership of the mechanism of law and finance. No doubt he'd doubled his locks, tripled his guards,

Definitely time to admit duty, face foe. Leave off with circling, knife drawn but hand hesitating. No more words but '*lay on*' then. I entered the grave-chamber vowing to defy whatever new theatre the family staged to entice my soul from practicality's path.

In a corner of the chamber rested the grave-stone where I'd lain spent of life as the bones beneath. Then awakened to feast with Flower and Brick, Lucy Dog of Mystery, and the ancient mariner Light. Folk strange as their designations. No; stranger.

Now upon the cold-stone feast-table lay an armored knight. Candles set about, but the armor shone not. That armor declined to shine. It brooded, stained by dent and fire, by blood and years of wet furious strife. No paladin's story-book armor. Behold a construction of steel plate forged in the smithies of Hell. Not for heroics but butchery. The sword lying across the chest: a heavy straight-razor of a butcher's axe. Jagged as a steel lion's jaws, stained as floor and soul of a slaughter-house.

I waited for the knight to rise enraged at disturbance. I disliked the cut of that butcher's edge. When he rose I'd move back, let the fiend twirl till I could rush within the blade's circle, reach the back, inserting knife between helmet and plate...

Anger glanced at me, my change of footing. "Man, be at peace. There's naught inside that but shadow, but dust." Perhaps.

I approached the thing, knife defiant against shadow, against dust. Listening behind in case Anger attacked me, or the person that trailed the tunnels attacked him. Unless this knight of dust and shadow himself rose, slashing his butcher-blade at all, furious for his disturbed eternity.

Strange armor, that. I have seen all the parts and pieces our grand-fathers decked upon themselves, before bolt and musket-ball made steel less battle-worthy than cotton. Suits of armor make stylish ornaments for mansion corners. But no knight of old wore aught like this spiked and jointed devil's shell.

The helmet bore the shape of a blunt dragon's head, black and grinning. I tried to picture battle wearing such. One would stumble half-seeing, slashing butcher-blade through friend and foe. Until heat and weariness won the tourney, drove the walking fortress to the ground. Then would come a dagger twixt helmet and breast-plate.

Granted, if such as this appeared on a modern battle-field a fresh-enlisted farm-boy with a musket would take one down first. Or a decent crossbow bolt, fired close. I lifted the visor with point of knife. Within, the prophesied dust and shadow.

"He's over there," said Anger.

I turned, looked about. Chamber, statue, dust, empty armor. Sun beam through which dust motes did their planetary dance. The very symbol of eternal, restless beauty. The motes moving, shifting, forever almost forming a figure, even a face...

"Ah," I said.

* * *

Nobility is not of breeding. A truth witnessed in war, and the politics of peace waged as war. Ambitious breeding reaches for the ideal of nobility; settles for manners. A worthy thing, manners, when not a bother. But the real Nobility goes where it will, having naught to do with cloth or class. I have seen it in a horse delivering a dead rider to camp. In an ancient farmer standing on a stool, reaching down a tin box, offering a wanderer a biscuit. In an Irish maid championing a stray dog before a bully of a butcher.

And I have beheld nobility in a sun beam. I stood before a noble. Of that I was certain. For all he shimmered mere dust in sun's shine. Bright remainder of dead centuries, this tomb his castle, this light his throne.

The spirit spoke in whispered words of incomprehensible wisdom. Which is to say, in no language of sense. Almost, I laughed. Yet another speech to hear and not comprehend? Some cousin to Latin. Antique French? No, German hid within as well.

So I stood solemn-faced, nodding at words I could not follow, considering what thoughts could come from motes spiraling a beam of sun. Which composed the mind: the dust or the light? The dance of both, perhaps. What wisdom could such have for me, a thick thing of clay and cloth, blood and wedding band? Well, what wisdom did I possess for him?

I pondered what truths I might share with a shaft of light. I am damned wise in this world, in the sorrows and joys of life. Yet others forever impose their wisdom upon me. Surely I possessed my own revelation? Not that I knew my revelation. But I vowed in that gray chamber to find it. I'd declare it to the world as angelic messenger. Is not *seraph* an order of the heavens? I'd shout my unique meaning to myself and to all shadows of light and dust that had ears to hear.

Anger raised hand, turned to interrupt these important thoughts.

"Sieur De Coursey says you have an enemy within the city above."

I shewed him empty hands and honest eyes, to declare *no foe of mine is fault of mine*. These things happen. An honest man will beget enemies, if he walk by day, by night or stay home a'bed.

Anger snorted. "He says this particular foe is a descendent of his line. Blood, flesh, heart of his."

I stared at the stone slab upon which the armor rested, the epitaph worn not from rain or wind, but mere dust of years. *Sieur Claire d. Courcy*

Well, then. Another relative. What does a spadassin do for excitement before he meets his in-laws? But the Decourseys wore the Harlequin Tartan nowadays. And this spirit, some ancient shadow of that despised line? I tapped hand to knife, considered how one best fought a sun-beam. Nonsense, of course. Only the family kept leading me to such considerations.

And one of the family led more oft than all others. The very creature who'd drawn me here today. Past time she made her entrance onstage. I turned to the dark of the chamber exit.

"It is rude to eavesdrop," I observed.

There followed silence, while Anger, sun-beam and blind angel waited. At last a high voice declared from the dark "Am not."

183

"Flower," I said. "If you would care to join the assembly?"

She said naught. I recalled her new laurel-crown of a name. "If the *Demoiselle* would deign to grant us her presence, we would welcome her wisdom."

After long dignified pause, in marched the gangly, proper puritan page, former Flower, present Demoiselle. She sniffed to say '*I enter because I choose so do. I was never caught.*'

More gabble of ghostly tongue. Anger leaned against the blind angel and laughed, highly entertained. The angelic statue kept his silence. Perhaps it grinned slightly. The Demoiselle bowed to Cousin Sun-light, greeted Anger as *Enguerrand*; courtly as please-a-prince. Ignored me entirely. She spoke rapid in the same tongue. Wretched little polyglot.

Anger translated for both. "De Coursey says, there is little time for speech. The sun will shift. He says, his present line stinks with shit and folly. Your foe is a white-faced dancing-master, a blood-dreaming mischief-maker. He comes to the city to destroy you." Anger, sun-beam and Demoiselle considered me. I considered myself, recalling the mimic haranguing the crowd in the church above.

"There is a fellow running about the city who makes himself seem me," I informed all. "As a Mac Tier might adopt the form of a wolf."

More dust-mote whispers. "Yes, that is the *Pierrot*," translated Anger. "Father to the late-passed Harlequin. Bastard blames you for his son's death."

"The ass attacked my wife," I observed. "That were best counted suicide, not murder. But how does wearing my face do aught but amuse?"

Anger shrugged. The *Demoiselle* bit her lip as though asking 'what *could* it all mean?' I thought that pose. She knew. There followed conversation between the three. Another family conference, myself loitering outside the language door. And just when I had begun to pick up a bit of Gaelic. Of course the creatures would switch to tongue of sunlight. Or antique Frankish.

What was Anger? I wondered. Specter or man? For that matter, what the sunbeam, what the girl? I felt reduced to considering Anger's hat. I knew the hat, its nature and history and purpose. I could tell long tales of that hat. That was something.

At last, "The Pierrot sought your city-foes," declared Anger. "They cook some plan to use your face and name, cause a slaughter. The Pierrot wishes harm to you, shame to your wife's clan. Your enemies gain by blacking the flag of your beliefs. De Coursey says the rot must be cut from the Harlequin line. You must take his old armor, wear it in battle against the Pierrot."

I considered the hell-and-blood construction of steel. Wear that? How to politely decline. "Ah, it is not how people fight nowadays."

185

Anger smiled, said something aside to the sun beam. "How would you fight a foe that stands before you, master of all your strengths?"

I considered jesting that I'd turn and run. But it was no jest. I would not wish to face a man who fought as well as I. There lies no boast in that admission, only the measured judgement of a master craftsman to his mirror.

I settled for polite demur. "I will not war with my wife's clan-cousins. My fight is with the Aldermen's Council and the Magisterium. If they have taken a Harlequin into employee or alliance, I shall settle with my sort, and leave him to his."

Anger shook his head. "Your Aldermen and Magisters are lesser foes. The Pierrot toys with them. It is he you must face, else fall."

I laughed. "To the family, only family matters. All others, *plaything people*, as your play goes. But I count Black and Green my greater enemies. I will not turn aside yet again to deal in matters of clan quarrel."

The room grew grave-silent. Natural enough, it being tomb. Anger considered. The Demoiselle sighed, shook head. The sun-beam shivered, motes dancing. The blind angel studied infinity, leaving us to deal with the finite. Leaving me to reveal the powers of reality. Which is to say, banks and law, coin and king.

"As to how I shall fight my enemy?" I asked the assembly. "Why, I will pierce my foe's heart through his ledger books. I know for a fact he smuggles lives and

186

rum, guns and coffee. Annoying, as he also works to raise the tariffs on these things. "

Ghost-guide, girl and sunbeam gifted me a look of measured consideration. Clearly I babbled. Sunbeam or ghost-guide or girl, what mattered to *them* was ancient feud, magic duels and hell-forged armor. Mills, banks, ships and laws weighed less than family dust and shadow.

I did my best to explain. "My enemy's chief clerk is the weak point in his mercantile armor. A careful kidnapping, and I have the books in hand. As I am presently pardoned, I can safely present them to the Magisterium. Proof positive of Alderman Black's thefts and treasons. That fire lit, I hunt down Stephano, regain my fortune, hire a few associates and we begin dismantling Black's cabal."

A perfectly sensible plan. More sensible than my usual 'Go to his house, climb in the window and kill him' which lacked in style what it possessed in simplicity. But what did the family know of sense? Their strategy was for me to don a ghost's ancient armor, God's sake. There came a long conversation in the speech of sun-beam and dust. Or old Frankish, I remain uncertain. I tapped a foot impatient. At length family consensus was reached.

"An excellent plan," declared the Demoiselle, picking up Anger's lamp. "Let's to the bank house."

Chapter 19
On elephants and Silk Rope.

Londonish is a holy city. The wider streets bloom
with marble-and-brick boxes consecrated to the gods of
Law and Throne, Coin and War, Healing and Death,
Theatre and Music. And Heaven's official Deity as well,
of course. If you prefer, name these shrines courthouse
and counting-house, ministry, bank and armory, theatre,
hospital and garrison, gaol, church and chapel. Label them
as you will, the things remain the same. Fanes consecrated
to some archon of law or sword, pain or healing, coin or
spirit. Each has its priests in ordered robe, the daily
sacrament. And daily sacrifice, oft as not.

My unfaithful friend Dealer envisioned a public
temple consecrated to Art. A low reason to betray a
friend, yet within the holy traditions of the city.
Londonish dreams of grand edifices dedicated to
ceremonies of desire and awe, greed and sacrament,
laughter and jurisprudence, worship and sorrow. As many
houses as the clans of the family, I suppose. These
platonic ideals will insist their way equally into tartan-
cloth or chiseled stone.

The Demoiselle and I sat in a simple chapel devoted
to Coffee, close by the temple of Mammon known as the
City Bank. There we slurped thick brew from clay cups,
ate honeyed bread that crunched stale. I now wore a
wide-brimmed hat. Not Anger's hat. Behold a lesser

chapeau of no destiny. Mere adornment to my periwig, company to the fool bifocals that blocked my sight.

"We shall buy a carriage," decided the girl. "Douse it with oil and flame. I shall enrage the horses, drive them crashing through the doors of the bank." She considered, eyes shining with impending flame. "I shall fire braces of pistols from either hand. Meanwhile *you* have climbed the cathedral spire, shot an arrow to the roof of the bank. An arrow with rope attached of finest Chinese silk. You shall circus-walk the rope over heads of astonished citizens. Then jump through sky-lights to locate your ledger books. That done, you leap into my blazing carriage and we ride away."

I weighed this plan, the hot coffee, the stale bread. The plan had the advantage of style and direct action. The coffee bubbled hot, but bitter; needing cream. The stale bread had no advantages I could find at all.

The servant-girl came with a pot of cream decayed as any bone-marrow in the catacombs below. I complained, the keeper came, agreed to charge nothing for ancient cream, but more for fresh. I reviewed my diminishing coin-purse, extracted copper, deposited sighs.

Before boarding ship, Lalena gifted me a purse heavy with silver. I'd accepted with gritted smile. Pride makes a fine hat; but what point in leaving only to fail my quest for lack of bread? The journey south had cost. Inns, horses, simple meals. Today I'd abandoned a new rapier and half my clothes in an alley. I debated returning now, searching for it. 'Course it would be gone.

I considered how difficult it is to loiter in disguise, robbing banks and avenging oneself upon merchant-pirates, when limited by slightness of purse. A *spadassin* without coin is scarce better than *lurking ruffian*. Perhaps I'd best track down my wayward valet Stephano first. Take back the jewels, coin and letters of credit he'd removed from my closet upon my arrest. In return, I'd gift him with a revelation of eternity; or at least a vision of Hell's infinity.

I returned mind to present challenge. I lacked funds to purchase carriage, horses, oil, pistols and fine Chinese silk ropes. I might afford fresh cream.

"We watch, we wait," I proposed. "The man comes forth, I step close behind with a dagger. Menacing words follow. We proceed to an alley, where I threaten. He promises Black's books, intending to cheat, of course. But they must be in the bank offices themselves, or in Black's house, or one of the warehouses. I will watch his eyes for the answer he fears."

"Pffff," sniffed the Demoiselle. "How do you see his eyes when you hold a knife at his back?"

"A proper spadassin has eyes in front," I explained. "Just as a mere duelist has eyes behind."

"What?" asked the Demoiselle. 'Everyone has eyes in front."

"No, I speak of extra eyes in front, staring back. Picture a mirror some five steps before me, which I gaze upon at need to see myself and all about. Quite useful in tavern and alley."

She narrowed her own up-front moon-orbs. "Then who's behind you now?" she demanded.

"The girl with the fresh cream," I said. And indeed this prophesied creature appeared, placed the pot before us.

"You heard her step," scoffed the Demoiselle. "You smelled the cream."

"Are you going to rob the City Bank?" asked the girl. An eavesdropper, of course. No matter. I was a school-proctor with my young charge. Nothing more natural than we should plot the robbing of the bank next-door.

The servant-girl was a skinny thing scarce older than Flower/Demoiselle. Aproned, and hair in prim bonnet. She stomped great work-boots seemingly made of lead. One would hear her tiptoe in China. She stared into dreams farther from here than the Orient. "I do love to stand by the window figuring how I'd get into their gold."

I checked the pot. No cadaver-cheese, but fresh lace of cream. Excellent. I added it to my coffee, stirred with a dirty spoon. "And how would you commit this terrible crime?"

She smiled into dream-distance. "An elephant. I'd befriend one, and we'd come by night. Oh, your elephant is wonderful strong and quick. He'd tug those great iron bars off a window with his trunk. Then I'd climb in, climb out, piling his back with bags of gold. Then off we'd ride, ha!"

The Demoiselle sighed. "You can't sneak up the street with an elephant. You can't slip away on an elephant. The whole city would follow you down the street to watch you rob a bank with an elephant."

The girl opened eyes wide. "I'd *want* everyone to watch. What pudding-head would rob a bank on an elephant without wanting anyone watching? Might as well sing a beautiful song with your head in a bucket."

The Demoiselle covered face with hands, embarrassed that one of her sex and age should so fail to see the impracticality of elephant burglary, as opposed to blazing carriages and braces of pistols. I smiled, caught myself doing so, and frowned. Flower-Demoiselle acted entirely her age. Suspicion moved me to look twice. The Demoiselle peeked through fingers, as fox in brambles. I turned to the servant-girl. Pale, freckled; blond hair a shade red. Overlarge eyes that reminded me of wolves and sea-maids, nights of ghosts, ghosts of knights. Bonnet covering head; covering *ears*. I reached to reveal these tell-tale objects but she stomped away, affronted at our failure to see the point of robbery as high theatre.

The old ones. Dance with them once, and life smolders forever-after in fever-dream. No one is quite what they seem, and the moments seeming most prosaic suddenly

192

shimmer with message and meaning, just beyond sight. Beyond even the extra eyes of a spadassin.

I missed my wife. She made these things normal, she being beyond mere madness as the moon above the tangled woods. I sighed, finished my coffee, rose to rob a bank. But visions of flaming carriages and elephant banditry had shifted my thoughts along a different path. I decided not to waylay bankers. My new plan was simpler. I'd just walk in and ask for the money.

* * *

"The theory is sound," I explained to the Demoiselle, as we crossed the street. "Clearly I am again a citizen in good standing. No reward on my head now. Hell-fire, I give speeches in church. Ergo my account must be in good standing as well. I present myself, withdraw my funds, thus replenishing my diminished coin. While doing this, I inquire as to Master Furst, the chief accountant. He is an acquaintance of long standing and the keeper of Black's books. I may obtain what I want without so much as a knife to his back."

The Demoiselle bit lip, considering. "Not bad. Few must know the other *you* is fraud. And those who know, likely believe the real Gray dead. Elsewise, they'd fear to clear your name. Perhaps only the Pierrot himself knows both the fraud, and that you live. But he will not share family quarrel-and-gossip with your muckety muck banker-bandits."

That absurd tale of Jacobins freeing me from my cell; the royal pardon for my idiot return. Arranging such presented no difficulty for Black and Green. Combine that with a mad Harlequin mimicking me. The question screamed a question to the heavens: *what the hell and why?*

I considered the crowd of tradesmen and burghers at the church. The hope of the New Charter had not foundered for my absence. Sad conceit, to suppose the wind of justice depended on my continued breathing.

'They arrange a slaughter', the Sun-beam de Coursey said. Simple enough. The Pierrot would enrage a crowd in favor of the New Charter. An arranged riot ensue, perhaps a call to uprising. Aldermen and Magisterium would declare no choice but drastic steps; which is to say, slash away with cavalry saber. Firing muskets and crossbows into crowds. Hanging leaders along the high-street for holiday flags.

Mine was no longer a mission of revenge; but staying hundreds of deaths, perhaps thousands. To prevent the river of human decision from being directed towards a future ruled by bankers and gaolers, merchant pirates; all the priesthood of Mammon, Baal and Moloch. I accepted this higher duty meekly. It still came to the same throats to cut.

Only that business of fighting a mad Harlequin with my face... I recalled his mild smile upon the two sailors beaten into the street. I shrugged. If a man could not defeat himself in fair fight, why then the other was the better. Was that true? Was it even sense? We reached the steps of the bank.

"I will now instruct you to wait here where it is safe," I informed the Demoiselle.

She nodded. "While I scowl, then agree sulking. Of course I follow behind anyway."

"Right," I sighed. "Well, be ready to run when the shout rings out: 'that man is not a fraud.'."

She grinned, and the sight wrenched my heart. For I beheld her toothed resemblance to Lalena. Cousins in spirit, if not in form. She'd need far more old-cloth stuffing.

And so we entered the great oak and steel doors of the bank. As promised before, Flower/Demoiselle and I then waited in line for a cashier to acknowledge our existence. The most dull and daily thing in the world.

Chapter 20

Of Human Cages, and Heaven's Rages

"That man is a rogue in disguise," declared a voice across the hall. I turned to see Banker Furst standing by the door to inner treasure-rooms. Pointing an accusing finger. Cashiers, clerks and fellow customers, not to mention guards, all followed finger to consider me. I gave a slight bow, lifting up my glasses to peer in comic blinks. At which, Furst gave a bankerish laugh.

We were never friends. And yet oft enough sat the same table. Black's dinners, usually. Sometimes Dealer's. Furst abhorred my affirmation of labor laws, my desire for justice to reach even unto mansion doors and banker's desks. But he did so openly; making no fool demand I yield to king and class as to the passing carriage of God. No, Furst simply declared his own pocket's interest lay in society as it was, and more of the same. So we mocked one another, in words more honest than I'd exchanged with Black or Green since the war. Better an honest opponent, than a false friend.

He'd sat to the back of my trial. I recalled studying the different faces of acquaintances, the averted eyes, the solemn frowns, the sly smiles. But Furst showed no glee, nor fraud of sorrow. His look declared puzzlement to see the world turn so upon a man. Well, it had puzzled me too.

Furst gestured us out of line. He summoned no guards. The Demoiselle followed behind, erect and proper as a prince's page. I approached the man, removing the idiot contraption of glass and wire that hindered sight. I studied Furst, wondering whether he saw Rayne Gray, or *Rayne Grayish*.

"Here to burn my bank, I suppose," sighed Furst. "For the good of Irish loungers everywhere." So then, he thought I was me. Which was true, I was me. But had I been another and he knew so, it seemed unlikely he'd jest so. I returned what riposte I would tender at a fine state dinner, were I me and not pretending to be another feigning me. Which is to say, I recited Blake.

"A Robin Red breast in a Cage
Puts all Heaven in a Rage
A dog starved at his Masters Gate
Predicts the ruin of the State."

He tendered a fiduciary snort. I deposited a polite bow. "But no burning of your bank," I vowed. Added for afterthought, "At least, not before I make a full withdrawal of funds."

Furst laughed, turned eye to the solemn personage of the Demoiselle behind me. She wore face blank as fresh ledger paper. Furst tapped finger to the side of his nose, in sign he knew a secret. "Ah. You've come for the contents of your private box."

197

I nodded to say '*but of course*'. In fact I'd kept no private box. Not in the past. I'd trusted in a secret closet. Alas, not secret to my valet Stephano, in whom I'd also trusted. Well, let us see what *Rayne Grayish* kept under lock. Furst turned. I followed, down halls, past guards and doors that would deny retreat if things turned violent. And when in my life did they ever not? But no choice now but forward charge.

A hall where a guard sat bored. A door of bars, a turn of key in lock. "I shall wait you here," said Furst. "I have less desire to see what horrors a *spadassin* keeps under lock, than you have to share such mysteries."

"Quite right," I approved. "The key, if you please?"

He looked surprised. "Why should you want that?"

"Of late, I have the most awful dreams of being locked in a cell. I decline to enter such unless I hold the key."

Furst laughed. "What suspicious minds lovers of the downtrodden own. So less able to trust than innocent bankers. You think I intend slamming the door, locking you within, just so I may harangue you for five hours on the natural right of the strong to rule the weak?"

In reply I held out hand for key. He sighed. "Well, as it happens I *did* so intend. But my sermon was brevity itself. Nothing like your jeremiads. 'Would have run two hours, no more." He tended me the key. Demoiselle and I entered the lock-room. I dreaded the iron slam of the door, but none came.

Within waited a bare cell of stone. Narrow niche windows cast faint light, reminiscent of today's earlier tomb. But no dust here, no ghost. Just a chest upon a table. Unlocked. I lifted the top, and if snakes and flames had burst forth I'd have smiled, none surprised.

But within waited a dozen silk pouches, an assortment of small boxes and wrapped items. Papers of various important seal and weight. Emptying a pouch upon the table spilled sparkles into the room, shining faint as the lesser stars of dusk. Diamonds, mostly, but an equal assortment of rubies. Some few sapphires. Stones cut in styles seen in old portraits of kings.

The Demoiselle whistled. "This all yours?"

I shook my head. "Some of these items are mine. That pouch of poisons. God's sake don't touch. I use those leather gloves. These letters of credit are mine." Items taken by Stephano. Had he surrendered them to my double, thinking him me?

I traced a finger through scattered diamonds. "But these stones are a dozen times what I owned. A hundred times." I pulled a teak box out from the chest. The weight told of gold before I opened to release the yellow shine.

I considered the careful balance of weight and size for each silk bag. "This is payment, prepared," I decided. "Your Harlequin cousin intends the purchase of some action." Something expensive, clearly. *They intend a slaughter,* the noble sun-beam said.

I searched the chest further. Upon the bottom, wrapped in cloth, waited a knife. An ornamented dagger, curved in a cruel claw. I stared at it a long time, daring to run a finger along the blade. A dull brown stain upon the steel. My knife. An expensive toy. I'd never use it for fighting. Stephano had used it to kill Elspeth. But that had scarce been fight; mere murder.

"Stop," said the Demoiselle. She grabbed my arm, did her best to shake me. Stop what? I wondered. I did naught, only stared at a knife. Perhaps I trembled a bit, but wasn't the child shaking me?

"Best we leave," she whispered.

Leave? Of course. Training came to fore. We were scouts in enemy territory. This bank was the field of foes, more than any French woods by night. I placed the knife in my coat pocket. Exchanged my silvers and coppers for gold. Passed a bag of jewels to the Demoiselle. Closed the chest. Summoned Furst, instructed that we required a porter to assist. Also a carriage, if he would be kind enough to summon one.

"Are you well, Gray?" he asked. He peered close to study my face. I tensed to break his neck. But then I'd need slay the guard in the chair. Blood and screams. We'd battle just to reach the street. Best let him live. Let every man live, save one. No, excepting four. Furst continued to study me. A horrid idea occurred to his lock-box scruples. "Was there aught missing?"

I shook my head. Enemy camp, suspicious foe. I needed a jest.

"I kept my heart locked in the box awhile. Now I must carry it about a bit. Of course it weighs on me."

Dry laugh, then sympathetic smile. "Hearts," Furst sighed. "No vault long keeps that treasure safe." I recalled this man had wife, children. Were they well? But a year past, he'd worn a black ribbon about his sleeve. I could not recall why. But doubtless his life extended beyond this play-stage of Bank and Coin. What sorrows made him weep? What joys made him laugh? I remembered the coffee-house servant girl, wondering if she was mystic family posing as common clay. Why not Furst as well?

Bah. Have done and just relegate all men and women, all beasts and stars to be brothers and sisters of one magic, secret, mystic family. Leave out only me, to walk the world staring at shadows of faces and the tips of ears. Diogenes without a lamp. I do not wish a lamp. I do not wish to see.

A porter brought wheeled cart, though I judged I could carry the box. But hardly fight as well. Not that I'd do better fencing while pushing a cart. But no guards cried *Halt*. And no play-theatre coincidence of my twin entered the stage, so that we faced one another while onlookers gasped.

All instincts cried out for flight. No different than in enemy fields. We marched calm, eyes and ears twitching for ambush. Only in the main hall before the door to the street, I recalled my mission. To locate Black's ledger books. I weighed grabbing Furst, shoving knife-point beneath his chin. Absurd. We were two gentlemen in a place of business, peers of long acquaintance.

"I wish to review my accounts with Alderman Black," I told Furst. God's truth in those words. "Shall I ambush him in his house, or is he now scribbling his merchant prayers in your temple?"

Furst laughed. "Since a certain conflagration of mysterious origin, he performs his legerdemain entirely at home. Surrounded by pots of water, no doubt."

The Demoiselle laughed. Furst looked pleased. I stared puzzled. "*Legerdemain*," he repeated. I nodded as though understanding.

"I did not send for a carriage," sighed Furst, giving up on whatever idiocy he meant. "Your manservant awaits outside, holding your horses. Or did you intend some clever ruse out the back?" He tapped the side of his nose again in sign he understood the secret ways of spadassins. Would I were so wise.

"My manservant," I repeated. "You don't mean Stephano?"

"Do two creatures walk the earth with such devil faces?"

The Demoiselle put hand to my arm again. Unnecessary. I smiled to Furst. "I have all that I came for," I said, shaking his hand. "For which I thank robber-barons everywhere."

202

We exited the bank, entered the evening light. I took the chest from the porter. The Demoiselle and I stood staring at the carriage in the street before us. Two horses and one driver, who leaned back to stare at the sky, berating cruel heaven with the face it gave him.

Exactly as months before. At the Church of all Saints. Flower and I, staring at this same carriage, this same man.

"What will you do?" whispered the child beside me.

What I did was smile. Shaking a bit, but as a man fresh from honeymoon I attest that pleasure shakes a man, as much as pain or rage. And what I felt now was hot, heart-beat pleasure. It twitched fingers, gave tongue a taste of red salt.

"Did I never tell of when I infiltrated the French command?" I asked. "Or do you of the family believe only yourselves play separate parts? Master Shakespeare would disagree."

At my voice, Stephano looked down to earth, beheld us, and leaped from the carriage. I prepared to throw the box in his face as he drew knife. But no, he moved to open the door, making his crooked bow.

The Demoiselle and I studied that open door, the man before us. Within waited a fresh cloak, my best rapier. A silver flask. I turned from this sight to study Stephano's neck. He wore a scarf, covering any scar across throat. He did well to hide it. An insufficient scar, as he yet breathed. At some point he realized we did not rush to enter the carriage, and gave up the bow.

"Is all well, Master Gray?" he growled. He frowned his fist of a face. "I am early. But so also, you." I shook head, did not meet eyes. Not yet. So then, the Harlequin must be on his way, finished his sermonizing to those he Judas-goated towards the slaughter-house.

Had my impostor re-taken Stephano into service? It would aid the fraud, to have this source of knowledge of my person. But did Stephano know the ruse, or did he believe the Harlequin me? Perhaps the Harlequin had spoken of forgiveness in my kindly voice, smiling out my kindly eyes.

But how could Stephano believe? *He killed Elspeth.* And let others believe I did. Betrayed me when I was wounded, running, hiding. He was the final man I trusted; and he'd sold me to my enemies. Stole my fortune, making his pathetic pretense of a throat-slash apology… Did the Harlequin smile and say 'I forgive'? No actor could deliver those words in my voice to this man, and play the part proper.

So I considered, while the man stood respectful, head tilted in slightest mockery. I'd once taken that mocking tilt as respect. It said, *You are master, I servant, but we both are fighters.* Years of recollection flooded my mind. Feelings I'd left in the dark of my cell, chained.

In war one feels love for the men who fight besides you, the faces circling the fire the night before battle, knowing tomorrow's circle will be smaller. Stephano, Elspeth and I had been three soldiers in the war against life's solitude. We'd made a home, as much as any nation of clans that Lalena could boast.

Stephano had betrayed that home. As had Elspeth. Perhaps I had as well, though I could not see how. I do not brood on such. I wondered if the Harlequin, rejected by their blood-kin, blamed themselves. No, they must see their cousins as the betrayers. Mere human nature.

"Well, let's away," I declared at last. My voice calm. No teeth gritted, no fists clenched. "You know where I need be next?" If he said 'no', I would direct him I-didn't-know-where. But a good valet strives to know such things. Stephano had been such. Before. Before.

"Of course," he nodded. I placed the box in the carriage, sat myself beside it. The Demoiselle remained hesitating on the walk, biting lip. Wise child, she disliked entering the same trap twice. Yet took step to so do, moon-eyes wide. But I shook my head, smiled in farewell and shut the carriage door. Leaving her behind. What must come next, would not make theatre for child's eyes.

Chapter 21

Of Heaven's Cages, and Human Rages

I kept eye to the windows for signs of our destination, for sudden attack. I opened the silver flask, sniffed what waited within. When last I drank from this, the drugged contents knocked me to the floor and half across the Styx. I'd only resurrected by the slaps and kicks of arresting guards. Whiskey that tasted flat? A spadassin should know better. But I had trusted the source. Again, a spadassin should know better.

I detected nothing now but the aroma of fine amber fire. No matter. I capped it untasted. There are cups one does not sip from twice. I unsheathed the rapier. A good one, well balanced, no nonsense of ornamentation with the hilt. I considered the top forward panel of the carriage. A good thrust through, and I might skewer the driver.

It was a peculiarity of Stephano that he spoke succinct when addressing another. But when merely *with* another, he milled out dialogue not meant for reply. He might go on for hours, while I read, while Elspeth sewed, while the fire crackled. I do not believe he chattered so when alone. The habit had no use in solitude. It was his way of saying to others, *here I still am*. Affirmation that he was, indeed, not alone. El and I understood. God's blood but we understood. We smiled, named him *Mr. Talkative*, let his chatter become the pleasant noise of falling water, the bird-twitter of dusk. He did so now, from his seat atop the carriage.

"More protests in the street. You've stirred them proper. Handbills enough to burn all winter, keep one warm. Who reads the damned things? Only street-dogs and the king's spies. Church-bells. No matter how the world burns, the bells get rung. Birth, death, marriage. Ha, there's the great bell my mam called Old Tom. And his cathedral sisters. They have names, those other bells. Named after angels. Luciel, Kariel, Oriel. Pretty names. I'd name cats so, could I abide a cat."

I wondered whether he thought me the real Rayne Gray, or took me for the Harlequin imitation. He acted no different now than any other day in my service. This coach, his chatter… as if we were back a year, and he my faithful pirate-valet again. The man I most trusted in all the untrustworthy world. This carriage would take me to my unburnt home, where Elspeth kept dinner warm for us, humming hymns by the fireside.

I puzzled over the cloak folded beside me. Nothing from my old wardrobe. This was black, hooded, long of hem and arm. A monkish domino for Latin chants in midnight service. Well, I had been absent from society since my death-sentence. Perhaps gothic defined the latest evening-style in Londonish? Nothing more likely.

"Ship came to the docks today with dead men. Near foundered on the sea wall. Throats torn out. Not normal sailors, I hear. That was sea-mischief, devil's gospel on it.

Been a gentleman of fortune on the water myself. Once watched an island follow our ship for a week. Nothing of your whales. This had trees clear as day, and a mountain and a lighthouse. Captain wouldn't go near, so it chased us three days. At last the thing grew bored and turned tale up and dived below the waves. Sent a wash that sent the captain overboard."

If the Harlequin told Stephano to await him at the bank, he may well have arrived as we left. Only to find his treasure removed. Would he scream of thieves and doubles? I doubted. Furst would hardly believe I'd been an impostor; nor would the Harlequin wish to discuss such matters. No, the *Pierrot* would pursue the carriage. Or rush to where he believed it fled. By sense I'd be off to Paris. Let him seek me there. So long as I ran a step ahead of him, he failed to enter the picture. Serving merely as cover to approach my enemies.

I reconsidered. Recalled the warning of the Knight of Light and Dust. *Your Aldermen and Magisters are lesser foes. The Pierrot is whom you must face, else fall.* I was judging the Pierrot as I would Black or Green. But he was not. He was of the mad, clever family. Forever *where they wished*; always *who they wished*. Masters of lounging on the path ahead, for all the random steps one took to flee what came behind.

What resources did this Harlequin lord have? All of a magic pirate clan, I supposed. The prince Lalena and I dropped to Hell commanded confederates in black clothes, white faces. *Servants*, she'd called them. I was unsure if they were family, or mere minions. Perhaps a lesser mix, as the *aberrations* of the Mac Tier. Creatures of the family who lost command of their gifts. The Harlequin servants had not impressed me with any great skill at fighting; but I had caught them off-guard. The fantastical family undervalued common-clay outsiders. Unlikely they'd so slip again.

"There are beasts beneath the seas like to what you see with eyes closed. Ghost lights, and fog-forms. Ha, I once walked the city fog lost till I came to the river. Well and there was a great creature poking head out the dirty water, exact as lost as I. We stared at each wondering how either could ask the other directions home. Had a great horse's head, it did. Eyes big as cartwheels. It honked like a bugle, then sank down into the mucky river. Hope the monster sailed safe home. It's all any sailor wants."

Watching the passing city-scenes I realized our destination. And smiled. Did I still need Stephano? No. Ah, but let him drive on. Let him breathe, let him chatter. For a bit longer. It made a pleasant reminder of old days, feeding oil to the fire now warming my heart, setting it to beat double-time. I considered what tools I would need tonight; extracted a glass vial from the treasure-box's wallet of poisons. I still carried Elspeth's dagger... not a thing to sully with another's blood. I put it with the treasure.

Beneath the seat I keep a concealed compartment. I empting the contents of the box within. Not a sure hiding-place. But I disliked leaving a treasure chest lying about. And there was no carrying it with me tonight. A fortune in gold and jewels weighs heavy when one needs run or fight. I anticipated both, and soon.

Treasure hid, I studied the sunset view of tailored lawns and ornate gates. Quite pleasant, but my gaze kept returning to the panel behind the driver. To the steel rapier. But quick thrust made poor revenge. It allowed too little time for remorse. For final words of hate, a vision of Hell's hot floor from Earth's cool dirt. No, I'd grant my Stephano the dignity of a fight. Perfect. He could have the dagger he used to kill Elspeth. For my weapon I'd take… a candle-stick. Had he not claimed she'd meant to bash his head with one? We would settle with the same weaponry. Stephano was a man of scar and skill. Excellent. I would make him feel as an Irish maid facing a devil's scowl.

"That's a ring round the moon tonight, for storm. But moons will show different rings for your different weather. There's a sharp white ring for a summer storm. A blue circle for lightning. Best take cover then. A rainbow halo marks a mean storm, all cold wind and wave. God help a ship then. Tonight's ring is blue. Lightning it is."

Storm warning declared, we approached Alderman Jeremiah Black's manse. River-fronted, a walled estate of comfort and elegance. A secret kingdom of wide lawns, polished stone, glass windows, bright lights and splashing fountains. I compared it with my own dark castle, my cold dusty lair of shadow and ghost, exiled to the edge of the world. Shook my head. What a *practical* wedding present a wealthy urban estate made. Yet people must forever fob off on newlyweds their cracked vases, their unwanted spoons, their demon-haunted Scott castles.

And yet, were I of calmer blood than this moment, I would exchange all the city, the treasure beneath me and all the earth about me, just to be there.

Stephano halted the carriage beneath the portico. Servants rushed to the carriage door. But loyal man, he leaped first, halting all with a grin to frighten Satan's mirror. And so won the honor of opening my door. Thus honored, I stepped forth, rapier unsheathed.

"Will I be accompanying you tonight, sir?" asked Stephano. He considered the unsheathed blade, devil's eyes widening.

I stared up at the bright manse of Alderman Black. Liveried servants holding wide the doors. Party laughter echoed forth, soft music and tinkling glass. Within would wait a clan proud as any tartan of the family. And far more prone to aberration, to abomination. Behold a tribe united neither by blood nor love. No, the ties here were account and credit, title and deed, debt and servitude.

Usurious bankers, unctuous bishops, unjust judges. Legislators, lawyers, lackeys. Slavers, whore-masters, arms-dealers and aldermen. Lords of vast lands seized from poor neighbors. Factory-masters who measured beggars and prisoners for a proper wheel to turn. Dim princes and inbred lords, ministers of office competent in no art but flattery. Officers in bright uniform and unscarred skin, trained to see living men as pins on maps. Clerics, priests and vicars of no creed but what softened a nest, fattened a belly, flattered a mirror. All the clever and the cruel and the fortunate; lords of the world who chewed at other men's lives, greedy and confident as rats in a babe's crib.

In the mad northern island I had faced monsters. Fascinating and terrifying, yet I never felt they had much to do with me. Ah, but the monsters in this house were *mine.*

Satisfaction made me shiver. Not for surety of my goal. Too many enemies, too little time to scout. Just from this point I could see Black had increased his guard triple-fold. Signs of dogs; shadows of watchers within the trees. Armed servants, cautious eyes from windows. I had less chance of returning alive from this bright house than from a French encampment. But at last I stood on the doorstep of my duty. No more words, but forward charge.

"Best stay with the coach, Stephano," I said. I sheathed the rapier. Yes, I would save my traitorous servant's throat for last. As I had my commander's. The memory made me smile. In return he bowed, handed me the strange black cloak.

"Must I wear this?" I sighed. Exactly as I did before every formal dinner, while he presented each separate fool article of elegant idiocy. And he'd reply in mock sorrow, *'Afraid so, sir.'* Ever the proper valet, fussing at each slightest detail of fold and comb and ornament. I considered my wedding ring.

"Alas yes, sir. *Clothes maketh man.*" Just so. I struggled into the cloak, disliking how it hindered arm and leg. Stephano fussed with the folds. Finally reached and pulled the hood up, leaving me a cave-mouth of cloth to peer forth from.

"Very good, sir," he said. "You look a right conspirator."

I gave him a look from out my cave. He sent one back. My look meant last goodbye to the companion my ruffian-valet had been. I had no idea what the returned face intended. I found I did not much care.

"Tend the horses, stay close by the coach," I said. "I may wish to leave the party early." I had come to the city to kill a man. I now turned and walked up the steps of his house.

Chapter 22
While I am, Death is not

I stared at Death. He stared at me. I nodded to acknowledge we were old friends. He shook head, meaning he disagreed. He blocked the entrance to the ballroom. I moved to step past. He turned his scythe sideways, blocking entry.

"And I was just thinking fondly of you," I sighed.

He reached a white-gloved hand, pushed back my hood. I considered doing the same to him. Tit for tat and add a bit, for spit and spat. Shoving the scythe up his bony ass had strong appeal.

"Ah. Our *Gray*." He gave the name a certain emphasis. Did that mean he thought it not my real name, mere word for the copy of the thing?

"Ah. Their *Streng*," I replied, giving the name equal emphasis. Perfectly fair. He was not the real Death, just Black's chief of arms. Dressed *a la mort*. Dark cloak, white mask, scythe and weak irony.

I stared past him into the grand hall of Black's mansion. Within swirled a carnival crowd of devils and angels, milkmaids and mermaids, popes and prostitutes in matching silks. Figures of beauty and fear, desire and dementia, archetypes and archons of import. Or rather, the idea of these things. Attend a few family gatherings, one cannot take costume for more than cloth and pretense.

A masked ball. I sighed in relief. My cloak was only costume, not uniform. I had feared to find myself in line with other fools, marching in gothic formation down to secret caverns. There by torch-light to plot the downfall of kings, the burning of churches and the teaching of French to the innocent.

Do not smile. Londonish swarms with secret societies, brotherhoods, ancient orders. Alderman Black once described to whiskey and commiscration, his initiation into the Bavarian Illuminati. Hours of solemn oath and midnight ritual challenging all his soul not to laugh or yawn. A week later he was invited to join a second Bavarian Illuminati that denied the existence of the first. Then a third. He gave it up.

While Magister Green eternally fretted he could not rise above the lowest ranks of Free-Mason, though he sits by day with rulers of empire. He bitterly blamed a minor clerk in the Naval Department, who held grand rank by cloak and candle.

Dealer insists he faithfully attended the Hell-Fire Club all the years Green, Black and I merely attended war. Though I picture Dealer as more voyeur than partaker in masked grotto-orgy.

"This way," said Death. No, said *Streng*. No Grim Reaper, he. Mere murderous fool. The rudeness did not surprise. He disliked my soul years before Black and I fell out. Streng required a touch of fear in other's eyes when he smiled. He considered it cowardly of me to smile in return. As well, he sulked I gave myself airs by considering myself the peer of his master. I didn't, to be honest. I was and am far better man than Black. As for Streng; *well*.

But did he dislike me now for who I was, or for who I feigned? Both, no doubt. I could not picture a Harlequin lord bowing to such an ass as Streng, except in mockery. Streng turned and walked down the hall. Two liveried guards took position behind us, walking in careful pose of solemn service. Pistols to the side; dainty French flint-locks. I gave them a nod and followed Streng. They followed me.

From beyond, an orchestra began final tuning. What a wondrous sound, that last moment before the written music begins. A harmonious whisper of oboe and bugle, violin, cello, bassoon and bell softly testing through note and key, reed and string. Like birds at dawn, twittering and flittering in the all-but-hush. I wondered what music would rise tonight. Alderman Black liked loud pieces that shouted for joy of conquest. One had to give him that.

We entered a study. Lamp-lit, a place of business. Desks. Cabinets. Papers. Disappointing. Not Black's office, but Streng's. Still my eye surveyed what a canny spadassin might find useful. Streng went to the desk. The door shut behind. I did not need turn to verify that one guard remained outside, one remained observing, back to wall.

Streng removed his Death's mask, tossed it to the desk as though weary of mortality. He opened a cabinet, rifled within. If he drew pistol I'd best throw myself at him. No doubt while the man behind shot me. After fighting Chatterton I'd vowed never to underestimate a guard. A wise resolution, but the world does not always allow us to be wise. Streng found a parchment, folded and sealed. He threw it on the desk beside the mask of Death.

"Your last speech. For the final gathering of your peasant uprising, tomorrow on Echoing Common. See you deliver it so you move the masses to murder, or all this theatre has been wasteful as it has been tedious."

Theatre? Well. That settled who this man thought I was. I struck a pose. "Friends, Romans, city-folk, lend me your ears." I drew rapier from under the cloak, waved it to the heavens. The ceiling, anyway.

"Would the slaves lay aside their ruth,
And let me use my sword, I'll make a quarry
With thousands of these quarter'd lords, as high
As I could pick my lance."

Beyond the walls began the thunder of Handel's
'Music for the Royal Fireworks'. Trumpets and drums.
Excellent for itself; and twice-so to cover the coming thunder. I bowed. "Hamlet, act three, scene four," I shouted.

The guard behind me disagreed. "Coriolanus, you fool," he declared.

217

"And with words jumbled," agreed Streng, raising his voice to counter Handel's joy. As if he could. "It should be the slaves slaughtered for the nobles."

I nodded. "It depends on whom you name slave, whom heaven knows for noble. But I have the next line pat." And before any could argue the scene, I turned and ran the guard behind me through the throat. The blade pierced the door, nailing him where he stood.

"*A rat!*" I cried. His eyes stared shocked. My eyes returned no apology. I did not wait to see him fall, but seized his gun, withdrew my blade, whirled to face Streng.

He stared open-mouthed. Tried shouting over trumpet and bugle. I shook head, stepping closer. I never trust a pistol to strike even a wall except the barrel is shoved against a brick. Streng reached into the cupboard while drawing his rapier. Fool. It left him fumbling for pistol and sword at once. I kicked his knee. A time-honored tactic, if lacking style. He howled, dropped the pistol, retreated behind the desk.

"Sit," I ordered, waving pistol and blade at once. Streng snarled, face more murderous than any carnival Death. He did not fear me. But did not see a path to killing me. Rapier dropped, he limped to a chair, sat.

"Told Black you were a mad whoreson not for trusting," he observed.

"Quite mad," I agreed. "We'll skip my mother. Keep hands where I see them." I enjoyed the music a bit,

218

listening for shouts, for pounding at the door. Nothing. No alarm given.

I placed sword-point beneath Streng's chin. "Let us trade, truth for life. Why do you want an uprising? Why plot a slaughter of tradesmen? And why this false Seraph resurrected from Hell?"

Pain to pride and knee twisted his face. I was a robber in an alley, stealing his fat purse of self-worth. But he tried a smile. "You'd best ask Black the why's of the world. You were only hired to do the part left unfinished by that shite Gray getting slaughtered in his cell. Would God I could have seen it. Why do you care now, the work all but done?"

He stalled. Quite proper, I'd have done the same. The longer we chatted, more likely others would interfere. But I'd murdered the guard. Streng could hardly think I'd spare him. He'd tell me nothing. I sighed, reviewing *'Music for Royal Fireworks'*. Bugle and drum would shortly reach a crescendo suitable to cover a gasp or death-cry.

A flicker in his eyes, a gasp behind. I jumped aside, not waiting to turn. A knife thrust where I'd stood. The guard I'd impaled. He'd risen, drawn blade, crossed the room in what must have been a long day's journey. Blood pouring from his neck, breath gasping out the wound. I'd have heard but for Handel. He slashed again, I parried with the pistol. It fired, striking him in the stomach. A modest *bang*, a cloud of smoke.

219

I turned to Streng, who'd retrieved his blade. He thrust across the desk, shouting. Pointless. From the gardens cannon and crackers exploded. Fireworks to accompany the bugles and trumpets. I parried, ran him through the chest. He collapsed into his chair.

The guard lay on the floor, gasping, drowning in his own blood. Struggling bravely against the closing dark. I knelt down beside him. He looked up, eyes damned angry.

"You were right," I shouted above the fireworks. "It was Coriolanus." I covered his eyes and cut his throat. Sighed, stood, turned back to Streng.

The man slumped in the chair, blood trickling from his mouth. I lamented the guard, but not Streng. I spoke of human monsters and aberrations. Black's chief of arms championed such. I should have ended him years past. Returned, I saw my failure. I'd grown over-comfortable with mansions and monsters, bankers and bullies. Had I faced my duty before, the brave guard at my feet might yet breathe. And a thousand others. By God I should have gone through the city scything all such as Streng. These thoughts placed some mask of anger upon my face. Streng frowned.

"You aren't Pierrot," he whispered. "You are the real one. You should be dead. Torn apart in gaol." He drooled blood. I leaned down to the man, whispered from one ghost to another.

"But that I am forbid

To tell the secrets of my prison-house,

I could a tale unfold whose lightest word

Would harrow up thy soul, freeze thy pouring

blood."

"Macbeth, Act 3," I declared. I waited for Streng to argue it. He did not, having slipped down to hell. I searched his pockets, found a ring of keys. Excellent. I went through the desks and cupboards. No ledger books or incriminating letters against the king, of course. Still you never know. I found a fresh pistol, a layout of the house with useful notations. I studied it awhile. Clearly it would have been fatal to climb the dumbwaiter to Black's upper rooms. Also the terrace, the roof, the basement and the garden court.

On the other hand, the central stairs past the ballroom offered a quiet path to the upper floors of Black's private areas.

My eye fell upon the packet Streng had tossed. I tucked it away for later. I picked up the Death's mask, now graced with a red hand-print. It added a pleasing touch. Donned the gloves. Raised the hood. Gathered up the scythe. Our cloaks were much the same. With these props I might well hope to pass for Black's chief of arms.

Exit *Death,* stage left.

Chapter 23
The Girl in Fire and Smoke

I stood on the edge of a costumed ball, considering humanity in disguise. Plays are forever presenting twins and doubles, girls guised as boys, men mincing for women, male actors playing women feigning men. We see the king passing for the fool, princes wandering in peasant garb. Dungeon guards and moonlight lovers are entirely foxed by mere change of clothes, a stretch of voice. In full daylight the audience scoffs. How does that idiot take his buxom fiancé for a gray-beard lawyer? The mad monarch for sane jester? The clever villain for kindly brother?

But those plays are not writ for sunlight. They are for torch-lit halls and rush-light cells, for chambers and stages where every figure is a creature shaped from equal parts shadow and light, costume and voice. I have seen in Paris a room wonderfully lit by burning gas-lamps. So bright! Every last shadow banished. No disguise could pass, no villain in dark corners lurk unseen. When such lighting becomes the rule, every man will be seen for what he is, and playwrights must turn to honest work. Spadassins too, I suppose.

I crossed the crowded ball-room. Chandeliers cast shadowed glow, not illumination. So also the lanterns to the sides, the candelabrum. Entirely proper for a dance of masks. I noted guards who straightened at Death's approach, thinking him Streng. Death nodded, approving their attention to duty.

A figure pranced past. A zebra-man in stripes of silk, shaking his diamond-sparkle mane. A laughing lion-woman pursued, painted finger-nails extended for claws. They dodged between dancers, to the consternation of feather-bedecked bankers and fish-headed financiers, snake-coiled-courtesans, tiger-striped aldermen. Generals guised as gazelles, bishops in ceremonial vestment of devouring lions. Death stopped, surveyed the crowd. Beast-pattern costumes dominated the dance. Nature stood in style tonight. Why not; last year it was Greco-Roman.

The quartet at the balcony began Mozart. I didn't recognize the piece. But no masking Amadeus's laughing notes. So well-played Death himself paused in his hurry, bone-mask face turned up in appreciation.

The violinist gazed off, bovine eyes contemplating bucolic afternoons of green and sky. A bull-mask. The oboe player sported fox's ears, black nose, yellow gown. The cello master dressed in fantastical tiger-skin and silk brocade. Last, hark to viola manned by wolf.

I stared. Those were costume and mask, each. And yet, how could they so feign the things, and not be the things? Death shivered. He'd thought himself part of the audience. But no, he was a player, confused by costume and shadow as any other. Still, the music was masterful. No disguising that.

The oboe player spotted me. Her eyes opened wide. She stood, rushed to the balcony, leaned down. Her fox-hair hung red-gold curls. Her black fox-ears twitched to be free of those tangles and I near laughed...but stopped. That face showed older than Vixen's. Not coquettish, but womanly. The form thinner, taller. Family, no doubt; but more like to Lalena's vampiric governess... I struggled to recall the name Rowena. And this fox-girl wore dress yellow as butter, patterned with black diamonds. Harlequin tartan? No Mac Tier would deign to wear that.

"I know you, m'lord'," she called down, and smiled, and it near broke heart, for I received a token of love in that smile meant for another. And of a sudden I longed to be on a sane stone at the edge of the world again, and not in the center of a mad dancing city.

Did she know me? I scarce knew myself. Was the person she saw Streng, Grayish, or Gray? Perhaps she meant Death. The thing itself, and not the costume of the thing. Who to say but these personifications do not form some clan of their own? Picture Death, Time, Harvest, War, Peace, Sleep and Night, all in kilt and family conference.

I put finger to Death's lips, if skulls had such in place of bony grin. In reply the fox-woman laughed, twirled. Plucked a red rose from a garland about the balcony, tossed it down to me. I had no choice but to catch it. She raised hand to her red-ripe lips, kissed the gold band she

224

found there. Then returned to the orchestra, piping away to raise the spirit of Amadeus.

Dancers about me laughed to see Music flirt with Death. No greater interest than that. I pocketed the rose, continued on. I came to a door guarded by liveried servants, waved an imperious hand. They rushed to open the door. I passed between their bows. They closed it behind. Excellent. I decided to make Death's costume my spadassin dress. How dull, all that climbing of walls, crawling sewers, skulking in shadow to reach one's goal. Good exercise, I grant.

Stairs, a hall, more stairs. I was familiar with much of Black's mansion; not these back-passages. Yet I felt a sense of déjà vu... this wandering of dangerous halls recalled the haunted castle. I wondered what mad relatives knocked at the castle-door today. What my wife did tonight. Was she thinking of me? In her eyes when we'd parted, I'd seen her fear. She didn't think I would return. A dark voice in her heart told her *I would not want to.*

Did I so want? I had a fortune in my carriage, no bounty on my head. I was free as the old ones, to be whom I wanted, go where I wished. I could set fire to Black's house now, call our feud even. Where then next? North to warm wife, or East to warm France?

I wondered if the guard I'd killed had a wife. Tonight she'd wait impatient for his step at the door. Scripting angry dialogue in the theatre-stage of her mind. *Then he'll say; then I'll say.* Only no cue comes to begin her lines. At last she'd undress for bed, calling herself a fool to fret. In the dark, she'd reach to the empty place beside her, draw hand back before it grew used to emptiness. Her man had been right about Coriolanus. I didn't recall that he wore a wedding ring. Not every man does. I considered again how Stephano had not remarked on mine.

A hallway ending with a locked door. But keys jangled my pocket to counter every lock. How this night shone with favorable stars! Would make a wary man suspect fortune's intent. Another stair, another locked door. I opened soft to see a large room of wealth and ornament. Surely Black's private chamber. Fireplace purred, a great warm cat of flame. Before it stood Satan. I smiled in recognition. My once-friend Dealer, in scarlet tights and doublet, sporting a horned cap, silk mask. A red rope of a pointed tail. He stared at the painting above the mantel. Dealer always studied just so, hands at back, face thrust forwards into the storm-wind of art and style.

I entered the room, closing the door behind. Locked it. Satan turned, started. As actors should when Death takes stage, scythe at shoulder. But then he returned gaze to the painting. "Mister Streng," he drawled. I understood. He gave Death a name, to declare form and limitation. Ah, but wherefore should he fear? Had he not traded his soul to live? Death came and stood beside Satan, shoulder to shoulder, and together they contemplated the portrait.

226

It was large, near life-size for the subject. A young girl on the path to womanhood, breasts still more pointed than the half-spheres of adult. One could tell by the round cheeks, plump thighs and sparse hairs to the groin, that but a year or two past she skipped rope, played chase on the green. Red burned her hair and alive, more living fire than the flame in the hearth, or the fires below the earth. Flames from hell, roaring up now, embracing me.

I stared at a young Elspeth. Well, Dealer had mocked me in my chains, telling me of this portrait. Declaring from the safety of the gaol hallway, how she'd been a spy for my enemies, and Black's mistress first. And indeed her ghost had confessed to me in dream the truth to some of it. To some of it.

Granted, Black bore me such malice it were believable he'd commissioned this work just to mock my ghost. Why should he not? He owned a flowing river of misbegot wealth. The man must spend it on something, else piled coins would pour out his windows to the profit of the poor again. I searched for a mole near the navel. There, just where I'd oft played. I sighed. Poor El.

"Go away, Streng," said Dealer. "You don't know at what you leer."

"No?" Death whispered.

"You see a naked girl," sighed Dealer, thinking me a dull bully. Which I was. Just not the one he supposed. "You don't understand what you see." He sniffed. "The reality is invisible to you."

227

Ah, here came a lecture upon Art. No bore's droning, but genuine opinion. Dealer was a master of composition and sign. He delighted to explain, not in mere pride but in joy to share. Only the sheer generosity of that sharing ever wearied the ear, over-filled the ear's cup. I felt a rush of love, rage and affection for my lost friend, just as I had when listening to Stephano's lonely babble in the carriage.

"Oh?" Death whispered.

"No," he affirmed. "This is a soul captured. Once it was light shining upon a young girl. Lying vulnerable upon rich sheets. Her ephemeral glow has been transposed to paint and canvas. Captured, and so a moment of the soul as well. Look at the eyes, man. They are wide open, pupils dark. Green windows showing desire, and fear of that desire. She is a girl-creature whose body has changed, shifted about her soul. She lays frightened of what she now is. Her breasts terrify her, so she thrusts them forwards. Her legs want, and in fear of that want she twists them restless about the sheets. Hair unbound, mouth unbound. Freed to be a naked vision of herself, she becomes a soul unbound. Behold a girl captured in light."

Death tilted his head, considered this testimony. Rendered final judgement. "No."

"Pffff," said Dealer. Then, yielding to curiosity, "What then do you see, except something to fuck?"

Death gave reply. In verse of Blake, of course.

"Love seeketh only self to please,
To bind another to its delight,
Joys in another's loss of ease,
And builds a Hell in Heaven's despite."

Dealer had been standing at ease. Now he stiffened, ceased to breathe. Whereas the fire flickered brighter, suddenly interested. Or perhaps my eyes were of a sudden more inclined to flame. Certainly I felt flames rising through the floor, igniting what smoldered behind my eyes, within my heart. Fire; so close a cousin to desire. Clan and sept, to *ire*.

And yet Death stood at ease, fingers tapping a tune on his scythe. In no hurry, and his turn to declaim.

"I see a young girl," said Death. "Stripped naked before a painter and her patron and god knows who else. Told to lie still in the bed where she is probably taken nightly, willing or no. Where you see *object d'art*, I see a person. You note her fear, but mistake the cause. She is already wise to her body and her desires. She was born with that wisdom, as flower to the sun. What she fears stands before the canvas, where you and I stand now. She fears the change of body turns her to an object of art, an object of rape, a thing of use to cruel hands and minds. Of naming as *thing* and *whore* and *tool* and *spy* and *obsession*, and no more be a person."

Very slowly did Dealer turn to me. Ah, no. Turned to Death.

229

"Pierrot," he whispered. Well, then he shared in that part of the play? One could guess his role. Black knew me well as any; but Dealer had the eye for detail. No doubt he'd been recruited to train the impostor. Fascinating lessons of '*No, Gray always slurped his soup. Don't walk so straight. Hunch forwards as a bear, two legs or four. And scratch your privates as you talk.*' I could have learned more from Dealer about the idea of myself, than from twenty mirrors.

I removed the mask, threw back the hood. Grinned. I'd need mirror to affirm I grinned so well as Death. Still, I've seen corpses enough to grasp the idea. I drew lips far back, presented teeth, eyes wide. Dealer broke for the door. Predictable. I grabbed his trailing tail, near pulling him from his pants. Then tripped him with the scythe handle. As he attempted to rise I kicked him flat again.

"That isn't El's soul, you twit," I noted. I put aside the scythe, drew a handier knife. Dealer whimpered. But I reached up not down, to slice along the sides of the canvas. Dealer opened mouth to scream for guards to come rescue art. I pointed knife to his own mortal canvas; he silenced.

"Elspeth's soul was never bound," I declared, hoping it true. I returned to the picture. "And if you'd ever had the love of beauty enough to see her spirit, it would not be laying on damned pink sheets. It'd be in the kitchen singing the sun's light, else when she sewed by the rain, fed scraps to stray dogs in the alley. Took a basket of bread and flowers to sad neighbors. Made Stephano feel he was a brother. Made me think myself man, no beast."

With that, I peeled the canvas from the frame, rolled it to a scroll, fed it to the fire. The flames brightened to the red-gold of a colleen's hair. Smoke rose, and I breathed in, hoping for scent of warm skin, kitchen soap. I coughed, Dealer cursed. I bent down, lifted him from the floor by his scarlet ruffles.

"Pierrot," he repeated, but he didn't believe.

When last we'd talked, I'd been chained to a wall. He'd kept his distance. Now we could be *close*. I put my face to his. "You wouldn't enter my cell, so I've come to yours." He paled at that. Not a fact any but he and I would know.

I shook him, though he trembled enough by his own. "Tell me, old friend. What does Black plot with my happy face? Why all this work to tarnish the name of the dead?"

He started to babble. I slapped him, so his devil's mask flew aside. Revealing man's eyes bulging in terror. A joy to see. El wouldn't have approved. She yearned for me to turn eyes to Heaven, foreswear Earth's strife. For which I'd burned her portrait first, lest her eyes behold from Heaven what I intended pouring upon the thirsty Earth.

She'd always returned a kind smile to Dealer's flirtation. Said it was a lonely life, living among beautiful pictures. But it was what he chose. *This* was what he chose. I as well, I suppose. I shook Dealer again, for what pleasure remained. But now he'd collected himself.

"*It isn't about you,*" Dealer hissed. Anger gave his voice strength. "It was never about you, you arrogant, posturing shite. Green and the Magisterium wanted a failed uprising, to shift power to civil courts. Black and the Aldermen just worked to be free of king's law. When you died it set it all back. Then they happened on the *Pierrot.* They made a fable of your return, convinced the mad King to grant you pardon. Your double shall lead a weak uprising in the name of the New Charter. The King will be blamed for your pardon, the Charterists hung for treason. Magisterium and Aldermen's Council sweep up the pieces, and royal prerogative and worker's rights finish together."

I wanted to argue. *Of course it was about me. I am the Seraph.* And yet, the business made more sense as plot against King and Law, than slight to Rayne Gray's ghost. Humbling, but there it is. The last crackle of canvas settled to ash and smoke. What else to ask, before the inevitable dramatic interruption? "How did the *Pierrot* enter this grand conspiracy?"

Dealer took breath, recovering, considering. He eyed the door. He also foresaw inevitable interruption, drama and rescue. At least a chance to dart off-scene. Black would come, or Streng or guards or maids with mops. Until then, best chat with me.

"Black noticed Pierrot in a play. Thought he was you, at first. Though up close he's older and thinner. Wan of face as a ghost." Dealer looked aside. "Something wrong about that creature. Day by day he *became* you. More witchcraft than theatre-craft. It frighted everyone. Particularly Green."

I could have shared recent frights of transformation, but declined. A shame. I would have delighted to share my recent adventures with this man. He'd have explained much of the meaning I'd overlooked. One can see the performance, yet miss the message. "What play was Pierrot in?" I asked. "What role?" No, I had no reason to ask. It was just something that interested me.

Dealer actually laughed. "You are the real Gray returned. We thought you torn apart by a mob. Waked you even, with honest toasts. Well, Pierrot had no leading role. Mere Cassio."

"Julius Caesar?" I recalled the role, a bit of line. "Poor man. I know he would not be a wolf."

"No, no, that is Cassius. Cassio, of *Othello*." He took a breath, quoted, "*To be now a sensible man, by and by a fool*".

"*And presently a beast*," I recalled. We both stilled. Recalling nights when he'd come to dine. Inevitable but we'd pull out Shakespeare, choose our lines to recite by light of fire and lamp. What parts had we done last in friendship? Ah. Bits of Macbeth from me. Over-flourished Romeo from Dealer, ever an eye to the balcony of Juliette's breasts. But what had Elspeth recited? I'd been drunk, could only recall my wonder that the words so moved her. I recalled tears in her eyes, shining by the captured light.

"*There's rosemary,*" I recalled her saying. "*That's for remembrance. Pray you, love, remember. And there is pansies, that's for thoughts. There's fennel for you, and columbines. There's rue for you, and here's some for me…*" How did the rest go? Why had it moved her so?

Dealer finished the quote. "*O, you must wear your rue with a difference. There's a daisy. I would give you some violets, but they withered all.*"

Dealer and I granted the shared memory its due of silence, neither of us giving glance to the fire, the girl lost within. Or freed within. At length I released his shirt. "You have an eye for detail, and for secrets. Where does Black keep his ledger books?"

He straightened his outraged horns, preened his insulted tail. "No idea." He eyed the door. The moment of recalled friendship was over. For me, well over. Enough of the man.

I put a friendly hand to his shoulder, drew him close for dear friend. I pressed knife-point to his friend's cheek, began to cut an 'F'. Not for *Friend* but *Fraud*. As well it stood for *False*, and *Failed*. He lashed with his fists, making the *F* crooked.

"Scream and I truly hurt you," I remarked. He held still, blood streaming down his cheek. I pushed him away.

234

"I've no time. *You've* no time. Trade. Your life, for Black's books."

Dealer staggered, took out handkerchief, mopped blood from face. He eyed doors and windows. Time past for guards to hear our struggle, rescue the brave *connoisseur.* Death growled. He flinched.

"How do I know you won't kill me after?" he demanded.

"My word is good," I pointed out. "You are the treacher here, Satan. Lest we forget."

He spat at that. I sighed. Meet a man wearing your coat while riding your horse and jingling your coin purse. Now call him *thief.* Like enough he will bristle with outrage, cheeks reddening at the slander. How easily we accept the reality of ourselves, but not the honest naming.

Then he laughed. "An eye for detail and secrets? Best say, I'm not blind as some." He waved the bloody handkerchief towards the mantel, where the ragged circle of canvas remained. Within the circle, a square panel inset with colored squares.

Well, he had a point. I had not noticed a cupboard hid behind the picture. Mind elsewhere, I suppose. Freeing Elspeth's spirit, recalling the mole beside her navel. I put away knife, kept scythe handy lest he break for the door again. I approached. Six colored squares, each of a different color. Red, Gold, Yellow, Blue, Silver, Bronze.

Tedious. A puzzle box. No doubt when wrongly solved, it fired a pistol, rang a bell, released a tiger. As said, a prosperous villain can only spend so much of his money on oriental rugs and gold plates.

I nodded to Dealer. "Lead on, Pandora."

Dealer mopped his bleeding cheek. "How would I know the trick? Do you suppose Black opens this before his guests and the chamber maid?"

That did seem doubtful. I stepped close, considering. Six squares separated from the panel. No doubt they moved when pushed inwards. A small handle to the side. Push the correct square, say '*sesame*' and it opens *sans* tiger or gunshot.

I looked for scratches upon the squares, to tell me which were most touched. Nothing so easy. I sighed, reached to tap the gold. I prepared myself for tigers and pistol-shots.

"Oh, get out of the way, you clumsy bear," sighed Dealer. Just the tone and phrase he'd used in days past, when I studied some addition to his inventory, attempting to judge form and color, age and composition. Meekly did I move my *leonine* self aside. He stepped before the fire, reached up, pushed the red square. It moved inwards. He did the same with yellow and blue. Then tugged the handle. The cabinet clicked open.

"Ha," I laughed. "The paint colors that mix to *Black*."

"Exactly," said Dealer. He pulled open the panel, reached in, extracted a pistol. Turned to me. Death blinked. No, I blinked. Suddenly I was not Death, merely someone about to die. A position I've held before. Still, a reduction in rank. A deserved demotion for failing guard-duty.

"Rayne Gray," drawled Dealer. "Our *Seraph*. Spadassin. Killer, butcher, bully. Self-styled hero to the downtrodden," he recited, naming me names. I did not bristle at a one, nor ever will. "Do you know how weary I am of you?" I had no idea. I considered the pistol. French, double-barreled. Two cocks, two triggers, two shots. He aimed at my chest. Dealer's hand shook, but not remarkably. We stood quite close. I watched his fingers twitch, anxious for tongue to finish formalities.

"I spent years enduring your ownership of the most precious thing of grace and beauty I have ever beheld," he declaimed. Straightened his backbone to align it with honest rectitude, prior to my murder. "I endured, because we were friends." He mopped the bleeding *F* on his cheek. "Good friends. And then in your idiot, childish, meaningless feud with Black you murdered her."

Touching that he acknowledged past friendship. Holding the gun he had no reason to flatter. "Stephano killed Elspeth," I told him. "I mentioned so, I believe." Dealer took no note, his attention on himself. He was performing a scene writ to regain his mirror's applause. A hard thing, to have flawed soul and honest eye.

"Liar," he spat. "Murderer. You learned what everyone already knew. That she spied for Black. You realized she only ever tolerated your brute person to serve Black. So you cut her down. It's what you do, butcher." Well, he required me to be a beast. It justified his betrayal, his spite, his coveting. No doubt he'd practiced these words putting on his devil costume.

"Is there nothing left here but hate?" I asked. And yes, I spoke aloud to us both. For even as I spoke, I watched the steadying of the pistol, the narrowing of the eyes. "We were friends." My final appeal to Blake.

I grew angry with my friend,
I told my wrath, my wrath did end."

He shook head. "All love I had left, you just burned in front of me." He thrust the pistol forwards, pulled upon triggers.

"The cocks are only half-set," I explained. "You must thumb them fully back." He stared down at the mechanism, thumbs fumbling. Smiled as one 'clicked' full back. I swung the scythe. With rapier drawn I might have sliced surgically across his wrist. He might have lost the hand. But I held no scalpel, only a farm-tool for cutting swaths of grain.

I've killed with saber and axe. Never beheaded a friend before. Not a perfect cut. Ragged towards the end. Past bone the slice slowed. But once begun, I did not feel it right to stop. All said, that was a tool of excellent edge.

238

I watched the neck fountain as the body collapsed. I'd seen that before. A living man's a liquid thing. We are founts set to run at proper time. The head thumped, rolled, came to rest as any round object weary of rolling. *F* now branded the cheek for *Fin.*

Ah, Dealer. I looked down and trembled. Was I become such a beast? Whatever words anger shouted, my heart had hoped at act's end the last lines would be of pardon. And it would, but for gun-click and scythe and moment's decision. *F* would have been *Forgive.* Him for me, me for him. And last and best, he'd forgive himself, then I'd do same for me.

Chapter 24
And with thy bloody and invisible hand

Blood and flame are kith and kin. I watched spilt blood seep towards the fire, making their family greeting. They only seemed to hiss. In truth, they shared fond, familial kiss. I regretted this blood. Dealer's betrayal meant little to me. Even his mocking had been theatre for self-pride and unrequited love. I bent down, tried to meet the eyes. They considered strange new art, beyond this world. I wondered if Dealer yet saw my face, heard my words. They say the guillotined blink on request. Perhaps I should whisper *forgiven*. No. Bad theatre, and he was connoisseur enough to deserve better. But I pulled away his costume hat of devil's horns, tossed it to the flames.

I wanted to explain I'd acted to save myself, not for vengeance. Why kill Dealer, yet let Stephano live? That nonsense of saving my former valet's throat till last, was milk-sop avoidance of duty. I knew my chances in this fortress. Too many enemy, too many shadows.

Chatterton's Angel declared my wedding day, "You cannot come out this alive, Rayne Gray. Too many seek the prize you've set to bed. And the prize herself is a drinker of life, same as you. Can a man challenge his reflection?"

Since then I awaited the sudden knife, the over-loving bite. No different than fields of war or the night-alleys of peace-time. But I had changed in the last months. Seen a world past the idiot curtain of daily expectation. Marriage changes a man, sure as the moon.

"If the world is magic, why then so am I," I told Dealer's head. "I am part of the world, am I not?" Spirits of Erasmus, Spinoza and Lucretius stood to argue but I spoke to the open eyes. "I have changed. I could be forgiving."

'*Do you want to forgive*'? asked the flames. '*Black burned your home. Stephano murdered Elspeth. Betrayed you, more than any.*' Dealer's eyelids rested low, thinking cynical thoughts. Easy to read his opinion. End of conference. I declined to argue further. "No. Never forgive," I informed head and flame and blood. "If I live, they die. I must make sure to live then."

I rose, shaking mad thoughts from my unsevered head. Went to the safe, found a leather satchel with three large books. Spell books, grimoires of financial magic. Behold ships and men, barrels and crops, mines and mills turned to arcane symbols. Numbers for lives, sums for thefts, curses cast upon farms, turning them to fairy gold. What a wonder of column and equation, name and notation. I could not help but smile. Behold the very books I'd sought the night I met a master fencer sitting lonely by a candle. Not yet a year past.

Of what worth now? If both Magisterium and Aldermen's Council aligned in Black's plots, what magistrate would declare trial for treason? Still, as Black gathered power, the number of his enemies must grow apace. Mere human nature. Some office close to the King might make use of these. The sad, mad king.

I faced the far door. I guessed it led to the terrace overlooking garden and fireworks. In which case, I knew who I would next meet. I went back, took the pistol, placed it in the satchel. Slung it about my shoulder, disliking the weight. Lowered the mask of Death, scythe in left hand, knife in right. Readied my soul for what would come, glad the Demoiselle remained off-stage. I then struggled to open the door with full hands, spoiling the exit somewhat.

Stairs, spiraling up. My honeymoon castle had just such stair within a tower. Lalena and I had tread careful lest it end in air. But no, it came to sea-wind and rain. We'd been searching for the gallery of family images. We never found it. At day's end she stamped foot, declared I'd made it up to mock her family. I stamped foot, suggesting her mad family dreamed it to mock me. Then we'd argued about my French officer's coat.

"It's a good coat," I told the winding stairs. "Still has the buttons. Most of the buttons." I came to a guard before a door, holding pistol and lamp. He took Death for dead Streng, lowered the pistol. "Doesn't a man have the right to choose his own coat?" I asked him. He nodded unsure. I became Death, nodding sure. I dragged the dying body down the steps, out of view of the door. Returned to the top, unlocked the door to night air and the sound of music, the battle-field smell of fireworks.

A garden terrace centered by a dinner-table. Candelabrum flickered in night-wind, setting crystal goblets glittering. Silver dishes, golden bowls, porcelain plate. At table-head sat Hades on ebony throne, decked in funeral velvet. Crowned with iron bone and thorn, devil's mask of black silk. Behold Jeremiah Black as *Hades, Lord of the Underworld*. One had to admire the commitment of his imagination to the worship of his soul.

The somber effete beside him: by day's light Magister Green; by tonight's holy moon the Pope. It took all my strength not to laugh in joy at his triple-tiered hat. How did he keep it from falling in the soup? I wondered at the other three. Conspirators of lesser import; good for a scene, serving as foil or spear-carrier. A Neptune in emerald green. Ah, but I'd seen a real sea-lord. A Punch of excellent ugly face, nose curling down to touch up-curling chin. A Roman toga'd Caesar, oak-wreath crowned. I rendered Caesar a second look. The judge who'd presided over my capital trial. I forgot his name. Months past he'd intoned '*hang till dead*'. Far more interesting things had happened since.

A fine and private meeting. In my years of knowing Black, I had never been upon this terrace. Only eyed it from the garden three stories below. In hindsight, the man could hardly lead me past Elspeth's portrait. Four terrace corners, each sheltering pots of cypress and well-hidden guard. The door behind me the only apparent access. I found the key and locked it.

243

"Streng," intoned Hades. "Where is Dealer?"

In reply Death bowed, jerked a bony hand to the floor. They took the meaning for the chamber below. Truly, Death pointed far, farther down.

Caesar laughed. "He is still moaning and mooing at Gray's whore."

"His heart overcomes his art," said Neptune. "Why lust for a used Proserpine, after Hades has tired of the ravishing?" This received some laughter, appreciative nod from Hades. Death thought it weak jest. Better something simple like '*Why go to Hell for a dead mistress*'? But they could pursue the proper *bon mot* in Hell themselves. Soon.

As chief of arms, I dutifully began my rounds, strode to the guard in the first shadow-corner. He straightened at my approach, nodded in respect. I nodded, waited for the next round of fireworks, then stepped on his foot to hold him still. I put hand against his mouth and cut his throat. He jerked, stilled. I propped him in the corner, peered at the terrace and table. No notice taken.

"Master Streng," called Black. "Fetch us the next round from the basket."

I puzzled what he meant. But I must not show myself unsure. No servants here, nor servant's entrance. From where did the feast come? Ah, he had some system of pulley set by the balcony, to send up fresh drink and food. I emerged from shadows, went to the railing, found the mechanism. A basket of proper claret. I struggled to uncork two bottles. Damn all corkscrew. I emptied my powder-vial into the first bottle, feeling remorse. Fine French claret. *Haut Brion*, undeserving of addition.

"What of that devil Pierrot?" asked Caesar, looking about as I filled his glass. "Not joining us?"

Black snorted. "I dislike his company. He gives himself near as many airs as the previous Gray. And he sets our Alderman friend to twitching."

The papal Green sighed. "Gray had right to wear what pride he chose. This other fellow shows a different pride. He takes our orders and smiles. Follows our direction and smiles. That smile mocks us. He means mischief."

Green accepted a re-filled cup, stared into it without slightest tilt to his tower of a hat. I felt an urge to goad him to look down, toppling that wonderful crown. I did not. I finished pouring wine, then continued inspection of the guards. The second struggled. Perhaps the smell of blood on my cloak alerted him. But the orchestra in the garden had begun a Haydn trumpet concerto. *Allegro*, and I could have cut an elephant's throat without notice. Not that I would. Let all beasts live. Merely remove from us those who consider themselves men yet act as beasts... said the man with hot blood soaking his cloak. '*Do you know how awful it feels to stand in clothes dripping with blood?*' Lalena had asked. I knew right well.

"Well, Pierrot is only an actor. And the script calls for him to hang, by and by, by and by," said Neptune. He wobbled slightly, as the sea-god's tide began to ebb. Punch laughed, shook his great ugly head at the idea of Jack Ketch. I watched as he maneuvered the wine glass between nose and chin to reach red lips.

I inspected another guard. This one straightened warily at my approach. I smelled smoke, tobacco not fireworks. A pipe smoldered on the ground. I shook my head in disapproval. He flinched. I pointed to it, he bent down and I struck hard on the back of his neck. He collapsed. I bent to cut his throat. Stopped at sight of the ring on his left hand. Sighed, and let him lie.

I went to inspect the last guard, listening to Haydn and the dinner conversation. I had never heard this piece performed. I had heard the conversation performed, many times.

"We would be fools to remove the king," observed Green. "We only wish him to sit in his throne, and let us be about the business of administering his kingdom."

"I thought we did so now," laughed Punch. I knew his voice. The Assistant Minister of War. Very keen to modernize. A visionary of molten steel rivers flowing into molds for rifle and cannon and swords, engines and ships. One listened to his prophecy and smelled hot iron, blinked at fiery glow.

I returned to the table, inspection of guards complete. I put down the leather satchel of over-heavy books, throwing off the blood-soaked cloak, but keeping mask. I sat myself in Dealer's seat. I did not expect he'd join tonight. But suppose his head rolled from the shadows, asking me to pour a cup? Suppose it followed me forever after, lecturing on art? I recalled the lines I'd recited with Elspeth and Dealer.

Come, sealing night, scarf up the tender eye of pitiful day;
And with thy bloody and invisible hand
Cancel and tear to pieces that great bond which keeps me pale.

Well, I'd killed no friend. Let no man born of woman, name me Macbeth. Dealer had been no Banquo. I poured a glass of claret, hoping I chose the safe bottle. Which was right? I felt fevered, trembling. Sipped a bit of claret, which helped. Unless it was poisoned.

"Too many laws still bind our hands," declared Hades. "And always this howl from the mob, for more votes, more rights, more share in the fruits of their master's fields."

"I can hear what Gray would say to that," remarked Green.

"The field belongs to those who labor in the field," I declared to the company, setting down cup. "Fruit and harvest belongs to he who sows, he who reaps." I leaned Death's scythe against the table, *prima facie* evidence. The harvest blade shown fresh red.

"Yes," laughed Caesar. "Exactly how Gray talked. What a mad Robin Hood." He began to cough, oak-leaves slipping down.

Punch's hands fumbled, searching for the face behind his mask. Fingers fluttered frightened over the elongated nose and chin. Caesar trembled. Hades considered me, turned eyes to his half-empty goblet. Green drank his deep, a proper gourmand. And yet his hat did not tilt! Amazing. He set down cup and sighed.

"Adam Smith's '*The Wealth of Nations*' says that a nation prospers by an invisible hand of market forces," he declared. "How shall the hand guide, except by ownership?"

"You misunderstand Smith," I retorted. "Or say rather you hope to make others misunderstand. His work points out that the prosperity of a nation is inhibited by monopoly and cabal, privilege and oppression."

Caesar fell forwards, gasping. His oak-leaf circlet rolled across the table. Punch sagged backwards in his chair, puppet suddenly deprived of puppeteer. Just an empty thing. Poseidon picked up the bronze circlet, let it drop again. Then let his head sink. The sea-tide ebbed, bearing him away to oceanic depths or the caves of hell.

Green observed these departures, but ignored them. "Smith shows that prosperity is the result of sensible division of labor unrestrained by government. There can be no division, if there is no divider. Ownership is the most fundamental and necessary division of labor."

Hades threw his cup to the ground, stood from his throne. "Guards," he croaked. He pointed at me. Had we been in bonny Scotland, their ghosts would dutifully appear. Alas, we were in Londonish where the dead stir not. Well, seldom anyway.

I pulled the double-barrel pistol from the satchel. Thumbed back both cocks. A pleasant '*click*', '*click*'. Then laid it upon my dinner plate, to appreciate the coming course.

"Labor is divided by different types of *work*," I pointed out. "How shall those you call masters do the least work, and yet claim the largest share of prosperity?" I took off Death's mask, laid it next to Caesar's crown.

There came silence at the table. Not surprising as half the guests lay dead. But Hayden's music continued. What a wonder is music. Composers must perish, and every last musician. Yet the music continues.

"Pierrot," spat Black.

"No, it is not," corrected Green. "Behold the man himself." He stared into his empty cup. At last the papal tower tilted forward! I held breath, inwardly cheering. Green put words into the cup, to mix with dregs. "It does no good to remove princelings from ownership. Hand farmers and tinkers the deed to castle and farm. Now they are the masters, now they shout for their share of the labor of others. You keep confusing economic reality with a story, Rayne, wherein humble orphans triumph over proud princes. Why, if they ever do, then they become proud and princely themselves."

"Nonsense," I retorted. Sipping my claret. Unpoisoned, else I'd be dead as Caesar, Poseidon and

Punch. "You are the one making a story, pretending the rational call to social balance is mere battle of prince and peasant. Consider Plato's Republic. You –"

"Balance!" laughed Green, head tilting back. Again I watched for the tower to fall. "You play with words. I think the late Caesar had it right. You play at Robin Hood. But Sherwood Forest makes no economic model for Britain."

"Will you both be silent!" shouted Alderman Black. "Are you mad? He is Rayne Gray. He has just poisoned us all."

Green and I stared at Hades, our looks chiding untoward interruption.

"These, certainly," said Green, waving at the three corpses. "But I feel only the usual indigestion caused by your cook, who is far less than you claim. And Gray also drank. No, he served us from separate bottles."

Black picked up a carving knife, considered its edge, my pistol, my smile. Sighed, put the knife down.

"Sit," I invited him. I ran a finger along the polished wood of the gun, studying the man. "And may I invite you to take off that ridiculous mask? It embarrasses."

Hades returned to his throne. He reached up, took away the mask. I studied the face. My age, and much of my humor. But no scars, except worry-lines of financial sorrow. More handsome, if a bit blank. To be fair, I'd grown used of late to *interesting* faces.

When last I saw Black's, he'd come to my cell to chat a final bit, fire a crossbow into my head. My future wife had interrupted, bless her.

Before that he'd been burning the books of my library, sending guards to their deaths chasing me about my garden. And entire years before that, he'd sent Elspeth into my life. To spy? For what, we'd been allies then. It could only be to have someone in my house he considered *his*. I studied the raging eyes, the proud chin, the idiot crown. We'd sat at table like this a thousand times. Laughing, arguing politics and women, wine and the world. Men who saw eye to eye on little, yet acknowledged the worth of the other. Peers. And all that time, he'd hated me so much he'd been slightly mad with hate?

Fair enough, and understandable to my present heart. I now felt the same for him.

"Hades," I laughed. "Seriously?"

He flushed, weighing my mood, the pistol, the door, the balcony, the attendant corpses. In the garden below swarmed a multitude of guards and friends. He might rush to the railing, call for aid. That would be comic. I half-hoped he would.

I watched lest his hand slip to pocket for pistol. It would be like the man to keep one about. One should not dress as Hades yet dine unarmed. But he knew me. He would not draw till my eye was elsewhere. I poured more claret, but only sipped.

"The late Punch made excellent point," I said. "You and yours already rule the world. Look at this idiot estate. Servants and fireworks, fountains and orchestra. You hire clerks to seek luxuries not yet overfilling your closets." Sip. "Why this idiot plot to lead tradesmen to revolt and slaughter?"

Black kept proud silence. He saw no profit in bantering at his death-scene. Whereas I had chatted brightly as he visited my cell, drawing back the crossbow. The man lacked style except in victory. Green answered for him.

"You never considered the consequences, Rayne. If you grant votes to men of no property, then you turn the kingdom upside down. Farmers are not philosophers. They are experts in dung and dirt. Shop-clerks know their shelves, not the needs of a mercantile empire."

I considered the guard I'd left breathing for his wedding band. He might be awake already, tiptoeing behind me now. Damn me for a milksop assassin, exact as Green accused. No more dawdling. I pushed away the cup, picked up the pistol.

"Farmers and shop-clerks know the worth of sense," I replied, standing. "Unlike twisted bankers and drunken princes who think it *statecraft* leading men to hope of freedom, just so they may be crushed."

"If I may quote Machiavelli?" retorted Green.

"No you may not," I declared as Black groaned, "No, absolutely not."

Green smiled, ignored pistol and groan. "That wise Italian said, '*Politics has no relation to Morality*'. Your heart is in the past, Master Robin Hood. But the coming age is one of wheels. Financial wheels, political wheels, factory wheels. When they turn well, they shall profit all. But wheels do not turn on kindness, but practical rule."

I considered shooting Green first. A reply conforming to his definition of *practical*. That is, *mechanical disregard of life*. Why had I fallen into all our old arguments? I felt a longing to share the wonders of the past months. '*Listen!*' I'd shout. *I've walked a haunted castle, talked to beings with faces shaped by dream. Opened a tomb of light, drank tea with a mad doll. I've discovered a second reality hidden behind the façade of the day-lit world. I've married.* That last wonder alone equaled a thousand magic castles, and all the wheels of the world.

How to explain? Even to enemies, worth the try. Except, I'd need put to words why I stood here now with those I hated, and not with her I loved… And those were words I did not want to hear, even from myself.

"You make the usual error of the wicked," I sighed to Green. "You confuse what is practical, with what is cruel."

"Indeed they do," said a voice across the terrace. "But who cares a shit for the turn of practical wheels? More enjoyable to watch the blood flow."

I leaped aside, turned pistol to the voice. There at the door. Unlocked so silent? A tall man, wide of chest.

253

Jaunty hat, cloak thrown back to ripple with night-wind. Rapier drawn, tapping the ground impatient to kill, for all the kindly smile on the face of *Rayne Grayish*.

He bowed to the table guests, living and dead. "I've come to kill a man," he said, and looked to me.

Chapter 25

When Death is, I am not

"Well, this should be interesting," declared Alderman Black. He found a goblet. "Gray, are the other bottles safe to drink?" Now he bantered, the posturing fop. I watched the approaching Grayish. His Harlequin son had once cast my mind into dream and memory. A mistake. My memories are not places for another to make casual visit.

"How is this done?" I asked Grayish, passing hand about my face. "This seeming to be me. Is it a picture you draw in other minds, or a true change of form like unto the Mac Tier?"

Grayish paused to consider the question. "Recall we of the family are who we wish to be. Your moon-clan shape-changers work upon their own spirits, to craft themselves another nature. But the Decoursey enter others' minds, direct their perception of reality. Consider me a dream of yourself."

"Fascinating," I admired. "Thank you for explaining." I turned to Hades sitting on his throne pouring fresh cup, and shot him.

Black cried out, goblet toppling untasted except by the ever-thirsty earth. He clutched his chest, holding back the outpouring life. I turned the pistol towards Grayish, whose rapier lunged towards my heart. I parried with the gun, which fired, hitting no one. I threw the gun in his face, leaped back drawing rapier in time to parry the second thrust.

"Does it require silver to kill you?" I asked. "Holy water?" Worth asking, I maintain.

"Not at all," replied Grayish. "It merely requires you defeat yourself in dream."

Sounded easy enough. But "*can a man challenge his own reflection?*" I recalled.

"Exactly," said Grayish, and corkscrewed my blade aside and near skewered me, but that I foresaw the move. An advantage to fencing the mirror, I suppose. I kicked to his knee but his turn to anticipate. He swept down knife to slice. The boot missed his knee, the knife slashed the boot. I feinted towards his head, he anticipated the move and suddenly his fist struck, knocked me flat. Hadn't foreseen that.

I lay on the ground looking up at that mild-smiling face. As many a man has done before. That is, looked up at *my* face. Not their own face. That's far more unusual, and very disorienting. This face staring down. How to describe?

A visage of no strong passion; broken nose, kindly eyes casting easy-going charm. A self-amused interest that sapped all my confidence. When another intends your death, by God they should show more fire than a man mending socks. Was this what others had faced? Horrible. I was a monster, who'd thought himself man.

"You killed my son," observed Grayish. "You, an outsider. A vampire's pet lording over the degraded clans. I was quite angry. But also curious."

I lay still, also angry, if uncurious. How defeat an enemy who is yourself in dream? Would he even bleed? I now saw sane purpose in hell-forged armor. Yet his fist had felt real. The Harlequin son had not fought this way... suddenly that seemed important.

Black moaned low for aid and pity. Shot through the lungs. He'd last the night, wheezing blood. Grayish slashed, I parried from the ground. I've practiced fencing upon my back. He stepped away, circling towards my head. He had all my practice, perhaps. I shifted to follow him.

"I was curious," he repeated. "Why did the blood-thirsting Sanglair tolerate you? Why would the last of the Blade clan befriend you? Why should the old ones gift your common clay with honors denied the family?"

"I have a leonine charm," I confessed. "You must have noticed in the mirror."

Grayish shook head. "More ursine, I think." A kick to my ribs. I gasped, slashed, missed.

"So I sought to learn of Rayne Gray," he continued. Did I always drawl so? It annoyed. "Who was he? A kindly, philosophical killer. Lover of art and music. Even a champion of the poor."

"And raconteur," I reminded. I pulled Streng's pistol, fired. He leaped back unscathed. I resolved to practice shooting while lying down. Still it allowed me to roll, rise to my feet. Grayish continued as if this shifting about was so much childish antic.

"I didn't foresee you returning, pretending to be me pretending to be you," he confessed. His chatter had a way of distracting. Suddenly he lunged, slashed, cutting my face. I cried out, riposted empty air. "Clever of you to steal my funds," he continued. "I require them back."

And now we fenced in earnest. He lunged, I parried, he swept his cloak in my face just as I moved to do the same. I dropped rapier and grabbed the cloak, threw myself sideways, near pulling him from his feet. He dropped the rapier, we grappled close, seeking throats and ribs with fists and knee. I drew knife, allowing him to place hands about my throat. I gave him a slash to that handsome face, matching my new scar. He leaped back, laughed and drew pistol. He'd had a pistol all this time? Confident fellow.

I considered throwing the knife, decided to retreat towards the shadowed corner. I struggled not to focus on the illusion of myself, standing before me. He stooped, recovered a rapier, approached idly swishing blade, still holding pistol. Was this illusion? Was he even real? Should I close eyes, listen for his breath and step?

"What did you intend with a box of diamonds?" I asked. I considered throwing myself off the balcony. I could not see that ending well.

"Oh, that. Well, a failed revolt lacks style. More fun to make it succeed. The treasure you absconded is payment to army and city garrison. To back the revolt, not crush it."

He halted my murder to brood. "Hurtful, how the family that reject the Decourseys, accepted you. Even the Mac Tier, who reject me…" He stopped himself, something like fury passing his face, erasing the casual smile.

"So," he continued, recovered. "I declare: enough is enough. The clans shall re-unite. I will take control of the common-blooded, and direct them in a great purge of all my beloved family. I shall hunt down my erring cousins in every last valley, every hidden cave, every isle and mountain top. The purified remainder will rejoin in a single nation again. Free to be ourselves, to live in love and respect, no longer the idiot playthings of rivalry, spite, and the plots of mad elders."

The face-slash burned. The kicked ribs ached. I backed into the terrace corner. The figure of Rayne Grayish no longer stood before me. No more masquerade, but the true self. Behold a tall man, older than I. Dark eyes, proud red lips scowling in hate. White of face as Death, as the moon…

"You're no Harlequin," I realized. "They don't fight this way. This is no dream-casting. You are a Mac Tier, taking my form as another would a wolf."

"Form and nature," corrected the Pierrot. "My mother was Mac Tier. What of it? The Moon Tartan only play with lesser natures. What art in that? The despised Harlequin dare higher."

"Not higher," I corrected. "You turned yourself into a beast, same as any wolf or bear," I noted. "And so lost the wisdom of being a man,"

The Pierrot laughed. "You insult your mirror, man,"

"I am not my mirror," I replied. "I am the thing itself."

He shook head. "You've been around the old ones too long. It addles the brain."

We both smiled at that. He had a point. Also a gun, pointed at me.

"You came to kill a man," he declared. "So also, I. My son was all to me. Far more than your whore to you." He raised pistol to kill, in no hurry. Family, enjoying the stage. I prepared to leap for his throat. Too far a leap. What did Lalena do now? I'd take the shot, continue the strike and then die. Any other foe I'd take to hell with me. Not this one. How hung my wife's hair now? Did she think of me?

"Elspeth O'Claire was no whore," a voice corrected. Not my voice. Alderman Green's. "She was a charming young woman misused by creatures much like you." The Pierrot whirled to see the papal Green, swinging Death's scythe. Pierrot dodged, waved pistol, unwilling to use the shot on this lesser foe.

"What is going on?" asked a voice beside me. I turned to see the guard I'd spared, for the wedding bands we shared. He rubbed aching head, waved his crossbow.

"A moment," I told him. I borrowed his crossbow, checked bolt and wire, and fired.

The shot took the Pierrot in the back. He staggered, turned to shoot me. Green swung the scythe into the man's back. They both cried out, the gun fell unfired. Green dropped the bloody scythe in horror. Poor Green. For all his endless chidings for me to be a practical killer, he'd never struck blade into another in his life.

Pierrot lay on the terrace floor, studying his part. Pierrot vanished, appeared as Grayish. Pierrot appeared again. Grayish appeared again. Disappeared. Reappeared. Stilled to a last sad Pierrot, staring up at the moon.

I returned the crossbow to the puzzled guard, walked to the dropped pistol, retrieved it with trembling hands. Pointed it at Green. He still wore the tall papal hat. "Lean forwards," I commanded, waving the pistol.

Green stared, sighed, leaned forwards. The hat tilted at a thirty-degree angle.

"Farther," I commanded. He did. The hat yet remained fast.

"How can that construction stay on your head?" I demanded. "Is it nailed on, man?"

Green ceased his bow, stood straight. He adjusted the hat slightly, approving its constant nature, refusing to explain. Typical. I went to the door, gun at ready. No shouts. Music in the garden, distant buzz of voices. It might well be that all took the shots for fireworks.

I walked past Green, picked up the leather satchel, emptied it upon the table. Hades sat slumped in his throne, wheezing, bubbling blood. His eyes considered me, the books. I waved Green over.

"These are the ledgers you sent me to find the night of the warehouse fire," I informed him. "Proof that Black was a traitor selling arms to French and Spanish, a slave-trading embezzling pirate thief who never paid his damned taxes."

Green looked from the ledgers to the blood-wheezing Black. "Seems a bit moot," he pointed out.

"No," I informed him. "I want his crimes brought to trial. His estate sold to repay the poor he robbed. I want him remembered as a thief brought to justice, not an Alderman dead in honest duty."

"I'm not dead," gasped Black. He struggled to raise a pistol from out the folds of his dark velvet cloak. I reached across, took it from his hand and shot him in the chest. Hades trembled, ceased. I put down the pistol, returned to the books.

"As I said, I want him remembered as a vicious pirate unredeemed by a single quality of character. Only notable for an extravagant opinion of his mirror."

"Rayne," said Green.

"I am sorry about Dealer," I added. "I cut his head off."

"Rayne," said Green.

"Thank you for your words about El," I added. "I saw her in a dream. Walking to Heaven. She so loved *Pilgrim's Progress*."

Green said nothing. I considered any last things.

"Ha, I'm married now," I said, waving my left hand. "She's very special. Oh, and thank you for saving my life. I'd intended to kill you. We'll forget that."

I struggled to pick my rapier from the ground, and puzzled why. My hand trembled. Well, I had cuts and bruises and corpses about me. These things will shake a man. I steadied, sheathed rapier, gave a last look to Black, shrugged, sighed.

"Someday I will ask you why Jeremy came to hate me so," I said. I turned to the body of the Pierrot. "In return, I will explain who and what you scythed. Goodbye, Green."

"Rayne," he said, but I was in a hurry to leave. I stopped at a thought.

"And see there is no slaughter of protesting tradesmen," I shouted back. "Else I return to this city, very vexed."

I walked towards the door, anxious to leave. A figure stood blinking confused. It was the guard. I'd forgot him, and now nearly shot him. Well, I was nervous. I kept seeing a head rolling across the ground, just on the edge of sight. The guard goggled at what nightmare he beheld: the table of feasting dead, the corpse of the Pierrot laid upon the ground.

"What in God's name happened?" he whispered.

"How long have you been married?" I replied.

He blinked. "Two years, now."

Two years. I'd been married not half that. And yet, I'd left my bride to come to this charnel play? I'd dared leave while her eyes said *he'll not be back*. I'd let my old life near devour my new. A crime. I near cried out at the crime.

"Does it get easier?" I asked of the man. "Better?"

He wobbled, head no doubt whirling. But honest man, he considered. At last answered. "It gets harder and better."

I considered. That seemed a likely enough answer.

"Thank you then," I said, and shook his hand. "Good luck to you and yours."

"To you and yours," he replied. I left then.

Chapter 26
A Place of Proper Ending

Guards should not concern themselves with those leaving a secured area. They stand vigil to prevent *entry*. But men with swords and guns will look for trouble. Guard-duty's a dull business. Though proper soldiers cherish dull business.

To leave I had to waylay a guest and a guard, exchanging cloak and mask. I did not kill, merely stunned, pushed into a closet, apologized, hurried on. I emerged in the ball-room where I mixed with the costumed gentry. The music had halted, the orchestra disappeared. Armed men ran in circles while guests gossiped. Rumors swirled of attack by bandits, assassins or the French.

I joined the stream fleeing to the clock's strike of twelve. Cinderellas rushing to our pumpkin coaches. Guards wove in and out without direction, searching for bandits, assassins and Frenchmen.

I found my carriage. Stephano stood with other drivers by a fire, warming hands and wine. He sighted me, rushed to open the door. I stared into the dark carriage and declined. Instead I leaped atop the driver's seat. He sighed and joined me, taking reins.

"You foresee trouble, sir," he declared. For it was my habit to ride beside him when expecting attack. It unnerves my spadassin nature to lurk where others know I lurk. In reply I drew the pistol, laid it upon my lap.

Stephano twisted his fist of a face for a grin, and we drove swift away. Swiftly, once the five dozen other carriages ahead had moved onto the road.

"Where to, Master Gray?" asked the man beside me. Sitting, humming, fearing nothing worse than a horse should throw a shoe.

"Take the North Road towards the river," I directed. "We do not return to the city."

Night air quiets my nerves. Not this night. I trembled in cold breeze, twitched at calls of owl and sedge warbler, crake and distant dogs barking. I had a vision of Dealer's head rolling after the carriage, calling out truths on art and love.

Mist took the road as we left cobbles and houses behind. I watched for a suitable place to halt the coach, kill the man beside me. I weighed what words I'd say first. Words to recall all the kindness of Elspeth to our rough souls. She'd been our light, encouraging us both to be men, not brutes.

I considered Howl's listing of preferences for family drama. A country-graveyard approached, moonlit and quiet by the roadside. That would serve: proper place to end the night's march of death. End the task for which I'd come: vengeance. The Pierrot had come to kill me, for killing his son. I wondered what feud the son had with the Mac Sanglair. Not a folk to casually attack.

"A question, Stephano," I said. "Why did you not note my wedding ring?"

He turned surprised. "What should I note, sir?" He looked down at my banded left hand, resting on the pistol. "Seems the same ring."

"You know I'm married," I declared. Not Stephano then, but *Stephanish*.

But he laughed surprised I should ask. "Was I not at your wedding a week past? At El's-" he stopped, stuttered, tried again. "At *her* old Church of All Saints?"

I blinked. I'd half decided the man was a Harlequin feigning my former valet. Why else ignore my wedding ring? That the false Grayish should have married himself with my face in my absence, had not occurred. Another widow somewhere then. It all made too mad and sad a business to follow.

But the explanation settled the identity of the man beside me. My former valet, my former friend. The man who murdered Elspeth, stole my fortune, betrayed me to the guard. And he *dared* sit with me now?

"Stop here," I directed as we rumbled beside the church-yard. He promptly halted the coach, looked uneasily towards the quiet rows of moonlit memorial. No, not all quiet. A service of strange purpose took place among the stones. By night?

"Resurrection men," decided Stephano. "Body-stealers defiling the dead."

I studied the scene, less sure. Four figures dressed so dark one could scarce see form, but that they wore moon-bright gloves, faces painted white as Elizabethan lords.

They worked furiously to dig… but I saw no shovels. I perceived the motions, could all but hear the turned earth, hear shovel edge scrape stones and bones. But their hands held air and moonshine. Harlequins acting out lunatic tableau. I recalled the attack on the bridge. The creatures performed mad nonsense with sane purpose: *to distract.*

I whirled. On the coach-roof behind crept a black-clad figure holding very real knife. I fired, he fell with a cry. I grabbed the knife in time to cut another clambering up the side. Stephano struck at dark forms below him. He goaded the horses, but white hands slashed the traces, leaving the reigns slack.

Stephano cursed, stood. Raised a pistol, fired at me. No, at another creeping along the coach roof. The figure fell, white face expressing mock astonishment. The horses shied in fear, the coach rocked, unable to move forward. If the attackers had shouted or screamed, the scene would have been less frightful. But they kept to eerie silence.

Till another gun spoke, Stephano gasped, fell. I leaped down beside him, found myself grabbed by a crowd of white-gloved hands. Knife to throat. I was pushed to my knees before a figure in pale dress, black diamond-patterned. Harlequin tartan. Behold the fox-faced musician at the ball, who'd tossed me a rose, a smile. With her stood others dressed in the same pattern. Their dark-clad servants milled about, capering mute, shadows of a dancing lamp.

268

"You killed my lord, clay-man," declared the fox-girl. I felt tempted to explain tonight had been a blood-bath. It required she name any particular corpse. But of course she meant the Harlequin Pierrot. It explained this angry ambush. Foolish to believe I could just exit stage, unpursued by bears or widows or severed heads. One cannot escape the family. They will await you on the path, for all your panicked turns and twists.

"Well, he stole my face," I pointed out. "And plotted my murder, among others." I stared at the body of Stephano beside me. He breathed in rough gasps. "One kills one man to avenge another, then family rise up to balance accounts. I begin to see a pattern of idiot dance, with the devil playing oboe."

She bent down, eyes near as mad as Lalena's, lips near as red. I felt an urge to kiss the resemblance, but refrained. She hissed. "I thought you him. How blind I was."

"More blind than you think, sister," said someone from the dark.

Now the Harlequin servants found voice, in cries of pain, surprise, fear. The weak moon shown down on a surrounding circle of glowing eyes. Fascinating creatures, these newcomers.

I watched a bull-headed man lift a Harlequin servant, toss him over the carriage. A wolf leaped upon another, bearing him to dirt. A doe-headed girl of slender form set about with a great spear, flailing the Harlequin like rugs

269

needing dusting. Still, this was less violence than they might have shown. Tooth, claw and spear sent them tumbling and flying, but not to death. The Tiger-man only waved sword, did not strike.

I pushed the knife from my throat, threw myself back, drew rapier. But all fighting had ended. Two sides of family stood glaring. Beast men against Harlequins, if you wish. Or Mac Tier against Decoursey. Cousins who glared, daring each to cross this line, defy that line, say this to that face.

There stood Vixen Mac Tier in Moon Tartan colors turned gray by moon's light. She faced the woman in Harlequin pattern, bright against the black-clad servants. "Sionnach Mac Tier. You join with the Decoursey madmen?" asked Vixen.

"I was driven out my house," replied her sister. For surely that was who she must be. "You as well. The other clans spat I carried the death-madness. They shut door to me, blood of their blood, heart to their heart. Only the Pierrot offered me place by the hearth."

"Our father is passed," declared Vixen. "Howl is now Laird of the Moon Tartan. And the man you waylay has the favor of Mac Tier and Sanglair. And Fulgurous himself perhaps. It were not well to cross such."

Sionnach put hands to hips, threw head back, proud as five queens and a bishop. "So the gossip says. But I stand here widowed tonight, sister, and only a week married."

Vixen looked to the fallen Stephano. "A life for a life, cousins. Let that suffice. And so return with us, your brothers and sisters. Together we can heal the harms of our father's madness."

Sionnach turned to the gathered Harlequins. They kept silent, arms crossed in stubborn disinterest. *Decide as you will,* their stance said. At last she turned back to Vixen, shook head. "You believe I will leave my dead lord's people, run back to my childhood bed? You think so little of me?"

Vixen considered. "No," she said. "I can't think so." And suddenly she burst into tears. Sionnach stared, then did the same. They lifted faces to the moon and wept silver moon-streams. Then rushed forwards as to battle, and embraced. All stared, Mac Tier and Harlequin. Then wolf held out hand to fallen mummer, and bull-headed Bellow set a Harlequin servant upright, dusted him gentle as shepherd to lamb. Both clans stood as one, watching the sisters weep by moon's light, and wept with them.

I remained dry-eyed. I scrabbled about in the dirt, found a knife. Dark-painted, as the Harlequins preferred. I went to Stephano, who lay forgotten in the road. I knelt down beside him, examined his wound. Close to the heart, enough to run a strong fountain till the spring ran dry.

I considered the man. What a devil's face. A devil who'd done me great harm; more than any other in a life of war and blood. He looked up at me. "That's done it," he whispered. "Friends of yours come?"

I nodded, eyeing the assemblage enacting their idiot ritual of feud and affection. Behold: *family*. I returned gaze to the man who'd ended what I'd considered my family. I squeezed knife-handle till knuckles cracked. Stephano stared out his devil's face, content smile to lips.

"All well then," he whispered. "I never thanked you for forgiving me. Those were kind words you said, sir. I've not forgot 'em. Nor how you asked me to forgive you in return."

"*I did what?*" I asked.

He laughed, choking. "Aye, you did. And I found it hard to forgive, as be forgiven. I've been a beast most my life. But I'll be a man at the end. So I forgive you, Master Rayne."

Theatre. I turned and looked at the cousinry. Some watched us, wondering if this promised equal entertainment as the weeping fox-girls. No, not weeping. Vixen and Sionnach had returned to arguing, stamping feet, crossing arms, flouncing locks.

I turned from that nonsense back to reality. My reality. It was not too late to whisper to this dying man *I never forgave you. I never shall. Burn in Hell*. Then slice his throat so he shipped to Satan a full minute ahead of schedule. Instead I sighed, dropped knife, clasped his hand as he'd clasped El's.

272

"I think marriage is starting to change me," I said to him. He grinned in understanding at my complaint, as one man will do for another.

* * *

We sat by a fireside in the moonlit church-yard, trees sharing solemn secrets with the wind. Owls and night jars discussed our presence, making wise observations. The horses kept solemn watch by the carriage, refusing to judge. A few grave-stone angels observed, faces turning soft or stern, joyous or sad, as fire-shine and moon-shadow chose to cast expression. Standard setting for a family gathering.

I held hands to the fire-flames, watching them tremble. The hands, I mean, not the flames. Flames tremble not. They only dance. Flames fear not, and no fire ever shook in horror at visions of ashes. I'd slain more men tonight than when I infiltrated the French command. Some I'd known full years. I didn't feel a triumphant soldier. I felt a blood-spattered beast.

Beasts... I turned to consider the Mac Tier warming themselves by the same flames. Doe, Bellow, and Vixen. The tiger-man, Bram. A fellow with wolf-head, not the new Laird Mac Tier. They chatted, exchanging family gossip. Casting kind-but-worried glances at me, the drawn sword I kept at hand. Every time I sheathed it, I heard shots, saw Dealer's head roll towards the fire, the Pierrot laugh, a nameless guard gasp... and held sword unsheathed again. Hands and soul found it difficult to simply declare *'all done with death'*. The cemetery setting didn't help.

The Mac Tier said naught, as if they understood. Masters of multiple natures, perhaps they did understand. I eyed them astonished at my earlier ignorance. Beast-men? No. These sat human as I. More so. They faced the same risk all men do, of losing their humanity. Greater risk for the wisdom they sought in dream-natures. Yet clearly they triumphed. They lived and loved wise in life. They dared commit their hearts to a vast nation of family, whether in feud or love. All I dared love was one other heart, one other face. And I'd walked away from her, to seek out those I hated.

I'd returned to the city to kill a man. I was no longer sure who. Alderman Black? Dealer? Magister Green? Stephano? Perhaps Rayne Grayish. Or, why not, even Rayne Gray himself. *'Can a man challenge his own reflection?'* asked Chatterton's angel. She gifted me with wisdom of that sort on my wedding day. I'd have preferred new shirts.

"He who makes a beast of himself, escapes the pain of being a man," she'd advised. I wept with laughter to think I'd taken the warning for the wise Mac Tier, and not my mirror.

On a sudden, Doe clapped hands, bored with grave-yard whispers. She reached into a bag, handed Bellow violin and bow. He sighed a bucolic puff, accepted, considered, hummed, tuned, and began to play. Doe reached hand to Vixen, and they stood, began a dance to match the grace of the firelight's flame. The wolf-youth piped a flute. From beyond the fire's light, the aberration began to hum his strange purring song. The Tiger-man... what was his name? Bram. He began to sing, soft and solemn:

> *"The moon-shadow folk, joying together, standing alone.*
> *Choosing what faces we show, sharing hearts by star's light.*
> *The fire-shaped people, the candle-shadow company.*
> *We run laughing all night, chasing the call of heart's delight.*

I looked down the moon-lit road. Why not run all night with the moon, northwards seeking my heart's delight? If she would have me back. And if she said *nay,* why I'd sit outside her door, offer her bags of jewels, boxes of gold. If such still lay hid in the carriage. I hadn't checked. I jumped up, laughing for joy of the decision to run to Scotland this instant. What excellent advice one finds in song.

But on a sudden I felt too weary to take a step, near tumbling into the fire. Vixen and Doe caught my arms. I sat again. Bellow brought me an unpoisoned cup. The aberration came close, shared purr and warmth. Beast-forms with human hearts, they did their best to comfort me as fellow man, if not proper family. Pats to back, whispers of assurance: *all will be well.* I collected myself presently, as a Seraph will do.

"Home tomorrow," I promised the fire, myself and the moon, and then dared finally rest.

End of Book 2

About the author:

Raymond St. Elmo wandered into a degree in Spanish Literature, which gave no job, just a love of Magic Realism. Moving on to a degree in programming gave him a job and an interest in virtual reality and artificial intelligence, which lead him back into the world of magic realism. Author of several books (all first-person literary fictions, possibly comic). Quest of Five Clans is his first fantasy series.

Quest of the Five Clans shall continue in these exciting sequels:

The Harlequin Tartan
The Scaled Tartan
The Clockwork Tartan

Made in the USA
Middletown, DE
10 May 2023

30345789R00156